LOVE'S GUARDIAN

DAWN IRELAND

To Jeannie,
I hope you enjoy
Alex and Declan's
story. It was great
meeting you!!!
Dawn Ireland

SOUL MATE PUBLISHING

New York

LOVE'S GUARDIAN
Copyright©2011
DAWN IRELAND

Cover Design by Rae Monet, Inc.

This book is a work of fiction. The names, characters, places, and incidents are the products of the author's imagination or are used fictitiously. Any resemblance to actual events, business establishments, locales, or persons, living or dead, is entirely coincidental.

All rights reserved. No part of this publication may be reproduced, stored in a retrieval system, or transmitted in any form or by any means (electronic, mechanical, photocopying, recording, or otherwise) without the priority written permission of both the copyright owner and the publisher. The only exception is brief quotations in printed reviews.

The scanning, uploading, and distribution of this book via the Internet or via any other means without the permission of the publisher is illegal and punishable by law. Please purchase only authorized electronic editions, and do not participate in or encourage electronic piracy of copyrighted materials. Your support of the author's rights is appreciated.

Published in the United States of America by
Soul Mate Publishing
P.O. Box 24
Macedon, New York, 14502

ISBN: 978-1-61935-104-2
eBook ISBN: 978-1-61935-015-1

www.SoulMatePublishing.com

The publisher does not have any control over and does not assume any responsibility for author or third-party Web sites or their content.

This book is dedicated to my parents,

Alexander Baird and Frances Lanore Ireland,

who taught me that nothing is "impossible."

Acknowledgements

Mmmm. How do you thank all the people who made this book happen? Friends and family have spent hours listening to my story ideas, book excerpts and writing ramblings—and they stayed in my life. Amazing. My husband encouraged me to spend hours in front of the computer, even when housework beckoned. Certain people refused to let me quit. Pat Iacuzza., it's a good thing Tim Horton's is open late. Pat Ryan & Tim Wright, you set my feet on the proper path and nudged me forward. My friends at Central New York Romance Writers took me in and nurtured my skills.

And Debby Gilbert, without you none of this would be happening. You kept saying this book should be on a shelf, and now—IT IS. Thank You!.

Chapter 1

England 1783
County Kent

Alexandra Kendrick reached for the doorknob, her hand hovering above the luminous orb. If the library's occupant raised an alarm, her cousin Eleanor was sure to try and stop her. Alex took a deep breath, turned the brass knob, and prayed the creaky hinges on the door had been oiled recently.

She slipped into the book-lined room, then nudged the door closed with her heel as she watched for any sign of activity. A fire popped and danced in the hearth, but it was the dark hair just visible over the top of her grandfather's favorite wingback chair that caught her attention. Lord Worthington had already made himself at home.

The worn edge of her rapier handle pressed into her palm, as her mouth turned up in a humorless smile. Eleanor had dubbed Alex's special *talent* unacceptable in polite society, but her abilities might succeed where worry and arguing had failed. This stranger had no right to her estates. She'd rather die now, than see everything she loved destroyed.

With her right hand, she reached behind her back, then grasped the key that stood in the lock on the door. Keeping her attention on Lord Worthington, she turned the cool metal until she felt the click of the mechanism. In the quiet room, the noise sounded like a cannon. Alex's body tensed.

With one lithe motion, her guardian rose to his feet and turned, dagger in hand.

Alex admired his speed. Even she couldn't get to her blade so quickly. But admiration turned to horror when she realized who stood before her. "Get out!"

Declan slowly replaced the weapon in his boot, crossed to her grandfather's desk, then turned toward her. He gave a slight shrug, his broad shoulders straining the material. "I'm afraid I can't, even if I wanted to."

Where was her guardian? And what was Declan doing here? His timing couldn't be worse. The man hadn't visited in eight years–and then only long enough to leave her on her grandfather's front step and declare she was Lord Lochsdale's problem.

Her nemesis studied her for a moment, a slight smirk on his face. "Your attire still seems to lean toward the masculine. Though I must admit, you fill out breeches better at twenty than you did at twelve."

Heat flooded her face. She should be insulted, but a part of her couldn't help being pleased at his comment. She'd changed in the last eight years, but so had he.

His broad shoulders were encased in a dark blue velvet coat with a touch of lace at the wrists and throat. Black breeches, spattered with mud, accentuated his heavily muscled legs. He dressed like a man of wealth, but his clothing didn't change the common sailor she'd known as a child.

His chest did appear wider than she remembered, and the coal black hair she'd always admired now curled at his shoulders in defiance of the current fashion. But his Caribbean blue eyes were the same, and they narrowed as they studied her. No, he hadn't lost any of his allure, damn him.

He had to leave before her new guardian appeared. She had no doubt that Declan wouldn't help the situation. Hell, he'd probably side with the bastard.

"I trust I meet with your approval." He gave her a

knowing smile.

She flushed, the warmth creeping up her neck. She had been staring, but he didn't have to bring it to her attention.

He lowered his gaze to her hand. "Still have a penchant for sharp objects, or do you always carry a weapon when I'm in the room?"

Alex had forgotten all about the rapier that hung in her left hand. She transferred it to her right, then clenched the handle.

Declan caught her gaze once more, a smug expression on his face. "You may want to consider retiring your weapons. After all, we'll be spending a great deal of time together."

The man was entirely too arrogant. She raised her brow and gave him a mock salute with her rapier. "Why should I spend *any* time in your company? To be honest, I'd prefer not to be in a room that had you in it."

A flicker of surprise flashed in his eyes. "I do believe wards often spend a substantial amount of time with their guardians. In deference to your grandfather, I intend to see to your care myself."

She almost dropped the rapier. "No." Her response was barely audible. She cleared her throat and tried again. "No, that can't be! You're a sailor, nothing more."

The words rang false in her ears. What a fool she'd been.

Declan had always seemed different from the other men on her father's ship, *The Merry Elizabeth*. His mere presence and air of authority could dominate a room. Now she knew why.

Anger, hurt, and surprise vied for supremacy, causing her stomach to twist into a knot. Declan was the Earl of Worthington—and her guardian? Damnation. Of all men, why did her grandfather have to choose *him*?

She couldn't recall ever being told Declan's surname, but that wasn't unusual on *The Merry Elizabeth*. Many men had a past to hide. She'd always assumed he was the younger son of a noble family who'd run up against the law. She met his patronizing gaze and raised her chin.

"Actually, my Christian name is Declan Deveraux, but in most circles, I'm known as the Earl of Worthington." He rested one hip on her grandfather's desk, watching her every move, like a sailor watched for the first sign of land after a long voyage. "I hired on to *The Merry Elizabeth* at your grandfather's request. He wanted me to keep an eye on you."

So, he'd been spying on her. Bloody hell. She'd followed him around the ship, thinking he could do no wrong, and all the time he'd been deceiving her. "I should have guessed you knew my grandfather. He wasn't surprised when you showed up with me after my parents died."

"Your grandfather wanted me to keep him informed, nothing more." Declan's voice softened. "He was worried about you."

"Yes, well, Grandfather should have worried when he made you my guardian. If he'd asked me, I would have told him you are totally unsuitable." Declan wasn't going to ruin her life again. This time she was going to fight for the home she loved.

He crossed his arms and gave her a condescending smile. "I shall probably regret asking this, but why am I unsuitable?"

What kind of an insult would raise his ire? Declan had always been angry with her when she'd been a child. What had she done then?

She searched her memory. The taunts that had annoyed him the most had disparaged his abilities. "You are unsuitable as my guardian because you're inept." Alex hoped she sounded convincing.

Declan's eyes narrowed. The smile faltered.

"I remember your performance onboard my ship," Alex goaded. "You couldn't even best a child at climbing the rigging. Do you fare better on land?"

In truth, she'd never known a better sailor. He'd only been trying to rescue her that day, and in all fairness he'd had no way of knowing she'd been climbing before she could walk.

She could almost see the storm brew in his eyes. Alex trusted it was a tempest she could control. His well-drawn features became harsher, and his face could have been made of stone, except for the spasm of his jaw muscle.

Alex swallowed. An angry man didn't think things through, did he? She hoped not. Her plan depended on it.

"Regardless what you think of me, you are my charge. You will do as I say." His gaze raked over her body in an insolent manner. "Starting with wearing some decent clothing."

"On the contrary. This clothing is very appropriate for our duel."

Declan laughed. He couldn't help it. Alex, was challenging him to a *duel*? "What will it be? Pistols at dawn?"

"No, my lord. Rapiers. Now."

He stopped laughing. She was serious. His gaze dropped to the weapon at her side. That's why she'd brought her rapier with her. There were no other women of his acquaintance who preferred a rapier to feminine wiles. "Lady Lochsdale, most *men* wouldn't consider challenging me. What could you possibly hope to gain?"

"My freedom. If I win, I want to live my life, without interference. I can run my estates. I don't need supervision. You'll return to London, and leave us alone." Her small chin tilted up, reminding him of the stubborn child he'd known. "So what will it be, my lord?"

"And what do I get if I win?"

"I suppose...I mean...well, I'll follow your orders,

provided the request is reasonable."

He had to admire her confidence. She truly hadn't considered he might win, or she would have been prepared with a response that gave him less control.

"Done. And the rules of this contest?"

"The first one to disarm his opponent wins." Alex gave him a smug smile. "I wouldn't want to run the risk of killing you. The crown would only find someone else to take your place."

Declan glanced toward the wall. All manner of fencing equipment was on display. If he had to do this, she'd wear protective gear. He'd never forgive himself if she got hurt. "I have a request."

"Name it."

"I want you to wear protective padding."

"Are you that concerned about your skills? You do know how to fence, don't you?"

She hadn't lost her ability to anger him. He had so hoped she'd outgrown that. He folded his arms and waited.

"Oh, all right. But if I have to wear it, so do you."

He suspected he'd be sorry for agreeing to this. He really didn't have to take her challenge. The law required Alex to obey him, but he wouldn't point that out, not if winning this little contest would make her more tractable.

They moved the furniture to the perimeter of the room and rolled up the oriental carpet. He shrugged off his riding coat and cravat, then crossed to the display of weapons on the wall next to the fireplace.

He'd left his rapier upstairs with his belongings, but Alex seemed hell-bent to do this now, so he selected a blade and padding from the collection on the library wall. He waited for her to do the same.

The rapier he'd chosen felt well balanced, though its

ornate hilt appeared worn. Lord Lochsdale had been an expert with weapons. Declan smiled at the memory of the hours of practice he'd shared with Alex's grandfather. He doubted his old instructor would have approved of this duel.

Declan rolled up his sleeves, made a few test thrusts, then turned toward his ward. She was watching him with a determined expression in her deep green eyes. If crossing blades with her would make her easier to handle, he'd do it. His old friend would just have to forgive him.

After all, she didn't stand a chance.

The blades clanged, then slid along each other in an age-old dance of parry and thrust. Declan began to suspect he was wrong, very wrong, to think this would be an easy contest. When had she developed such finesse?

Alex tried to slip under his guard, her speed incredible. Declan was hard pressed to keep up. What Alex lacked in strength, she more than made up for in agility. Perspiration filmed her brow and dampened her curls as she turned each of his thrusts, trying to force him off balance.

Someone rapped on the door. Declan could hear people shouting, but their voices seemed distant, compared to the labored breathing in the room and the pounding of his heart.

The cacophony of frantic cries and banging outside the library continued to escalate, until it distracted him for an instant. Alex took the opportunity to cross over his blade, catching his upper arm. He heard the fabric tear and felt a slight sting. He'd been grazed by a blade more times than he could count. No matter, the injury was a nuisance, nothing more.

They worked their way in front of the banks of curtained windows. His sweat slicked the hilt of his weapon, making his grasp tenuous. He was glad they'd moved the furniture. With Alex's aggressiveness, he couldn't afford a misstep.

Her skill showed in every parry, but her movements had slowed. Declan noticed her eyes seemed drawn to his arm.

He felt the blood dampening his shirt and saw her stance relax slightly as she focused on his injury.

With a lightning thrust, he slipped his blade under hers, then caught her weapon near its hilt. Surprise crossed her features as he forced her rapier upward. Alex's hold faltered. Her weapon clattered to the floor, sliding across the polished wood.

Declan placed the tip of his blade at the base of her throat. For what seemed like an eternity, he gazed into emerald eyes, black flecks swirling in their depths, the tension rife between them.

Alex lowered her gaze first. Only then did he remove the point from her neck. "Now do we understand one another?"

"Yes." Her hands fisted at her sides, the knuckles white with strain. "Is there anything else, my lord?"

"Not at the moment." Declan tried not to let his satisfaction show. Being her guardian might be easier than he thought.

Alex made a quick turn and stumbled over the rolled carpet. She almost fell, but he grabbed her arm and drew her to him so that her cheek rested below his shoulder.

He'd only meant to steady her, but surprised himself when his arms came around her in an embrace. She felt soft and warm from their recent exertion. The air surrounding her was musky with a hint of vanilla. Declan breathed deeply. He liked the smell and the way her body fit to his.

For a moment, Alex relaxed against him, and he had the strangest urge to comfort her. When he attempted to bring her closer, she stiffened and backed away.

"Don't." Her posture ramrod straight, she turned and crossed to the corner of the room.

He tried not to notice her backside as she bent to collect her rapier. Male attire suited her, clinging in all the right places. Perhaps that was the reason for his uncharacteristic behavior. He'd have to find some way to get her in a dress.

Alex turned toward him. She checked her weapon for damage, then lovingly ran her hand over the intricate design on the hilt. When she raised her gaze to his, Declan saw dignity and pride in her eyes. "I'll obey you because I have to. You've won my cooperation. Nothing more."

She unlocked the door and opened it. With her chin held high, Alex faced the staff. Silence descended as they cleared a path for her. With graceful movements, she passed through them and ascended the stairs.

Declan unrolled the sleeves of his shirt, while trying to decide what to say to the onlookers. He couldn't tell them the truth. Even if he were believed, there was her reputation to consider. He shrugged into his coat, favoring his injured arm, and headed to the door. The astonished gathering watched him expectantly.

Damn. He'd thought Alex a menace as a child, but the woman promised to be much worse.

Chapter 2

"I hope you don't have any more *accidents,* my lord."

Declan eased out of his coat and laid it over the back of a chair. "I'll try to avoid them in future." Which might prove difficult, now that he was dealing with Alex.

Richards's eyes widened when he beheld the blood-soaked fabric, a frown of disapproval on his pale, thin face. "This shirt is beyond repair." The servant crossed to the mahogany wardrobe in the corner of the bedroom, then returned with fresh clothing.

Declan tensed as his valet briskly removed his shirt with no care for his wound. Obviously Richards felt a little pain was proper penance for destroying a fine garment. Declan sank onto the big poster bed to allow the servant to take off his boots.

A blond strand of hair escaped from under his valet's powdered wig. Richards was becoming lax, after less than twenty-four hours in the country. It was an edifying sign. In London, his servant never allowed anything on his person to be out of place.

He understood why his aunt had insisted he hire Richards. The man was a gem of the first water when it came to his position as a valet. But he could have done without a servant who felt an earl needed to be dressed appropriately at all times.

Testing his mobility, Declan rotated his shoulder, then stretched. His injury ached now that the shirt had been removed and the wound was bleeding again. "Have a maid bring up something to clean and bind this scratch."

"When I heard you'd had an accident, I took the liberty of doing so, my lord."

"Perhaps you should see what's keeping her." He gave his servant a small smile. "We wouldn't want me to bleed all over another shirt, would we?" Declan reached for the clean garment that had been laid out on the bed. Richards grabbed it and hurried from the room.

At any other time, he might have laughed. Threatening to damage clothing was a sure way to get Richards to move quickly.

Declan laid back on the bed. He would be slightly stiff in the morning, the wound sore, but in his twenty-eight years, he'd had much worse. The greatest injury was to his pride.

Members of the Ton would have months of entertainment, at his expense, if they ever found out he'd been wounded while fencing with his ward. He rubbed his sword arm, loosening the muscles, and closed his eyes.

Morgan, his glib-tongued friend, would be more amused by the fact that Alexandra didn't seem to be enthralled by Declan's looks or wealth. He'd probably say it would do Declan good, "teach him a bit o' patience"—if he ever stopped laughing.

The big Irishman could be a trial, but there was no one he'd rather have at his back in a fight. Just to play it safe, he wouldn't mention the little fencing incident when he returned to London.

Richards reappeared with a pretty little blonde in tow. Declan grimaced as he sat up, then waited for the woman to clean his wound. She stood there, her basin of water in hand, staring at his naked chest as though she'd never seen one before. Richards gave her a nudge, and she stepped forward to begin her task.

The cool water stung like hell. Declan clenched his teeth and focused on keeping his breathing even. In very short order, she bound the wound and rinsed the cloth, then using slow, sensuous stokes, she cleansed the dried blood that had trickled down his chest.

"My lord, I was to tell you dinner will be ready at six." The maid dropped the rag in the water and caressed his upper body with her damp hands as if checking for other injuries. She stopped, palms flat, at the base of his neck. "There now, I'm thinking they'll be hardly any scar. If you'll be needing anything, anything at all, just ask for Molly. I'm more than willing, day or night." She picked up her basin and gave him a saucy smile.

"Thank you, Molly, I'll remember that." Declan returned her smile, and she missed the door as she backed out of the room. Blushing a pretty pink, she turned and exited.

Declan shook his head. Ever since he was sixteen, every woman he'd met had acted like that around him. Every woman, that is, but Alex.

The memory of her bold challenge wove itself into his thoughts. He probably shouldn't find her brashness amusing, but he did. No other woman had tried to injure him, at least physically. She was direct, he'd give her that, but what to do with her?

"May I suggest the black velvet coat with gold embroidery for dinner, my lord?"

"Mmm?"

"The black coat, my lord?"

"Oh, yes." He would have preferred just his waistcoat. He suspected Alex wouldn't care, but Eleanor was another matter. "The black is fine."

"Perhaps a little powder for your hair, just for propriety's sake?

"No."

"But, my lord."

"You're well aware I hate powder." Declan adjusted his cravat in the mirror. He didn't dare let Richards do it, or he wouldn't be able to breathe for the rest of the evening.

Richards felt a knot just wasn't proper unless it choked the life out of you. "Try to remember, I'm not comfortable with frills."

"I try to make allowances, my lord."

"I know you do." Declan tugged at his wide cuffs as he headed for the door. "Oh, and Richards, I'll be riding very early in the morning. You won't be required."

"But, my lord—"

Declan turned and held up his hand. "I'm more than capable of dressing myself." With a sour look, his valet nodded and turned away.

Amused, Declan headed toward the dining room. Richards could be difficult, but at least he knew when to back down. Declan doubted the same could be said for Alex. From what he remembered, "giving up" wasn't in her vocabulary.

Alex slammed her brush against the polished wood of her dressing table, causing several crystal perfume bottles to dance. One flower-etched vial teetered on the edge, then crashed to the floor and shattered into a myriad of pieces.

Hell and damnation, was nothing going right today? She bent to gather the larger pieces, trying to avoid the sharp edges. At least it hadn't been the special vanilla fragrance she favored. She straightened and searched for a place to put the shards of glass.

Her cousin Eleanor burst into the bedroom. "What have you done?" The peach gown on her willowy form hung askew, her panniers having slipped off center. Small wisps of golden hair escaped the normally tidy bun.

Alex gave her childhood friend a rueful smile. "I knocked a bottle off my dresser. I'm afraid my room is going to smell like roses for the next week."

"That's not what I meant, and you know it." Eleanor

let out a long breath as she tried to straighten her panniers. "How could you? The household is in chaos. There's no telling what Lord Worthington will do now. You promised to at least sit down and discuss matters with him."

"Talking wouldn't have done any good." Alex placed the broken pieces on her dressing table, then searched her wardrobe for rags to mop up the mess. She found several, closed the door, and leaned back against the solid wood. "Lord Worthington's given name is Declan Deveraux."

Eleanor stopped her attempt to right her clothing and looked up. "Not *your* Declan."

"Yes." Alex knelt by the spill and selected a rag from the pile, then laid the others aside. Mindful that there might be glass remnants, she vigorously scrubbed the spot where the oil had soaked into the moss colored carpet.

"I'm sorry," Eleanor said softly. "Did your grandfather know how you felt about the man?"

Alex straightened and rested her backside on her heels. "He knew. I'd told him how Declan turned my father's men against me. I don't care if I was twelve. That didn't justify coercing Paddy into mixing laudanum in my tea so Declan could bring me here. My *guardian* took me away from the only home I'd ever known." Her throat felt tight. She wasn't sure she could bear her grandfather's betrayal on top of everything else.

Eleanor closed the door and turned toward her. "What happened in the library?"

She looked down at the outline of the spot, still visible amongst the pattern of the carpet. "I challenged him to a duel."

"Oh, Alex. Not again. It was bad enough that you tried to stab the man when you were twelve."

"I wasn't going to kill him. I simply needed to make it clear that he isn't wanted here."

"When will you learn that diplomacy is often the better

weapon."

Diplomacy? With Declan? Not bloody likely. She looked up at Eleanor who had restored her dignity and stood gazing at her with sorrowful blue eyes. "I had to do something." She returned to scouring the remainder of the spill.

Eleanor crossed the room, leaned down, and laid a hand on Alex's arm. "You should call a servant to take care of that."

If Grandfather were alive, he would have told her the same thing. Alex stopped and shut her eyes. She would give anything to hear the gentle chiding of his voice again. Wetness gathered in the corners of her eyes. She opened them and took a deep breath to gain control. Crying wouldn't solve anything.

She shrugged off Eleanor's hand, straightened, and snapped the used rag in the air with a force she hadn't intended. Her cousin backed up, attempting to avoid the spray. "The servants have other duties. They don't need to be cleaning up my mess." She dropped the rag to the floor and sighed. "You just don't understand."

Since her arrival here, her family had been unable to fathom her discomfort at having things done for her. But then again, her grandfather and cousin had been born to a life of privilege. She had not.

Over the years, the staff at Oakleigh had become accustomed to what they called her "uncivilized ways." In spite of that, she loved them. They were her life now—her responsibility. Fear trembled in her chest, making it hard to breathe. She could lose them, just as she'd lost the people she'd loved on *The Merry Elizabeth.*

She yanked a dry rag from the pile and continued cleaning. "It's 1783. God's teeth, at twenty I shouldn't be stuck with a guardian if I don't want one." With each word, she rubbed a little harder at the stain, ignoring her stinging hands. They wouldn't be lily-white, but there wasn't anyone she was endeavoring to impress. She paused and glanced at Eleanor. "Do you think he'd leave if I explained to him I'd been running the estate for Grandfather the last three years?"

"Even if you could convince him, what difference would that make?" Eleanor fidgeted with her pearl necklace, twisting the triple strands. "Alex, we've been over this again and again. You've spent hours pouring over your grandfather's will, and the answer is always the same. He left the estates and your care to Lord Worthington." Her cousin gave her a patient look. "You're going to have to find some way to get along with him."

"But the man is impossible." Alex stood, put the rags on the dressing table with the broken glass, and started to pace.

"Your grandfather knew what he was doing." Eleanor's voice held a note of conviction. "You must believe that."

Alex rolled her shoulders and glanced down. The last few weeks had not been kind to the Aubusson carpet. She'd worn a path from the dressing table to the bed. All those hours of worry, and she still didn't know what to do. If only she'd been some minor nobility, then she might have been overlooked. But as her estates were wealthy and extensive, there was no hope of that. "Damn Queen Elizabeth's dispensation."

"Stop swearing." Eleanor's automatic response made Alex gaze heavenward. Even at a time like this, her cousin worried about lady-like behavior.

"Without the queen's edict, I wouldn't be forced to marry." Alex shook her head. What good did it do to be the Countess of Lochsdale if she couldn't control her own life? "I'll wager Grandfather thought someone needed to approve my choice. That's why he appointed a guardian. As if I didn't have the sense to find a husband on my own."

"You don't really mean that. Without the dispensation,

you'd be at Luther's mercy." Eleanor hugged her arms to her body. Eyes wide, she whispered, "Imagine being in his power? I, for one, think it is fortunate Queen Elizabeth's decree was very specific that the title and lands could pass to a female, but only through direct descent. Since you're the only direct descendant left, it fell to you." She shivered. "Without her edict, who knows what might have happened."

"Luther's never forgiven me for being born." Alex gave a dry laugh. "The irony is, if I hadn't, everything might have reverted to the crown. King George would have decided on any claim made by Luther. I know there are whispers about the king's illness, but I doubt he'd allow Luther to inherit."

"Thank God."

"I don't need a guardian to choose whom I shall marry and when." She glanced at Eleanor. "Grandfather told me I could make the decision. After my dreadful Season in London, he realized I wasn't ready. I'm still not."

Alex sat on the edge of the bed and tried to keep the frustration out of her voice. "I'll find a husband, eventually, but right now I'm needed here. I can't go traipsing off to London. Even after months of dinner parties and balls during my first Season, I still hadn't met one lord I could respect, let alone love." She lay back on the counterpane with her hands behind her head. "Do you remember all those hopefuls falling over themselves at the ball we hosted?"

"Of course. Their ardor was quite comical. How many glasses of champagne did they bring you?" Her cousin smiled and settled beside her on the bed, fanning her skirts in a futile attempt to avoid wrinkles. "When you refused to choose a husband, I could feel the outrage in the room."

"I swear, if I hadn't promised Grandfather I'd behave, I would have challenged Lord Duprey at that ball." Alex sat up. "Did you know he kissed me?"

Her cousin's shocked expression made her want to laugh. Someday Eleanor would discover that not everyone lived by Society's rules.

"When?" Eleanor brought the tip of her fingers to her lower lip. "I thought you were well-chaperoned."

"I was, but I'd stepped out to the garden for some air, and he came up behind me. He's lucky I didn't have my dagger. If kissing is the reason men and women marry, it's most assuredly overrated."

Her cousin laughed, a joyous sound, so incongruous with the refined woman she presented to the world. "Maybe he's as poor at kissing as he is at everything else. As I recall, he only excelled in arrogance."

Alex got up, crossed to the dressing table, and tried to run a brush through her curls. Why couldn't she have Eleanor's wavy golden hair instead of auburn tresses that couldn't be tamed? Before she could do any more damage, Eleanor joined her and took the brush away.

"Here," Eleanor said, "sit at the dressing table. Be still. I can't arrange your hair if you keep fidgeting."

She tried not to move, gazed in the mirror, then stuck her tongue out at her reflection. "I wish I'd been born poor."

"Now if that isn't the most foolish thing I've ever heard you say. Most women would be thrilled with your station in life." Eleanor stopped the brush in mid-stroke. "What prompted this?"

"Thinking about the past." Alex rested her chin in her palm and caught Eleanor's gaze in the mirror. "On *The Merry Elizabeth*, it didn't matter what I looked like or who my family was. Now I constantly have to remind myself to act like a countess." She turned away and smoothed an imaginary wrinkle in the dresser scarf. "I guess I'm just missing the old days."

Eleanor's voice held amusement. "See, Lord Worthington did you a service. If you'd stayed on board ship, you never would have met me, and wouldn't that have been a shame?"

Grinning at Eleanor's reflection, Alex raised an eyebrow and tilted her head. "Do you mean to tell me you liked the snakes I put in your bed? I didn't even know I had a cousin. If you'll recall, I made a vow to hate you after we met."

"You hated a lot of things when you first arrived, but look how well it turned out." Eleanor patted a curl into place. "Why, I'll wager you've even become accustomed to those dresses we made you wear."

Alex joined in Eleanor's laughter. They both knew she wore her silk shirt and breeches whenever possible. She needed to fence and ride astride. Those activities made her feel truly alive, and they couldn't be done readily in dresses. Grandfather had understood, even if the rest of the world didn't. *God, she missed him.*

Eleanor tugged some curls loose around Alex's face and stepped back to admire her handiwork. "There, you look like a princess. Now all we have to do is pick out your dress for this evening." She crossed to Alex's wardrobe, opened the doors, and shook her head. "You really should have more dresses made." Eleanor studied the meager selection. "Why don't you wear the green silk? It looks so nice with your hair and eyes." She removed the gown and laid it on the bed.

"Fine." Alex didn't want to think about tonight, it made her head ache, but she couldn't think of anything else. If she didn't keep control of her estates, what would become of Eleanor and the others? They were her responsibility.

Did Declan think he could put in an appearance and usurp her place? This was her home. Not his. She'd kept the ledgers, instructed the servants, and decided on expenditures. He didn't know the first thing about Oakleigh Manor. Or her, for that matter, yet he would be allowed to choose her husband.

At best, he'd let her continue as before. At worst, he might force her into marriage with a man who could destroy the home she loved.

She couldn't let that happen. If rapiers hadn't worked, then she'd have to outmaneuver him another way.

To do that, she needed to study her enemy. Where had he been the last eight years? From the little information she'd gleaned, he'd kept to himself. In spite of this, or perhaps because of it, rumors of his exploits with women were legendary among the Ton. The gossipmongers in the *Gazette* were forever coming up with a new love interest for him, not that she believed anything in those columns.

Eleanor came up behind her, rested her hand on Alex's shoulder, then blurted out, "I hate to ask, but do you think you could curtail your riding and fencing while Lord Worthington's here? Maybe watch your language?" Her cousin's refined features appeared drawn. "It would be for your own good."

Alex stood and faced her. "You know me better than that. I'll not pretend for his benefit."

"It wouldn't be for his benefit. There's no need to make him think worse of you than he already does." Eleanor clutched her skirt in both hands, a sure sign she was upset.

Alex opened her mouth to respond, then realized the futility of trying to change her cousin's mind. They'd had this discussion many times before. People often mistook Eleanor's gentle nature for a weak will, but stubbornness ran in the family. She stepped forward and pried Eleanor's hands from her skirt, then clasped them in her own. "Stop worrying. Everything will be fine. I'll find a way."

A tremulous smile appeared on Eleanor's lips. "No one knows what changes Lord Worthington will make. All I ask is that you do your best to get along with him."

Her cousin seemed so forlorn, Alex didn't have the heart to argue any longer. "I'll try, but I can't promise anything."

Eleanor gave her a brief hug. "Things will work out, you'll see." She turned back before she reached the door. "If you'd like, I'll tell him you're resting till dinner."

"Actually, I'm not coming down for dinner this evening."

"Alex."

"I need some time to think things through. I promise, I won't continue to avoid him."

Eleanor sighed. "I'll tell him you're unwell. But sooner or later you're going to have to deal with him." Her cousin gave her a quick, sympathetic smile, then left.

Alex resumed pacing, reliving every moment she'd spent in Declan's company. He thought he had absolute power over her, but he was wrong. Somewhere, somehow, she'd discover the weapon that would prove most effective against him.

The wind whipped through Alex's hair, tangling her curls. They would take hours to comb out, but she didn't care. Right now, she wanted to feel the morning mist on her face and the power of her horse as they sped across the meadow.

Spears of sunlight filtered through the fog, promising a beautiful day. Why couldn't it have been gray and overcast to match her mood?

Dredging up memories of Declan had been painful and fruitless. She hadn't discovered a single weakness she could use to force his hand. The only surety was the bleak future that awaited her.

She'd been so confident yesterday, yet he'd defeated her easily. To make things worse, she'd walked straight into his arms. Her cheeks burned at the memory. Why couldn't she shake the feel of his arms around her, or her insane desire to explain how she felt? It's not as if he'd care. He'd probably laugh at her fears. Her hands tightened on the reins. Nothing made sense anymore.

At the edge of the meadow, she slowed, guiding Blade along the tree line at a trot. He sidestepped at the sound of an animal in the undergrowth, so she reached down to give him a reassuring pat. They were both a bit jittery this morning.

The quick rhythm of hooves pounding the earth drew her attention in the direction of the manor. A huge black stallion bore down on her. The rider, dressed in black, created the illusion that horse and man were one.

Declan.

With a sigh, Alex shoved aside a wayward curl that insisted on finding its way across her mouth. She really wasn't in the mood to match wits with him this morning, but it seemed he wasn't going to give her a choice.

She'd initiated the contest, now she had to live with the consequences. Grandfather had warned her about thinking things through before she acted. He was right.

As he drew closer, she could see Declan's scowl. She squared her shoulders and reined Blade to a standstill.

His stallion came to a halt several feet from her horse. "You weren't at dinner last night." His calm voice was at odds with the tension in his jaw. "We missed you."

Alex dropped her gaze. "I wasn't well." She toyed with the bracelet on her wrist, refusing to look up. Lying always showed on her face.

"May I ask what you're doing so far from the manor, alone, dressed like that?" He might have been asking how she liked the weather. His voice seemed conversational, pleasant.

She raised her head to meet his frosty blue gaze. "I'm riding, as I do every morning."

Declan's face became grim, and that damn twitch was back. He appeared upset, in spite of his casual tone. Why?

"I don't have to play the lady on my own estate." Alex swept the hair away from her face and held his gaze, refusing to back down from his regard. "And I prefer to ride alone."

Her solitary rides had never been a problem before. Not even her grandfather had feared for her on manor property. "If you're worried about me, don't be. I know this area.

Besides, I'm always armed." Alex patted her boot, drawing his attention to the hilt of her dagger, barely visible above her scuffed leather boots. "Nothing's going to happen on my own land." She turned her horse and started away from him.

"No!"

His pleasant facade snapped, like a ship ripped from its moorings by the wind. "I don't care what you have done in the past. From now on, someone will accompany you."

Her back stiffened. Was she to be a prisoner in her own home? In his present mood, she doubted Declan would be reasonable. Alex didn't want to argue with him, but it seemed inevitable, unless she left.

At a slight urging, Blade shot across the meadow. Where she went didn't matter, as long as it was away from *him*. They'd discuss what she could, or couldn't do, at another time.

Within moments, he was at her side, his stallion easily overtaking her mount. He hauled her off Blade's back and swung her around to face him. She tried to back away, but his arm locked around her, forcing her tightly against his chest. Alex managed to look up so she could breathe, and wished she hadn't.

Everything seemed different, more intense. The horse stopped, but anger, outrage, and anticipation spun thru her at an amazing pace. The moment hung in the air, like a gull in flight. Damp earth and heated horseflesh mixed with the smells of a new spring day. Declan's eyes reminded her of blue crystal under his thunderous black brows, yet it wasn't fear that made her search his gaze. There was something compelling in the way he looked at her.

His breath warmed her face, making wisps of her hair dance around her forehead, as his unyielding body pressed against her.

He leaned forward, his ice blue gaze narrowed. "This is what could happen." His mouth came down hard on hers.

At first, the pressure was painful. His hand tangled in the curls at the nape of her neck, holding her head immobile. Her whole body tensed, as she tried to twist away. Then, without warning, he softened the assault on her lips, until small sounds escaped from the back of her throat.

He still held her captive, but the seductive movement of his mouth against hers made her question her wish to be free. What was he doing to her?

Desire stabbed at Declan as he ran his palm against Alex's silky hair. Her soft moans vibrated against his lips, causing him to harden. The honeyed taste of her mouth blended with the scent of vanilla floating on the spring breeze.

He teased her lips with the barest of caresses, while he dropped his hand from her neck to her shoulders. Her body felt warm, soft, and he suspected her skin would feel smoother than the silk garment beneath his palm. The need to touch her without the thin barrier overwhelmed him.

While still exploring her mouth, he leaned back slightly and loosened her shirt from her pants. He shouldn't be doing this, she was his ward for God's sake, but his infamous control seemed to have taken this moment to desert him.

His movements freed her arms, which wrapped around his shoulders as if she would never let go. It was all the encouragement he needed. He wasted no time letting one of his hands wander under her shirt, while the other caressed the back of her neck. He could feel the firmness of her flesh as it stretched over her ribs, sloping to the curve of her waist.

Her hands kneaded his shoulders, and the leather saddle creaked as she tried to draw him closer.

His fingertips slipped upward over silken skin until he cupped one full breast. Thank God her manly attire allowed such easy access. His thumb and forefinger gently tugged on the hardening tip.

With an indrawn breath, she jerked backward, breaking

the kiss. She stared at him, her eyes huge, then twisted back and forth, trying to free herself from his grasp. Unfortunately, she only succeeded in thrusting the lower part of their bodies closer together.

Declan bit his lip, his arousal almost painful where it rubbed against her. He grabbed her wrist, then lowered her arm between them, noting her rapid pulse under his fingertips.

Shaken, he removed his other hand from under her shirt, then raked it through his hair. She had every right to be upset, but he wouldn't apologize. If he had been a highwayman intent on rape, the consequences would have been much worse.

"We must be making progress." Declan tightened his hold on her wrist when she tried to break away. "At least you didn't reach for your dagger."

"Let go of me." Alex tried to pry his fingers loose. Her eyes wild, she reminded him of a hare he'd seen once, trapped by a pack of hunting dogs.

"You're despicable. Why can't you leave me alone?" Alex stopped struggling, but bitterness edged her voice. "Of course, if you left, the courts would find another guardian." She gave a laugh devoid of joy. "I'm sure my cousin Luther, Viscount Addington, would volunteer. Even you're preferable to him."

He felt her shudder. "Well, I'm glad to know I'm not last on your list." Before she could guess his intent, he reached over, removed her dagger, then slipped it in his boot, next to his own. "Just in case," he remarked, and let go of her wrist.

Freed, she scrambled from his horse, as if pursued by wolves. She whistled to Blade, who grazed nearby, then jumped into her saddle and wheeled around to face him.

"Alex, listen to me," Declan said. "It's not safe for you to be riding astride dressed like that. For your own sake, I'm asking you to reconsider. A lady wouldn't act this way."

"You want me to act like a lady?" Alex tossed her curls, the sun picking out the copper highlights. "Then I suggest you start acting like a gentleman." A slight tug on Blade's reins, and they were off, racing back toward the manor.

He let her go. She was right. What had possessed him to practically attack her? The women he knew in London considered him a devil because he wouldn't allow himself to become enamored of them.

He'd never met a "Lady" he liked, until now. Why couldn't Alex act like the other women of his experience? He'd found the Ladies of the Ton tedious, at best. They were all the same, interested in fashion, gossip, and what male they could catch in the matrimonial noose. If it weren't for his damn title, he'd happily settle for the occasional mistress, and avoid married bliss.

In trying to teach his ward a lesson, he'd learned one. She was too much of a temptation to have around. Aside from Alex's beauty, he admired her spirit and determination. If this kept up, he might actually come to like her. God forbid.

A mental picture of his mother's portrait came to mind. He squeezed his eyes shut, trying to eradicate the memory. No matter how appealing he found Alex, he would not fall prey to his father's sin.

He shook his head, then turned Knight back toward the manor. The only solution was to marry Alex off quickly. She wasn't going to like his decision. Thank heavens the little hoyden didn't know she had weapons that would be much more effective than her dagger.

Chapter 3

Alex leapt off Blade's back before the horse had come to a halt, then flung the reins at John. The propensity of the groom's straw-colored hair to stick straight up exaggerated the look of surprise on his face.

"You'll not be rubbin' Blade down?" John's mouth hung open. "But ya always..."

"Not today," Alex called over her shoulder as she headed toward the gardens. She lengthened her strides on the well-worn paths edged in boxwood. Spring flowers, not yet in bloom, created a haze of new green everywhere she looked, but she didn't stop to admire the beauty her mother had designed.

Her dismal thoughts were like the tangled climbing roses whose barren abundance overwhelmed the statue of Pan looming before her. Alex crossed to a stone bench at Pan's feet, sat down, and hugged her arms to her chest.

What the hell was she going to do? Her face grew warm remembering how her arms had brazenly encircled Declan. She had wanted his kiss, relished it.

Bringing her hand to her lips, she felt the tenderness and swelling that were physical proof of her wantonness. Why had she responded to him like that? Lord Duprey's kiss had been a mere parody of what she'd felt when Declan had kissed her. How did she expect to gain control of her life, if she couldn't even control her emotions? She had to find a way to convince Declan to return to London and leave her in peace.

As if her thoughts conjured him, Declan appeared,

silent, like some dark spirit, intent on destroying her world.

Every muscle in her body tensed. He hadn't given her time to come up with a plan.

He just stood there, looking at her. She kept her gaze riveted on him. Handsome, detached, untouchable: all those descriptions fit.

"What do you want?"

He raised one finely arched black brow and inclined his head. "We never finished our conversation."

"Maybe you didn't." She clasped her hands in her lap, trying to show composure she didn't feel. "I have nothing further to say."

He crossed to the bench. "May I sit?"

She didn't want him that close, but he'd do what he wanted anyway. "As you wish." She moved as far from him as possible. His smirk told her he'd noticed.

He pinned her with his gaze. "About the kiss."

She looked down. "We don't need to discuss that." Her voice sounded strained. "You made your point." Her errant hair insisted on blowing across her face, so she tucked it behind one ear with a sharp movement.

The silence stretched between them like a solid entity. She could hear the wind in the rose canes overhead, the dry rustle fraying her nerves. Why was he bothering her if he wasn't going to talk?

Alex focused on the dirt she'd just discovered under her thumbnail. "What did you want?"

"Look at me."

She scraped at the offending soil with her index finger.

Declan slid across the distance between them and grasped her chin with his fingers. She resisted, but he gently brought her around to face him.

"You and I seem to differ on how you should live your life." She started to interrupt, but he held up a hand to stop her. "As we can't agree, I suggest we find someone else to watch over you."

Her sentiments exactly. Would he really just return to London, and she'd never hear from him again? Damn the sinking feeling in her stomach. This is what she wanted, wasn't it? Alex clenched her fists. "I can take care of myself."

He gave her a tolerant smile, disbelief evident on his handsome face.

She took a deep breath. "If *you* think this is best, may I at least choose who controls my life?" There were several friends of her grandfather's she could ask, maybe Lord Ellington. She liked him.

"That's exactly what I had in mind. I'm glad you're going to be agreeable." Declan's genuine smile momentarily made her forget what they were discussing.

He stood and walked away, but he'd gone only a few paces before turning back to her. "I imagine we could leave for London in a week or two. I still have a few things to clear up here.

"London?" Alex shook her head, all at once suspecting she'd missed something. "We don't need to go to London to find a replacement."

"For your grandfather's sake, I want you to have many men to choose from." He gave her a wry smile. "I have to admit, I'd like you to make your selection and marry as soon as possible, but I realize these things take time."

"Marry?" Alex couldn't believe what she was hearing.

"It will be the height of the Season, so choosing a husband shouldn't be too difficult." Declan shrugged. "I'm sure you'll find someone to your liking."

The man was daft. "I'll not do this!"

Declan seemed perplexed, then his brow cleared in understanding. "Ah, you're afraid you are too old." He studied her with an assessing gaze. She wasn't sure, but she thought she saw admiration on his face.

Abruptly he turned from her, his voice strange, deeper

than before. "I don't think you need worry about your age. Most men will find you attractive enough."

Clearly, he wasn't one of them. Alex bristled, forcing her voice to remain calm, despite the stab of hurt. "I'm going to say this again, so even *you* can understand. I don't wish to marry, at least not now. You can't force me." She reached for her dagger, only to remember he had it.

He raked his fingers through his hair. "You will obey me in this, Alexandra. It's the best solution to an intolerable situation." He strode to the bench, towering over her. "Aside from the guardianship, I won a wager in which you agreed to follow my wishes." He held her gaze, the assurance in his voice scraping up her spine like the tip of a knife. "Have you forgotten?"

Worthington was a snake to bring that up now. Alex held his gaze and kept her voice steady. "I honor my wagers."

"Good, then you will go inside, get into some decent clothing, and start to plan what you'll need for our trip. We'll leave in a fortnight."

Alex rose to her feet. She felt dwarfed by his size, but refused to be intimidated. "As you wish, *my lord*." She turned on her heel, and strode back toward the manor. Once out of sight, she broke into a run.

A resounding thud filled the air as Alex threw the front door open with enough force to hit the wall. She headed for the stairs, taking them two at a time. Eleanor came out of her room, a startled expression on her face. Alex gave her a stiff smile, then headed for the sanctuary of her bedroom.

Her insufferable guardian dared to bring up the wager. She paced between the dressing table and bed, her arms crossed. Marriage was not the answer. What had given him that ridiculous notion?

The door opened, and Eleanor stuck her head in. "Are

you all right?"

"No, I'm not all right. Nothing will ever be all right again." She realized she was shouting and lowered her voice. "That, that man wants to marry me off."

Eleanor entered the room and shut the door behind her. "We discussed this. You knew it was a possibility." She settled in the window seat and smoothed her violet gown. "Stop pacing. Wearing out the rug won't help."

Alex sighed and curled up, feet under her, in the spot next to her cousin. "What am I going to do about him?" She turned her diamond bracelet around her wrist. The gems sparkled as they caught the light.

"It's not so bad," Eleanor sighed, her face pinched with worry in spite of her assurance. "You've always managed to come up with a solution. You will this time, too."

"I hope so. Last time I crossed Lord Worthington, I lost everything, my home and the people I held dear. I thought I'd never be happy again, then I met Grandfather." Her lips turned upward in a slight smile. "It took a while for me to realize how much he loved me. In spite of everything I did, he never gave up." Alex clasped Eleanor's hands in hers. "You both made me feel part of a family. I'll not lose you as well!"

"Don't be silly." Eleanor grinned. "I'm not that easy to get rid of."

Alex squeezed Eleanor's hands. "I'm not going to let Lord Worthington do this to me. A husband would expect me to always behave like a lady. Can you imagine, never wearing breeches again?"

Eleanor raised an eyebrow. "If you recall—"

"Regardless. My guardian would be condemning me to a life of pretending. I could live with that, if I had to, but what would happen here?"

"We'd survive." Eleanor gently broke their clasped hands and leaned back against the casing. "Stop worrying about us. Besides, it would be in your future husband's best interest to take care of things here."

Alex shook her head. "If a man doesn't love his wife, he does what he thinks is right, regardless of her wishes. He might decide to send you away, or Edgar, or Berta. I wouldn't have the power to stop him."

"What makes you think your husband wouldn't love you?"

Alex's face grew warm. True, it wasn't impossible. She might someday find a man to love her. "Who's going to fall in love with me right away? Remember London? I spent a whole Season and didn't find anyone."

Of course, she hadn't really tried. It had seemed pointless. Not one of them would have accepted her if they'd known she favored breeches and could run an estate. They wanted women with dowries who would produce heirs, nothing more. None of them would have been able to best her in fencing, let alone accept her challenge, the way Declan had. She stood up and resumed her pacing. "No. I can't risk a hurried marriage, but how in the hell am I going to convince my guardian?"

Alex tugged at the uncooperative bodice of her green silk gown and sighed. *I hope Eleanor's right*. She squirmed again, trying to tease the scanty material over her breasts. This whole idea was ridiculous, but she'd promised. Her cousin's words still rang in her ears.

"You've let him see nothing but your temper. Of course he wants to be rid of you as soon as possible, wouldn't you? Try being nice to him for a change. If you're friendlier, he might even relent and allow you to go your own way."

"Being nice" in Eleanor's mind implied doing exactly what Declan asked. Well, she was wearing a dress, at his request. Maybe now he'd stop acting like she was a problem to be solved.

She remembered the day Grandfather had given her the elegant gown. He'd winked at her and stated that if it didn't bring the young bucks round, nothing could. What would Declan think of it? Not that it mattered. Right now, she wanted his cooperation, nothing more.

Smoothing the silk one last time, she squared her shoulders and left the room. As luck would have it, when she reached the stairs, Declan stood at the bottom, ready to ascend. Dressed for dinner, his impeccable appearance was marred only by the black lock of hair that tumbled over his forehead.

He brushed it back with a practiced motion, looked up, then froze. For an instant, Alex thought she read surprise and desire in his eyes. Just the possibility boosted her confidence.

Smiling, she descended the stairs and inclined her head in his direction. Before she passed him, Declan stopped her. His voice sounded deeper, somewhat uneven.

"I was coming to get you." His gaze skimmed her figure. "You need to eat. I'll not have you starve because of your dislike for me."

Her smile faltered. He didn't mention her appearance, and how dare he imply she was too thin. She wanted to tell him she didn't find him attractive either, even though it was a lie, but Eleanor's words echoed like a litany in her brain. *Be nice. Be nice.*

Alex forced what she hoped was a smile to her lips. "Whatever gave you the idea I dislike you?"

"Oh, I don't know. Perhaps it's because you keep trying to stick me with sharp objects."

"Grandfather used to tell me I was impulsive. I'm afraid he was right. It's not you, but the situation, I find abhorrent." Alex extended her hand. "Shall we?"

He hesitated, then turned and offered her his arm.

They said nothing on the way to the dining room, but he glanced her way more than once with a puzzled frown. Declan seated her across from Eleanor before taking her grandfather's place at the head of the table.

Alex couldn't believe she actually enjoyed dinner. Declan did most of the talking, and underneath the arrogant male demeanor she found a sense of humor. He regaled them with several stories concerning things he'd done as a youth; most of his tales involved his unsuspecting governess, but a few concerned her grandfather's butler.

She remembered Beal as a surly old man. He'd left her grandfather's employ shortly after she arrived. She'd been glad to see him go.

A shiver of fear touched her as Declan described how he'd managed to climb the steep roof of the manor in the dead of night. Picturing the twelve-year-old dangling a makeshift ghost in front of Beal's window, she couldn't resist a smile.

He must have scared the staid butler half to death. It served Beal right for always being so unpleasant.

So, Declan had grown up in the area. If he'd truly been that close with her grandfather, then perhaps Berta knew him. The gentle old woman had been her grandfather's *friend* ever since Alex could remember.

Shame and remorse washed over Alex. She'd briefly spoken to Berta at the funeral, but she should have gone to see her before now. She just hadn't been able to face the older woman. A lump formed in her throat, and she swallowed in an attempt to ease the tension. How much had changed since she'd last seen the twinkle in Berta's watery blue eyes.

She'd visit her tomorrow. If her adopted grandmother knew Declan, she might know why her grandfather had made him her guardian. Somehow, Berta always seemed to find a solution to life's problems; maybe *she'd* know what to do about Lord Worthington.

What was she up to? Pondering the question, Declan stretched his large form in the leather chair.

He'd been at the ledgers since six that morning. Thank God, Lord Lochsdale had been meticulous about all things pertaining to his estates. It wasn't at all like the shambles his own estates had been in when his father died.

He rose and opened a set of the French doors along one wall, then leaned against the frame with his shoulder. The Lady Alexandra of last night was more of a mystery than his rapier-welding hoyden. What did she hope to gain? He preferred her frontal attack. Charming females were dangerous.

Cool air flowed through the doors, molding the shirt to his chest. He closed his eyes and heard the heartbeat of the estate in the rhythmic pounding of the blacksmith. The noise outside didn't quite mask the rustle of material or click of high-heeled shoes as someone entered the library behind him.

Declan spun around and slipped his knife from its sheath. An unannounced guest didn't bode well in this manor if yesterday was any measure. The intruder was a man, dressed in the peacock fashion and wig affected by the Macaronis. His powdered face and elaborate finery enhanced his almost feminine beauty. One moon-shaped patch graced the corner of his hard-set mouth.

His visitor couldn't have expected Declan to have a weapon, yet no emotion glimmered in his cold, light-blue eyes. A man with that much control usually had something to hide. Declan tightened the grip on his weapon.

"Lord Worthington? I'm—"

"I'm sorry, my lord." The butler burst into the room, giving the intruder a reproving look. "I tried to stop him. I told Lord Addington you were occupied with accounts, but he insisted on seeing you."

"It's all right, Edgar." Declan lowered his blade and

positioned himself behind the ornate mahogany desk. "I don't mind the interruption. I'll ring if I need you."

The *peacock* gave the retreating butler a disdainful glance before he turned back to the conversation. "I'm sorry to disturb you, my lord. I'm Luther Fenton, Viscount Addington. Alex's second cousin, perhaps she's spoken of me?"

"Actually, she did mention you." *Even you're preferable to him.* Now he understood Alex's comment. He laid the dagger on the desk between them. "She seems to have some rather strong feelings for you."

Surprise flashed briefly in Addington's eyes. "Alex and I have always been close, though she may try to deny it. She isn't comfortable sharing her feelings with everyone." He lowered his voice and moved closer to the desk. "I've come to set your mind at ease concerning her welfare."

"Really." The man lied well. If Alex hadn't made that passing remark yesterday, Declan might have believed him. He took a seat and motioned for his guest to do the same. "I wasn't aware of any concerns."

"Perhaps I've been misinformed." Addington turned his hands palm upward and shrugged. "My sources indicated you were reluctant to become her guardian." He paused and gave Declan an inquiring look.

Declan merely met the man's gaze. The silence grew until he could hear the wind whispering through the curtains.

Addington appeared disconcerted, but continued. "Her future has been taken care of. There was an agreement between Lord Lochsdale and myself. Alex and I are to marry."

"It's odd Lord Lochsdale didn't make you guardian in my stead."

"It was only recently decided on. I'm sure he would have changed the will had he not died suddenly."

"Was she aware of the arrangement?"

"No, we felt it best if I won her over to the idea." He rested his hands on the chair arms and leaned forward, his voice edged with contempt. "For a woman, she seems to have a mind of her own."

That was the Alex he knew. She'd never agree to marry this popinjay.

"Do you have a written contract?"

"No, the agreement was verbal." Addington's lace cuff swayed as he extended one thin white hand. "We're reasonable men, my lord. I'm sure you have pressing matters in London."

With steepled fingers, he watched his guest, pursing his lips as if he were actually considering the man's claim. Lord Lochsdale would never have agreed to this match. He'd loved his granddaughter too much to marry her off to someone like Addington.

His visitor brushed an imaginary speck of lint from his blue embroidered waistcoat. "If it's agreeable, I'll go over affairs here and send you a full report. I imagine the marriage will take place quickly, and you'll be done with the whole affair."

Declan sat back in the desk chair. "I appreciate the offer Lord Addington, but as it happens, I have a fortnight before I need to return to London. If I remember correctly, the hunting in this area is exceptional. I thought to avail myself of the sport. Would you care to accompany me?"

"I'd be delighted." Addington produced an enameled snuffbox, then extended it toward Declan.

"No, thank you." How the habit had become fashionable, he'd never understand. "Shall we meet here tomorrow morning?" If Declan wasn't mistaken, he'd just made an enemy.

"That would be agreeable." Addington took a pinch of

snuff and returned the box to his pocket.

Declan stood and came around the desk. "Now if you'll excuse me," he said, folding his arms and leaning back against the desk edge, "I have a great many papers to go over."

Addington looked as if he wanted to ask something, but instead, he rose and walked to the door.

Before he left, Declan spoke, "Just one more thing. Regarding the Countess of Lochsdale, I'm afraid I promised the poor girl a Season in London with the express purpose of finding a husband." Declan would love to see Alex's reaction if she found out he'd called her a *poor girl*. "Of course, as you've been developing a fondness between you, I'm sure you'll be her choice."

Addington no longer appeared quite as accommodating. He gave a curt nod. "As you wish. Until tomorrow, my lord."

Luther Fenton, Viscount Addington, closed the door with care, although the urge to slam it almost overwhelmed him. The hall appeared empty, so he lovingly ran his hand over the smooth top of a Chippendale table, smearing the polished wood surface. This would be his, just as it should have been.

He glanced in the hall mirror and studied his reflection. *He looked like the lord of the manor.* A spot on his coat drew his attention. He brushed at the white patch with his fingertips, then adjusted his cravat. A Season in London would stretch his resources, but perhaps it wouldn't be necessary.

Sad, how many hunting accidents occurred each year. The earl would just be one of many. Tomorrow morning didn't leave him much time. It wasn't going to be easy, not like the others.

The initial meeting hadn't gone well, but the game

wasn't over yet. Luther felt like skipping down the front steps. He perused the well-tended estate and smiled at the black storm clouds gathering overhead. He truly did love a challenge.

Chapter 4

Alex lifted a sapphire-blue dress from the chest in her mother's bedroom. The silk, as soft and elusive at the memories it evoked, slipped through her fingers. Her mind grasped at the hazy childhood remembrance.

Wracked with fever, her mother had worn the gown as she lay on the bunk in her cabin. Alex hadn't been able to do anything but wait and watch as the forbidding shadows of evening threatened to steal her mother's life.

A small candle burned, mixing the smell of tar with tallow. The flame, sputtering with the sway of the lantern, barely illuminated her mother's sweat-sheened face. Her slight body thrashed in a way that had nothing to do with the storm beating at the ship.

Mother had called her name, over and over. Alex had tried to tell her she was there. She'd gripped her mother's frail hand in her pudgy round one and held on until...

"Alex!" Declan knocked louder. He would not be ignored. In spite of the storm wailing outside, his knocking drew servants from all parts of the house, though they all pretended to be busy with duties.

"If you don't answer this door, I'm coming in." Declan waited for several moments, then threw himself against the wooden timbers. The fastening mechanism snapped and the door swung inward. He glared at the servants' shocked faces, then crossed the threshold and closed the door behind him.

Even with the dimness of the room, he spotted her immediately, seated on the floor, surrounded by masses of colored silk gowns. She gripped the edge of a trunk, her head resting on her hands. He couldn't see her face; her glorious hair shielded it from view. Why didn't she acknowledge his presence?

He crossed the room in several long strides and bent down to take her shoulder. "Alex."

She started, turned, then looked up at him. "Lord Worthington, I didn't hear you come in."

"I knocked. Actually, I did more than that. If you check outside, I believe the entire staff came running." He reached down and touched the wet trail of a tear as it made its way over her cheek. "Crying?"

Alex brushed at her face with the back of her hand. "Dust." She stood, using the trunk for support, and squared her shoulders before looking at him. "We rarely use this room. I'll have to speak with the maids."

She bent and plucked a forest green gown from the pile, then crossed to the dressing table mirror. The garment slipped from her grasp several times before she managed to hold it up to check the fit.

The plain design of the gown didn't hold with the current fashion, but the style suited Alex. The powder, frills, and patches of the day would only detract from her beauty. His ward's vibrancy came from within. She didn't need jewels or lace.

"It would look lovely on you, but I didn't think you cared for gowns." Declan waited for a sharp retort.

"This was my mother's favorite." Alex crossed to the bed and laid the gown across the end with care, the taffeta rustling as she smoothed the wrinkles. "I decided to see if I could make due with any of these in London."

She fidgeted with the sleeves for long moments before turning to face him. "I'm certain you didn't search me out to discuss dresses." She gave him a smile that was a bit too bright and cheery. "Is there something I can help you with?"

He wished she'd stop trying to be charming. It didn't

suit her. "Did you know about a long-term betrothal between you and Lord Addington?"

Alex blanched.

"He arrived a few minutes ago to inform me of your upcoming nuptials."

"You didn't believe him!" She turned away, and began to pace the small space between the bed and dressing table. "Bloody hell, I knew he was underhanded, but this?" Alex paused for a moment. "He'd need it in writing. Grandfather would never have signed anything like that without telling me." She glanced his way. "You didn't agree to anything, did you?"

He was tempted to tell her he'd given her to the man with his blessings. For some reason, it bothered him that she didn't have any faith in his ability to discern Addington's motives. "It may come as a surprise to you, but my acquaintances consider me a careful man. I agree, your grandfather would not have encouraged the match, but Addington could cause trouble."

"That's all he's ever caused." Alex's pacing increased. "As a young man, he used to be more careful." She stopped and faced him, holding out her wrist to reveal a glittering diamond bracelet.

"See this. It's really a collar." Alex's voice softened. "It belonged to a long-haired white cat I called Misty. Grandfather gave her to me. I don't suppose you would know what an animal can mean to someone who feels lost and alone in the world." Alex fingered the band gently and went to sit on the edge of the bed.

His father had never allowed him to have a pet, but he understood loneliness. He'd learned to deal with it over the years. How much harder it must have been for Alex to cope after being part of a loving family.

"Misty got along well with everyone," Alex said, holding his gaze, her smile brittle, "except Luther. She hated him and would do everything she could to keep him away from me. Because of that, my cousin tormented her."

Alex lost any hint of a smile. "Late one afternoon I went to the stable where she often took a nap. Before I reached the entrance, I heard a terrible cry. By the time I'd arrived, she was...dead." Alex slid her hands down the tops of her thighs, clutching the day gown's thin material just above the knees. "Her neck had been broken."

She turned away, the gathering silence making him wish he'd not sought her out. He'd never comforted a woman before. Hell, he couldn't recall anyone ever looking to him for solace.

At last, she stood and went to the window, arms crossed, right hand rubbing up and down her upper arm. "I could never prove Luther did it, but I know he did." Bitterness etched her voice as she turned to stare at him. "I understand he's gone on to tormenting people. The servants are afraid of him, with good reason."

Anger coursed through Declan's veins. He wished he could right the wrong somehow, but it was an old wound.

He crossed to her and laid his hand on top of hers. She stilled at his touch and glanced down at the point where they were joined, then met his gaze. Anger replaced the vulnerability in her expression. She broke free, sidled past him, and returned to the trunk.

Alex hated that look in his eyes. She didn't need his pity. She hauled the remaining gowns from the trunk with rapid, jerky movements and piled them on the bed. Being nice to her guardian didn't mean she had to tell him about her past.

Damn Luther anyway.

If Declan felt he had to protect her, he'd never let her be. He may be insufferable, but he'd defend her, if for no other reason than his love for her grandfather. Loyalty, in this case, would definitely prove inconvenient.

She turned to see him watching her, a slight frown causing furrows between his dark brows. Stiffening her spine, she marched across the room and stopped within a foot of him. It was disconcerting to have to crane her neck to look up at him, but she held his attention with as direct a stare as she could muster.

Standing this close, she could see the fine laugh lines at the corners of his eyes. His nearness disturbed her, but she wanted him to take what she had to say seriously. "Don't worry, Lord Worthington. I can handle Luther. Death would be preferable to being married to him, and I enjoy living. I'd appreciate it if you'd decline his kind offer."

"I'm afraid I can't do that. I've already agreed to his calling on you."

"What?" Outside lightning flashed, immediately followed by a crack of thunder. She stepped back. Cold fear washed over her. How could he do this? Couldn't he see what Luther was?

"Lady Lochsdale, it's always a good idea to keep your enemy close." Declan had the audacity to smile. "You'll keep him off balance if you pretend friendship."

She almost choked.

Was this his way of telling her he knew what she was doing? Fidgeting with her bracelet, she refused to look him in the eye.

"Promise me you'll be courteous." He stepped toward her and tipped her face up to look at him. "Don't worry, I'd never allow him to hurt you. Addington and I are going hunting in the morning. I'll learn more of his plans then."

Declan pushed a lock of hair away from her face, hovering just a moment longer than necessary. The small space between them seemed more charged than the wild beat of the storm outside. Another moment, and she'd be burned like a tree scorched by lightning.

She backed away. "I'll be courteous, but no more."

"That's all I ask." Declan headed for the door.

"Lord Worthington?"

He paused, looking back over his shoulder.

"Be careful," she said. "I don't want anyone putting holes in that skin of yours, unless it's me of course."

He gave her a sudden grin, and was gone. She didn't need a guardian, but she wouldn't want anything to happen to him. Anyone who got in Luther's way tended to get hurt, and Declan was in the way.

Chapter 5

"Berta, he's forcing me to marry." Alex looked down from Blade's back into the calm face of the older woman. Her wispy white hair and lined face spoke of age, but her eyes were lively, active, and not the least surprised by Alex's news.

Getting to her feet, Berta threw a handful of weeds onto the pile at the end of her garden and wiped her hands on her apron. "You'll be staying for a cup of tea. It's been ages since we've had a chat. Not since..."

Ageless blue eyes met hers and mirrored the same pain. Alex suspected Berta and her grandfather had been closer than what society would have deemed proper. They'd never married, but Alex thought of her as a surrogate grandmother.

She dismounted and allowed Blade to graze, then followed Berta up a stone path interspersed with velvety moss. It led to a small, whitewashed cottage, nestled in a grove of pines.

As she crossed the threshold, familiar smells assailed her: dried herbs, wood-smoke, and over it all, the scent of wool. Piles were mounded in the corner to be carded and made into the shawls Berta was famous for. They were comfortable smells. For the first time in several weeks, Alex began to relax. Why hadn't she come sooner?

"Have a seat." Berta bustled around, filled the kettle with water, and hung it over the fire. She put loose tea in a flowered teapot, then came over and sat across from Alex. "The townsfolk say there have been a few changes up at the manor."

Words tumbled out, and Berta let her ramble on. Listening seemed to be what Berta did best. Maybe that's why so many people brought her their problems. Alex told her everything. Well, almost everything. She left out the kiss. That was her secret.

"So, Lord Addington's staking his claim at last. I wondered how long it would take." Berta got up, brewed the tea, then carried two steaming mugs back to the scarred wooden table. She set one in front of Alex, and resumed her seat.

"You knew he'd try this?"

"No, but he's been after you, or rather the manor, for years. His title came to him from an impoverished estate on his mother's side. He and your grandfather had many disagreements, as Lord Addington considered Oakleigh Manor to be his inheritance." Berta put sugar in her tea and stirred it thoughtfully. "The crown allows the title and estates to go to you. Few women are that lucky." Berta paused a moment, looking at Alex intently. "You *do* realize you must marry quickly."

"Why does everyone keep insisting I marry?" Berta had been her last hope. No one seemed to understand she was waiting for someone to share her life. They thought of marriage as a duty, but it was a decision that could make her miserable for the rest of her days.

Her grandfather had never pushed her to marry after that disastrous Season in London. He'd made her feel as if she'd had all the time in the world to settle down.

He was wrong.

"Why didn't Grandfather encourage me to marry sooner if he knew Luther was a threat?"

Berta sighed and sat back in her chair. "We all have a little selfishness in us. He just wasn't ready to lose you. He'd already lost your mother, and when you refused to marry, he was content to have you by his side." Berta patted Alex's hand. "Refusing to see the extent of Luther's ambition was a mistake. I suspect your grandfather thought you'd meet someone eventually."

Alex sat back in her chair. Her body felt oddly numb. All these years she had fought to choose her own destiny. She had decided early on to marry only when she found someone she could respect. She'd wanted a love like her parents. Now what was she to do? There wasn't a single man of her acquaintance she'd even consider.

Berta gave her a concerned look. "Lord Addington is going to continue his little games." The elderly woman dropped her gaze and fidgeted with her spoon, staring into her cup as if seeking answers. At last she met Alex's eyes. "You...please be careful. I've heard things about Addington. I feel better knowing your guardian is at the manor."

"Don't worry, Berta. I can take care of myself." Alex got up, went around to the older woman, and bent down to give her a hug.

"There now, child," Berta murmured. "Everything will be fine, you'll see." She patted Alex's back like she used to do when Alex was a young girl. "I hate to see you go all the way to London to find a husband. They tell me your guardian's a handsome devil. What about him?"

Alex broke the embrace and straightened. "He won't do at all."

"Why not? I remember him as a pleasant young man. Your grandfather spent a great deal of time with him after your mother left. He thought very highly of the boy."

"Obviously. But, boys grow into men." She strode to the window, and stared out at nothing in particular. "Oakleigh Manor and its people are my responsibility. My husband must let me care for them."

If she couldn't have love, then her future happiness hinged on marrying a man who would allow her to control her own life. "You've not met Lord Worthington. I can assure you, he'd never let me do as I please." She turned back to Berta. "Besides, he's already expressed a desire to marry me off as quickly as possible."

Was that a trace of disappointment in her voice? "It's getting late. I should go." She crossed to the old woman and gave her a quick peck on the cheek.

"Remember what I said," Berta admonished as she saw her to the door. "Watch yourself around Addington." She placed a dry, roughened palm against Alex's cheek. "I know you don't want a husband dearie, but it wouldn't be such a trial, if you found a man you could love."

Alex headed down the path. *What did love have to do with anything? She needed a man who would leave her alone.*

The last pink had just faded from the morning sky when Alex followed Declan and the others from the mews. Staying out of sight, she kept to the trees, until the small party came to a meadow a few miles from the manor.

She was spying. It was wrong, but maybe in this case, God would forgive her. Declan didn't know Luther the way she did. Her cousin could tell her guardian anything in order to get what he wanted. Although, Declan didn't seem much inclined to fall in with Luther's plan—whatever it was—judging from his aloof expression.

If only she could hear what they were saying, but they'd chosen a spot near the middle of the clearing. Keeping to the edge of the woods, she watched as most of the men tried to calm their respective falcons. Only Declan and his bird sat perfectly still. No doubt the animal felt the same mesmerizing compulsion she did in his presence.

The primal lure of the beautiful birds surrounded her. So delicate in appearance, yet she'd seen the scars the falconer bore from the talons of his beloved charges.

Unlike guns, this form of hunting appealed to her. It held a quiet dignity. Man and bird worked together in the age-old cycle of life and death.

The head falconer passed between Declan and Luther, giving them instructions Alex couldn't hear, stopping here and there to adjust the hoods on some of the other birds.

Declan let his falcon fly first. There was great beauty in the way it floated on the wind. She watched it soar, higher and higher. Very soon it would plummet to earth, breaking the back of its helpless prey. She never liked to watch the kill, so she focused on the forest nearby.

Sunlight glinted off something metallic not fifty feet from where she sat. There weren't any paths in that area, so it couldn't be a horse's bridle. She watched intently for several minutes, but saw nothing.

Nerves.

She was about to give up, when a shadowy figure stepped from behind an oak, raised what appeared to be a gun, and took aim directly at Declan.

Fear sliced through her. She shouted to get the attacker's attention and urged Blade forward. He plunged out into the open, angling in front of the small hunting party. With luck, she'd block the assailant's view of her guardian. A shot reverberated in the crisp air as she approached.

A sharp sting blossomed in her right arm. Every moment slowed, as if she needed to memorize events. Blade reared. She struggled not to lose her seat, her left arm straining as she yanked on Blade's reins. Declan raced passed her, placing himself between her and the would-be assassin, his gaze sweeping the horizon. The others seemed frozen, their faces twisted into various forms of surprise.

At last, Blade quieted, though he still quivered beneath her. The right sleeve of her shirt felt damp. She looked down at the red seeping into the white silk—so much blood.

Riders approached. She dropped her reins to place her hand over the wound, and through the pain, the men's voices seemed muffled, almost as if they spoke a foreign language. Then she heard nothing at all as darkness engulfed her.

Chapter 6

Alex's mouth tasted like cotton. What had she eaten last night? She threw off her coverlet and tried to rise, but the throbbing in her arm went from an annoyance to shooting pain.

She fell back and stared at a dark speck on the ceiling. Memory came rushing back, followed by panic. *My sword arm.* Alex glanced at the bandages on her upper arm. With cautious movements, she tried to roll her shoulder. It hurt like hell. With her good arm, she drew the covers to her chin and returned to staring at the ceiling. How long had she been asleep?

"Don't worry, you'll live to fence again."

Alex's gaze jerked toward the foot of the bed, where she met Declan's turbulent blue stare. He was stretched out in a chair. He'd removed his coat and rolled up his sleeves, revealing muscular brown arms. With his long hair free of restraint, and the shadow of a beard emphasizing his masculine jaw line, he seemed more like a pirate than a lord.

She remembered the stories Paddy used to tell on *The Merry Elizabeth*. Right now, she wouldn't be surprised if Declan dragged her out of here and sold her to the white slave traders the way pirates did with all unwanted captives.

"May I ask what possessed you to ride in front of a man with a loaded weapon?" Declan queried. "Better still, why were you there at all?" He got up, shoved the hair off his forehead, and started to pace at the end of her bed. "You could have been killed. Fine way for me to repay your grandfather's trust."

He stopped and looked directly at her. "I'm waiting."

What was this tirade about? He should be grateful. How dare he berate her for saving his life? Eleanor's theories be damned. This man was never going to be her friend, so she might as well stop trying. "In case you hadn't noticed, the gun was pointing in your direction. It seems there are others, beside myself, who would like you out of the way. Not that I need you out of the way now."

"Just what is that supposed to mean?"

"It means, I agree. I need to go to London and get married without delay. Addington has proven he'll do anything to get what he wants." She'd never believed her cousin would take things this far. He'd failed in his first attempt, but that didn't mean he wouldn't try again. And his target would be Declan. At least in London, her guardian would be in his own territory.

"You suddenly want to marry because you see Addington as a threat. To who, me?" Declan's brows drew together. "You needn't worry. I'll deal with your cousin."

"Why would I worry about you?" She picked at the pink ribbon on her night rail. "It's simply that Addington might discourage any other suitors I have in the area. It's best if I go to London."

"What happened to marrying when you're good and ready?"

She lifted her chin and held his gaze, attempting to give him a haughty look. "I'm ready now."

Declan actually smiled and shook his head. "I'm sorry, my dear. I don't believe you."

"Believe what you will. It's none of your business anyway. Let's just say we're on the same side now." Alex adjusted the covers, trying to look every bit the innocent, demure young lady, while keeping her smile in place to keep from wincing. "How soon before we leave for London?"

Declan couldn't keep up. He'd never known a woman

with such a mercurial temperament. *Did she have the slightest idea what she really wanted?*

He stared pointedly at her arm. "Our travel plans have been delayed due to unforeseen circumstances."

She had the grace to blush.

"The doctor says you should be up in a couple of days. You're lucky the bullet went through the fleshy part of your arm, missing the bone."

"Did you catch him?"

"No, but I had men scouring the woods right after you were shot. The intruder managed to get by them. It had to have been a local who knew the terrain." Declan gave a frustrated sigh. "Without your assailant, we have no way of tying this back to Addington. He, of course, maintains that it was an incompetent poacher."

Addington was lying. Declan didn't doubt his instincts. The gun had been pointed directly at him. The man must be more desperate than he first thought. Perhaps Adrian should do a little checking into Addington's affairs. His cousin had a talent for discovering the unsavory side of men like Alex's cousin.

He gripped the carved footboard and studied his ward. She didn't appear to have any signs of fever. But her pale face and delicate form were swallowed up in the covers of her oversized poster bed. He'd almost lost her, all because her courage put her in the wrong place at the wrong time. "Lady Alexandra, I want you to forget what I said earlier. Stay away from Addington." He raised a hand to keep her from speaking. "Let me deal with him. I'd also like you to remain close to the house until we leave for London."

"Is there anything *else*, my lord?"

He couldn't miss the sarcasm in her voice. *Good, the old Alex was back. He preferred her arguments.* When she was friendly, his thoughts strayed too often to the kiss they'd shared.

"Not right now. If I think of something, I know where to find you." He retrieved his black embroidered coat from the window seat and left the room. He hadn't gone far before he turned and stuck his head back through the doorway. "In case I didn't mention it, thank you for saving my life." He closed the door before Alex's pillow could hit him in the head.

No matter how Alex shifted, she couldn't get comfortable. She'd only been confined to bed for two hours, and she was already going mad. Relief washed over her at a tap on the door. Thank God, a visitor.

Her cousin's hushed voice sounded worried. "Alex, are you awake? I thought you might like something to eat."

"Come in, I'd love some company."

Eleanor entered carrying a tray, then made a startled sound when she stepped on a pillow.

Alex grimaced. Damn, she'd forgotten to retrieve it. She must have looked guilty because her cousin stared at her with that "what have you been up to" look. "Oh, all right. I threw it at him."

"Who?"

"Lord Worthington. The man is insufferable."

Eleanor set the tray on the bedside table. "I thought you were going to be nice." She bent down, picked up the feather pillow, and propped it behind Alex's shoulders. "He acted very worried about you. After the doctor left, he insisted on remaining by your bed. He seemed to be afraid that you could develop a fever."

"That's ridiculous." Alex settled back into the softness. "Lord Worthington's only concern was that I might die before he could kill me. He was furious I was there to save his bloody neck."

Eleanor frowned at her. "Don't swear."

Alex shook her head. "I'll never understand him. I agree with him, tell him I need to marry, and then he decides not to believe me."

Eleanor froze in the middle of shaking out a napkin. "You what?"

"I agreed with him."

"Why?" Eleanor sat on the edge of the bed and placed the filigree tray on Alex's lap. "You've never liked being told what to do. Now you're going to agree to his terms?" Eleanor glanced up from her task.

Alex held her gaze. "Luther's not going to stop. I don't want anyone to get hurt."

"Meaning, Lord Worthington."

"Meaning, anyone. Besides, this is my home." Alex glanced around at the room that had been hers for the last eight years. "My family, and many of the servant's families have lived here for generations." She picked up a piece of bread and concentrated on buttering it. "When I was taken from *The Merry Elizabeth*, I was devastated. No one gave me a choice. I was forced to leave the only security I'd known.

"But as much as I loved life onboard ship, my roots are here. This time I'm going to fight." Alex gave Eleanor a sudden grin. "Worthington's right. I'll have a greater selection of men to chose from in London. I don't have to marry just anyone. I need to find a special kind of man." She tapped her index finger against her lips. What did she want in a husband? "Eleanor, would you write a list for me?"

Eleanor appeared puzzled, but went to the writing desk in the corner, sat down, and laid out the quill, ink, and paper. "What do you want at the top of the page?"

"The perfect husband."

Eleanor made a choking sound. "You can't just list what you want, then shop for it like Cook does when she goes to market."

"Why not?" Alex thought for a moment. "My husband

must let me take care of the estate. Mark that down as number one."

"Alex, no man is going to allow you to run an estate. He'll be worried about its income, or your time away from him."

"Hmm." She fidgeted with her bracelet. Eleanor was right. "Fine, then item number two: he must have his own wealth. Number three: he can't be in love with me."

"What if you fall in love with him?"

"It won't happen. There's not a lord of my acquaintance I could fall in love with." The image of Declan's aristocratic features popped into her head, but she shoved it aside.

"What about Lord Worthington?"

"What about him?" *Had her thoughts shown on her face?*

"He's still your guardian," Eleanor pointed out. "He could reject your choice."

"Nonsense. What could Lord Worthington possibly object to?" Alex adjusted the covers. "He wants to be done with this as quickly as I do."

Finding a husband would be simple. Staying out of Declan's way until they went to London would be the difficult part. Once there, she'd be too busy to think about mocking blue eyes in a face that could make an angel swoon.

Chapter 7

Declan found the extent of Lord Lochsdale's holdings hard to believe. Alex's grandfather had carefully maintained ledgers on it all, just as he'd instructed a young Declan to do fifteen years ago.

He stood, glad to stretch his legs after sitting the last couple of hours. He'd prefer good, honest physical labor to going over accounts any day.

The door to the library opened and Alex entered. "I'm sorry. I didn't know you were in here."

She was a welcome distraction. They'd had a temporary truce the last few days. Alex hadn't been well enough to ride, and even wore dresses on a semi-regular basis. He, on the other hand, tried not to interfere in her day-to-day activities.

Alex glanced in his direction, but her gaze seemed to be held by the various items on the smooth surface in front of him.

"Did you need something?" Declan straightened the stacks of papers he'd been working on and came around to lean on the edge of the library table, avoiding the carved wooden wings of the mythical creatures that cavorted around the sides.

"I was looking for a quill and ink." Alex began to back away from him, one hand hidden in the folds of her skirt. "I'm sorry to have bothered you."

She acted as jumpy as a horse at the start of a race. Any minute he expected her to bolt out of the room. "What did you need them for?"

"It's not that I needed them. I just felt like writing."

His Alex, writing because she felt like it? Next she'd be telling him she'd taken up sewing. He raised an eyebrow until she continued in an exasperated tone.

"If you must know, I wanted to add to my list."

So that was what she'd been trying to hide. It must be of some importance for her to be so touchy. "List?"

"I'm making a list of the qualities I want in a husband. That way I'll just score each potential candidate. I'll marry whomever has the greatest number of points."

He should have expected something like this from Alex. "Admirable. But have you forgotten I have a say in whom you marry?" He would agree to most anyone who was suitable, just to put her out of temptation's way, but she didn't need to know that.

"No," she retorted. "I intend to choose someone you can't object to."

"So, what qualities do you find desirable in a male?" He'd never posed that question to any other woman, but he couldn't contain his curiosity as to what Alex found attractive in a man. "Perhaps, you'd like an intellectual." He pretended to ponder his choice, then gave a slight shrug. "Oh, but there wouldn't be any sport in that. You'd run the poor man through before he'd even raised his weapon."

"I suppose *no man* could match you in prowess with a rapier." Alex perused her list, making an elaborate production out of studying every item. "No, I don't find arrogance on here anywhere. You'd never be a choice."

"I wouldn't be a choice, because I choose not to marry until I must. When I do, it will be a business arrangement, nothing more." He didn't want to think about his inevitable marriage. Instead, he turned his attention to the rapier collection near the fireplace. "These weren't here when I was a child. When did your grandfather start collecting?"

He studied the rapiers with a critical eye. They were of the finest quality, about thirty in all, with various grips and blades. He didn't know much about antiquated weapons, but some appeared to be from the sixteenth and seventeenth centuries.

"They're mine." Alex came to stand next to him. "I would select what I wanted, and Grandfather would purchase them for me. Most vendors have an aversion to selling to women." She gave him a slight smirk. "Even if I could out-fence every one of them."

"Now who's being arrogant?"

"Not arrogant. Confident." Alex smiled up at him. "There's a difference."

"Is there?" Her teasing smile undid him. She was so close he could smell the vanilla fragrance she favored. "Might I find *confidence* on this list?"

He'd meant to grab only the paper, but somehow ended up taking her hand. Her pale fingers were devoid of jewelry but perfectly formed. Everything about her fascinated him. He lifted his gaze to her luminous green eyes.

She was exquisite. He'd known many beautiful women, but they'd never affected him like this. He desperately wanted to feel her pressed against him.

"I think I should warn you about arrogant men," Declan whispered. "They're liable to take advantage of a situation." He brought his other hand up to caress the silky hair at the back of her head, and slowly drew her mouth to his.

Alex wasn't sure when she dropped her list. She wasn't even sure how she came to be in his arms. One moment Declan gazed at her with a strange kind of intensity, and the next, she was being kissed with a passion she hadn't known existed.

Declan's hands roamed her back, trying to coax her closer. Her arms came up, encircling the muscled expanse of his shoulder. Everywhere she touched felt hard, but warm. The soft pressure of his lips continued down her neck, halting just long enough to nuzzle behind her ear.

She didn't want to do anything that might make him stop. This vortex of swirling feelings and emotions appealed to her in a way she never could have imagined.

He reclaimed her mouth with an urgency that seemed to have a direct line to the spot below her belly. She pressed against him, wanting, what?

The click of a door caused her to stiffen and break the kiss. She glanced up at Declan. A slight smile curled his lips as he glanced over her shoulder.

"Glory be, and I thought you would be bored in the country." A man's lilting Irish voice sounded from the entrance. "You, Worthington, could find a winning colleen on a desert isle."

Alex jerked out of Declan's embrace and turned around to see a grinning man filling the doorway. She tried to straighten the neckline that had slipped half off her shoulder and felt a flush heating her cheeks. Was it from the kiss, or embarrassment at being found in Declan's arms? Her guardian moved forward to greet their guest. Damn him for appearing so unruffled by their surprise visitor.

Declan inclined his head in Alex's direction at the man's questioning glance. "Lord Morgan, may I present the Countess of Lochsdale, Alexandra Kendrick, my ward."

The Irishman raised an eyebrow at Declan before coming forward and bowing over her hand. He had a grace she found surprising, considering his over six foot frame. "I'm charmed, Lady Lochsdale. If I'd known there was such beauty to be found in the country, I would have visited sooner."

Declan joined them and gave Morgan an exasperated look. "What the devil are you doing here? I thought you were looking after Catrina."

"Nice to see you, too." The ruggedly handsome Lord Morgan slapped Declan on the back. "I got tired of waiting."

A low sultry voice came from the doorway. "So did I."

Alex looked in the direction of the voice. A woman, who bore a strong resemblance to the statue of Aphrodite in her mother's garden, posed in the entrance. She was tall and willowy, making Alex feel like a child by comparison. Her features were classic, with the flawless skin and blond hair Eleanor told her were all the rage in London.

Dressed in a pale pink gown, she seemed to float toward Declan. She put her arm through his and lifted her cheek for a kiss.

Alex had a ridiculous impulse to cross the room and yank the *vision* off him.

"Lord Worthington, it really wasn't very kind of you to leave us in London without a word," she breathed. "I, that is, *we* were worried about you." She looked up at him, the image of a concerned lover.

Alex wished she could be anywhere but here. She reached down to retrieve her list, which brought her to the attention of the clinging vine.

"Who do we have here? Lord Worthington, this couldn't possibly be your charge. I was under the impression she was still in the schoolroom." She raised an eyebrow in Morgan's direction.

"How would *I* be knowing?" Morgan defended. "When Worthington said he'd be needing some time to clear up this business with his ward, I assumed she was a wee thing."

The *vision* looked Alex up and down. "Well, at least some of your assumptions were correct."

That did it. She refused to be talked about as if she were elsewhere, and if that was a set down about her height, well it was still *her* home. She could toss out whomever she pleased.

Before she could open her mouth, Declan spoke, "Lady Catrina Edwards, may I present Lady Alexandra Kendrick, the Countess of Lochsdale."

Lady Catrina inclined her head toward Alex, then

turned back to Declan. "You don't really have to remain here, do you, Lord Worthington?"

Declan glanced at Alex, before responding. "I had thought to stay for another week, but under the circumstances, I think we should leave in the next couple of days. You'll stay here, of course. We can travel back to London together."

Alex wanted to wipe the gloating smile off Catrina's face, but Declan's next comment did that for her.

"Lady Lochsdale will be accompanying us." Declan gave Catrina an assessing look. "Now that you're here, do you think you could help Lady Lochsdale with her wardrobe? It's early in the Season, so she will need several gowns." Declan must have noticed the slight pout of Catrina's mouth, because he added, "You have such elegant taste in clothing. With your guidance, Lady Lochsdale should have no difficulty finding a suitor."

Catrina positively glowed at the mention of a suitor. She crossed to Alex and studied her critically.

The royal blue day gown had seemed like such a good idea this morning, but under Catrina's scrutiny, Alex felt as if she were dressed in rags.

"It will be difficult," Catrina lamented. "But with some patches for her face, updated gowns and a wig, she should be presentable."

"No wig," Declan stated.

"But Lord Worthington, there are certain events which require—"

"I said no wigs," Declan commanded, "and leave her hair unpowdered."

Was anyone going to ask what she wanted? Catrina stood within striking range. It was a good thing Declan still had her knife.

Catrina crossed back to Declan. "As you wish, my lord. I'll do my best." She reached up to pat hair that didn't have a strand out of place. "Would you show me to my room, Lord

Worthington? I must be a dreadful sight." She took his arm and moved with him toward the library door.

Declan smiled down at her. "You're as beautiful as ever. I'd be pleased to escort you." They exited, leaving Alex to entertain Morgan.

"Does he always forget other people are in the room when Lady Catrina's around?" Alex asked dryly.

Morgan wore an odd expression as he shook his head. "It's not his way to be leaving like that. What have you done to him?"

"What have I done to *him?*" she fumed. "He's not the one being discussed and insulted."

Morgan crossed to her. He took her hand and bent over to kiss it. When he straightened, mischief danced in his sherry brown eyes. "When you know him better, wee one, you'll discover he was running away."

With that enigmatic statement, he dropped her hand and left the library.

"Lady Lochsdale," Luther said, "I trust you're fully recovered from the unfortunate incident last week." Luther glanced briefly in Declan's direction at the head of the table. "She gave us quite a scare. Didn't she, Lord Worthington?"

"Incident?" Morgan's voice held a note of interest. "You'd not be getting into more trouble, Worthington, and me not around." He gave his head a woeful shake. "You're always having all the fun."

Luther shrugged. "It was a poacher with bad aim, nothing more."

Declan picked up his crystal goblet and swirled the red wine around the inside before giving Luther an assessing stare. "Lady Lochsdale chose to be in the wrong place at the wrong time. The doctor assured us she's received a minor flesh wound."

"You were shot?" Catrina paled under her powder.

"It was nothing." Alex didn't want to talk about her injury. Why couldn't Luther leave it alone?

She should never have asked him to stay for dinner. His ingratiating manner annoyed her. Luther didn't believe in being nice, unless he wanted something. And *she* was the something he wanted.

This was all Declan's fault. It would never have happened if he hadn't been in the hallway, Lady Catrina still attached to his arm, when Luther arrived. The invitation had come out of her mouth before she could stop it. Now she had to contend with Luther and her uninvited guests.

Declan turned a cool gaze in Alex's direction. All night long, as he'd played the charming host to his friends, he'd barely noticed her. Why did he choose this moment to pay attention to her?

She was surrounded. Declan at the head of the table to her left, Luther to her right, and Lady Catrina across from her. Tomorrow, she'd be sure to sit between Eleanor and Morgan.

"Lord Worthington," Catrina purred.

Alex stabbed a glazed carrot with her fork. Was it her imagination, or was that woman's voice even breathier than before?

Catrina leaned toward Declan and placed her hand on his arm. "I had planned to go riding in the morning, but if the woods aren't safe, perhaps you should accompany me."

Catrina's low cut dress left little to the imagination. If that's what Declan liked in a woman, it was a good thing Alex had never considered him husband material.

"I'd be pleased to accompany you," Declan responded, then stared directly at Alex. "I'm sure Lady Lochsdale would like to join us. She has a fondness for early morning rides." Declan raised his glass in a mock salute to her. "I can't think of anyone who could give a better tour of the grounds."

Damn him. It had been a little over a week since her injury, and she'd finally healed enough to take Blade out. How had he guessed she'd planned to ride in the morning? "I don't think I'd make a very good guide."

She didn't want company, especially this company. The feeling was mutual, judging by the pout on Catrina's lips.

"But I insist." Declan smiled, showing even, white teeth. "The air will do you good."

He wasn't going to let this drop. Alex sighed. "I'll meet you in the stable at first light, but if you're not there, I'm leaving without you."

"Done. Oh, and you ladies will ride sidesaddle, of course."

Lady Catrina seemed puzzled. "How else would we ride?"

"Lady Alexandra has a habit of riding astride."

"Lord Worthington, you jest." Catrina looked scandalized until she realized Declan wasn't kidding. Then a knowing smile curved her lips.

"Is that one of the reasons you didn't find a husband at your first Season?" Catrina's voice was smug. "You poor dear. I understand, not having parents and being raised by your grandfather, you couldn't be expected to be well-versed in social etiquette. Not to worry, I'm sure I can find you a husband this time."

"Perhaps Lady Alexandra shouldn't go at all," Luther said. "What with her recent injury, she could look for a husband from amongst the local gentry."

"I've promised Lady Alexandra a Season in London." Declan's blue eyes narrowed as he studied Luther. "She deserves a large selection of suitors to choose from. Don't you agree?"

Luther raised his hands, palms upward in a gesture of submission. "I was just making a suggestion. I only want what will make Lady Alexandra happy."

They were doing it again, talking about her as though she wasn't in the room.

"Lady Alexandra, do you have any other habits that Society might consider unacceptable?" Catrina gave her a condescending look. "I need to know for your own good. We wouldn't want you scaring off suitors with scandalous behavior."

"I'm not sure." Alex pretended to ponder. She picked up the knife off the platter where Edgar had been carving the roast. The blade was well balanced. "Lord Worthington seems to think I have a problem with sharp objects."

"Lady Alexandra,"—Declan's voice carried a warning—"put the knife down."

"See, he seems to be concerned. He just doesn't know me well enough to understand I hit whatever I aim for."

In one quick flick of motion, Alex let the blade fly. It landed with a thud in the wooden relief above Catrina's head, its ornate handle embellishing the apple at the center of the still life.

Silence echoed in the room. Alex decided it was time to retreat. "If you'll excuse me. I seem to have lost my appetite."

She almost made it to the door before Lady Catrina erupted into hysterics. Alex could hear Eleanor trying to calm the distraught woman. Strangled sounds that seemed suspiciously like laughter were coming from Morgan, while Luther complained about her appalling lack of manners. Over it all, she heard Declan's roar. "Alex, get back here."

Alex had always had a good sense of self-preservation. She picked up her skirts and ran.

Blade's nose had a velvety softness that felt good against Alex's palm. She rubbed his favorite spot between the ears. Unlike people, animals never expected anything from you.

She buried her face against her horse's neck, inhaling his animal smell. It always made her think of her early years at Oakleigh. How many times had she hidden in the stable when she felt overwhelmed by the world outside?

But that was then. She was an adult now and the Countess of Lochsdale; it was past time for her to be cowering. She straightened and put a particularly unruly piece of hair behind her ear.

"So this is where you're hiding." Declan's voice came from the shadow of the doorway.

"I'm not hiding." Alex made a show of adjusting the blankets on Blade's back. "I came to check on my horse."

"At nine o'clock at night?" He walked into the glow of her lantern and stood, arms crossed, staring at her. "I think you owe Lady Catrina an apology."

Why did he have to look so magnificent? The light playing across the angles of his face gave him an air of authority. She suddenly felt like a child being reprimanded for picking on one of the other children.

"Apologize? Why? So she can continue to berate my family?" She probably sounded petulant, but that woman annoyed her beyond reason.

"I'll admit Lady Catrina's comments were unfortunate, but that was no reason to throw a knife at her."

"If I'd been throwing it *at* her, she'd be bleeding now. I was making a point."

"Let's just say the point's been taken."

She sat down on feedbags piled against the stall and leaned back against the rough boards. "I'm tired of people like her. I don't fit into Lady Catrina's world." She turned her attention to Declan. "Why are you forcing me to?"

"Because you must." He sat down next to her with a sigh. "You're different from most women."

She enjoyed being different, but she didn't want it thrown in her face. "You don't understand."

"I understand more than you think." Declan tugged a piece of straw from one of the bags and studied it. "Do you know how I met your grandfather?"

"No."

"He caught me hunting on his land about a mile from here."

"You were poaching?"

Declan smiled. "I was trying to get my father to notice... It doesn't matter now. The point is I had a rebellious youth. I didn't want anything to do with my title or society. I thought all lords were like my father." Declan stood and dragged his fingers through the lock of hair at his forehead. "Lord Lochsdale taught me it's not the title, but what you do with it that's important."

"You didn't want to be an earl?"

Declan gave her a small smile. "Contrary to what the common man believes, being an earl does have its limitations."

"That holds true for a *countess* as well." She went over to the lamp and adjusted the wick. The flame burned brighter, chasing away the shadows. "Grandfather used to tell me that with a privileged position comes responsibility. I never really understood what he meant until after he died."

Declan moved closer to her and wrapped a burnished curl around his index finger. "You don't need to change to fit in, Lady Lochsdale. Actually, I'd be disappointed if you did."

He smiled at her, and she felt as if they were two friends sharing a secret.

"Just go along with what Society expects. Ultimately it will help you accomplish your goals."

"I'll think about it."

"Will you promise me something?"

"What?"

Declan let go of the curl. "Act like a lady, but don't

ever become one."

She wrinkled her nose and glanced down. "I don't think you need worry." She plucked at the yards of material gathered at her waist. "The weight of a woman's skirts are enough to discourage that."

Declan laughed. "Good. Now I think we should get back inside before the others start to worry."

She picked up the lantern and gave Blade a last pat. Declan headed for the door, but she stopped him. "Lord Worthington, are you still riding in the morning?"

"Yes."

"Must I accompany you?"

"Think of it as practice with the sidesaddle. If you intend to ride in London, it will be expected. You do own a riding habit?"

"Of course." She grinned at him. "Well, actually I didn't, but Grandfather insisted."

"Thank God."

"It isn't the ride I object to." Alex hesitated a moment, searching for words. "The truth of the matter is I'd rather not spend much time with Lady Catrina."

"I know. I'll speak with her, but I wish you'd try to get along."

"Why?"

"Lady Catrina has influence with the Ton. Besides, I'm fairly certain I'm going to ask her to be my wife."

She almost dropped the lantern. Wife. He couldn't. Aside from Catrina's beauty, what else did she have to offer?

"I see."

"No, you don't see. She's the perfect wife for me." Declan crossed to her and took the lantern from her nerveless fingers. When she tried to turn away, he grabbed her arm and held her gaze. "Alex, why does it matter who I marry?"

Declan studied her face until she felt the heat rise in her cheeks. "Did you think we might..." He let go of her and stepped away. "This is ridiculous. I enjoy your company, but aside from a couple of impetuous kisses, we aren't involved."

"No, we aren't. You're my guardian and I'm your ward. For a moment I'd forgotten." She jerked out of his grasp. She had to escape. "Now, if you'll excuse me, I need to finish packing. The sooner we get to London, the sooner I can find a husband. Better yet, maybe I should reconsider my options here." She headed for the door, but wasn't quick enough.

"Lady Lochsdale."

She turned back. "Yes?"

"I'd never approve Addington as your husband. I meant what I said about staying away from him."

How dare he tell her with whom she should associate. "I intend to encourage all my suitors. My speedy wedding is one of the few things we agree on. Goodnight, my lord." She turned and walked out into the blackness.

Chapter 8

Alex adjusted her pillow for what seemed like the hundredth time that night. The light of a full moon streamed through her window, turning everything it touched to silver.

She gave up trying to sleep and slipped into a nightgown. Sitting cross-legged on the window seat, she dropped her chin in her hands and stared out the window, not seeing anything. She couldn't stop thinking about Declan's surprise announcement.

It wasn't as if his upcoming engagement had anything to do with her sleeplessness. That would be preposterous. She found him attractive, that was all. Certainly they had nothing to base a relationship on. He'd been overbearing and unpleasant since he arrived.

Her little inner voice warned she wasn't being fair. Declan hadn't been entirely unpleasant. When he'd smiled at her this evening, she'd felt like she could accomplish anything. Then there were the kisses.

Closing her eyes, she remembered how it felt to be in his arms. How different his kisses had been from the stolen kiss she'd shared with Lord Duprey. In Declan's arms, she was aware of every touch, and her body yearned for greater intimacy.

Her eyes snapped opened. This preoccupation with her guardian had to stop.

A movement in the garden drew her gaze. There, near the statue of Pan, stood a woman. Her dark cloak billowed out behind her as she paced back and forth in front of the statue. At one point she drew back her hood, and moonlight glinted off golden curls. Only one woman on the estate had hair like that.

Catrina.

A few minutes passed before a man dressed in dark clothing detached himself from the shadows and joined her. Alex couldn't make out his features, but after a brief conversation they strolled arm in arm out of sight.

It had to be Declan. He'd met his ladylove for a late night tryst.

That effectively cooled her romantic fancies. How foolish to think she was more to Declan than a responsibility. He probably kissed every woman he met. She straightened and squared her shoulders. She needed to forget about him and concentrate on her future.

Her future? With a sigh, she turned sideways and stretched her legs out on the window-seat. Was it asking too much to have respect and love in a marriage?

She remembered her mother standing on the prow of *The Merry Elizabeth* next to her father. They were always laughing, as if each moment together brought them great joy.

A part of her had hoped for that kind of life. She'd wanted someone to share with, but finding a husband had turned out to be just another responsibility she'd acquired since her grandfather's death.

Declan was right. She hated to admit it, but she needed Society. She'd have to try and fit in, at least until she married.

With her arms above her head, she stood and stretched, then relaxed and rolled her shoulders. She'd start trying to befriend Catrina in the morning. If she could accomplish that, the rest of the Ton would be easy.

She crossed the cool floor, slipped out of her nightgown, and got into bed. As she snuggled under the covers, she considered what Declan had told her about his youth.

Based on the stories she'd read in the *Gazette*, he appeared to be perfectly at ease with members of the Ton, and yet he'd implied he wasn't. Aside from his disdain for titles, why did he consider himself different? And why would Catrina be the perfect wife?

She was thinking about him again.

She tried to make her mind go blank, but the last image she saw before sleep claimed her was Declan's face. His smile warmed her in a way no blanket ever could.

"If it isn't our knife throwing hoyden. You decided to join us after all?" Catrina taunted Alex from atop one of the stable's gentler mares.

Alex slowed her stride as she came to the small group of riders and servants clustered near the stable. Catrina, a frothy creation in silk, clung to the horn of her sidesaddle, looking down at Alex like she was some kind of poor relative. But her eyes gave her away, she watched Alex's hands, as if afraid a knife may appear at any moment.

Perhaps it was just as well she'd secreted her blade in her boot. Eleanor said lack of sleep made her less than reasonable. Well, she'd had very little sleep last night, and if that woman made one more insulting comment—

"You're late." Declan sounded like a tutor reprimanding his charge.

She turned to find him glowering down at her. Strong hands reigned in his skittish mount. Man and animal struck her as very alike, leashed energy that fought to be free.

Alex swallowed. His raw magnetism beckoned, challenging her to accept him. Seduction in the form of devastating looks, and an assurance that threatened to make her forget that she wanted, no, needed, to control her life. Her stomach clenched as she studied his unrelenting visage. Had anyone ever truly bested him?

She lowered her gaze, and moved to scratch Declan's magnificent stallion between his ears, even though she had to stand on tiptoe to do so. It pleased her that the horse didn't move away. With a slight shift, she managed to look around the animal's large head. "What's his name?"

Declan raised an eyebrow, but answered the question. "Knight."

"As in *Arabian Nights*?"

"No, as in Arthur's knights of the Round Table. He has the heart of the destriers of old."

"I suppose the two of you ride off to rescue damsels in distress?"

The corners of Declan's mouth tugged upward. "We're hardly the rescuing kind."

Catrina adjusted a curl that had come loose from her chignon. "Nonsense, my lord. You rescued me from the pallor of London in spring." It was almost as if she struck a pose, perched on her sidesaddle, layers of cornflower blue silk skimming the side of the mare.

Declan raised an eyebrow at Catrina. "If you'll recall, I didn't invite you."

Catrina appeared nonplussed. "You knew I'd come." She adjusted the lace in the décolletage of her habit.

Didn't Catrina own any high-collared dresses? Alex looked down at her serviceable hunter green riding habit and decided it would never do for London. When she glanced back at Catrina, she noted the woman still watched her. Friendly was not the word she would use to describe the look.

She'd best make her apology and get it over with. Avoiding the inevitable wasn't going to make it any easier. She crossed to Catrina and gazed up at her. *Time to start pretending. Please God, don't let my true feelings show on my face, just this once.*

"Lady Catrina, I'm sorry about the knife incident. I'm not used to having someone of your caliber come to visit." Alex tried to look sincere. At least that part was true. She'd never had a guest who was so mean-spirited. "Can you ever forgive me?" She hung her head, trying to appear repentant, but her head snapped up at the sound of Morgan's cheery voice.

"Go on, forgive the chit." Morgan announced as he approached from the stable on a dappled gelding. "If you don't, we're liable to be here all morning."

He must be joining them. She gave Morgan a smile, and he grinned back. Relief washed over her that she'd have at least one ally on this unwanted expedition.

Catrina's smug voice sounded loud and clear on the crisp morning air. "If you're truly sorry, it would be wrong of me not to accept now, wouldn't it?"

The hairs on the back of Alex's neck stood up. It took all her control to look at Catrina with what she prayed was a hopeful expression. "Then you'll still help me with my Season in London? It would mean a lot to me."

"If Lord Worthington wishes it." Catrina smiled in Declan's direction, then turned back to her, the smile gone. "But you will do exactly as I tell you."

"Of course." Alex didn't dare glance at Declan. As it was, she caught a suspicious glint in Morgan's eye. Did he know she was lying?

John, the stable boy, brought Blade out. Alex knew John had been up for hours, but his hair made him look like he'd just rolled out of bed. He tried to saddle Blade, but the horse seemed to have an aversion to the sidesaddle. Alex came forward and made some adjustments to the straps as she whispered soothing words to her horse.

"Perhaps you shouldn't take Blade. We don't need any more accidents." Declan's voice held disapproval. "You aren't used to a sidesaddle."

Was Declan questioning her ability? She could ride almost as well as she fenced, in spite of this foolish saddle.

John brought Blade over to the mounting block and in

one smooth motion, Alex found her perch. How did women stand this uncomfortable position for very long? "I suggest we go north. The scenery is spectacular in that direction."

Declan gave her a look that told her he didn't like having his suggestion ignored, but he didn't say a word as he started down the path.

She'd love to challenge him to a race. Even riding sidesaddle, she'd hold her own. She started to call him back, but for once curbed her reckless nature. Racing probably wasn't on Catrina's list of acceptable pursuits for a lady.

Alex dropped back next to Morgan and allowed Catrina and Declan to lead. She watched the two for several minutes, but from what she could observe, Declan seemed, at best, to tolerate Catrina. Why would he want to marry her?

"Lord Morgan, have you known Lord Worthington long?"

"Several years. We were at Eaton together."

"And after that?"

"I was fool enough to follow Worthington into the military."

A friend of Alex's grandfather had described the horrors of war when she was thirteen. The man was a consummate storyteller, and the images he'd created hadn't faded with the years.

For some reason, the thought of Declan deliberately putting himself in harm's way disturbed her. "Were either of you hurt?"

"It's lucky we were."

The way he said it made her suspect they'd experienced firsthand the terrors she'd heard about. "How long were you there?"

"Long enough to wish we'd never joined." Morgan gave a mirthless laugh. "We were young and thought we needed a bit of adventure. At least that was my reason for enlisting." He shook his head. "Worthington's father was furious. The old earl tried to keep his only son from going—which, of course, meant he had to go."

"I take it they didn't get along?"

"You could say that." Morgan's expression held a pensive edge. "It's glad I am the old man's dead. If he hadn't died, Worthington would have killed himself in one outlandish stunt or another."

"And now?"

"I'm not sure. He's repaired his fortune, but I'm thinking scars to the soul don't heal as easily." Morgan pinned her with a look. "You like him, don't you, Wee One?"

"Why do you call me 'Wee One'?"

"Lady Lochsdale doesn't seem to fit. When we first met, you reminded me of pictures I'd seen of the fairies and other wee folk in my native Ireland." Morgan gave her a knowing smile. "Now I've answered your questions. It's only fair you'd be answering mine. You like him, don't you?"

"I haven't known him long enough to form an opinion."

"Mmm?"

"Oh, all right. He is the most exasperating, overbearing, headstrong man I've ever met. In spite of all that, I like him. God knows why."

"Same reason I do. He makes you feel at ease around him. I've never known him to be judgmental."

"That hasn't been my experience."

"Hasn't it?" A secretive smile lurked in Morgan's eyes. "Then perhaps you're the exception."

Declan searched all Alex's usual haunts and had a moment of panic at the thought she'd run away. She'd seemed agreeable, if rather quiet, on the ride this morning.

That might have been due to Catrina's badgering. He'd speak with her tonight. Her constant baiting of Alex had to stop. If it didn't, the trip to London would be a disaster.

Odds were good Catrina wouldn't last a day in an enclosed carriage with Alex.

They were leaving in the morning. He had so much to finalize concerning the estate. He'd hoped Alex could answer some questions. *Where was she?*

He went in search of Eleanor and found her in the room that had once belonged to Alex's mother. She was carefully storing away the gowns Alex wouldn't be taking with her to London.

"Eleanor, have you seen Lady Lochsdale?"

"Did you need her for something?" She brushed imaginary dust from her gown.

"I have a few questions."

"Perhaps I can answer them for you?"

"No, I need to speak with her." Declan watched in fascination as Eleanor gripped her skirt with her hands. She probably wasn't even aware of her actions. Why would Alex's whereabouts cause her distress?

"I need some information about the estate." Declan held up a hand. "Information only she can answer." He tried not to let the irritation he felt at Alex's disappearance show. "Where is she?"

Eleanor fumbled with the cameo at her neck, closed her eyes, and let out a long sigh. "Alex asked me not to tell. Please don't be angry." She opened her eyes and gave him a pleading look, then laid her hand on his arm. "It's her last day on the estate as a free woman. She wanted it to be the way it was in the old days."

"I'm not angry." Did Eleanor think he was an ogre? Is that how Alex viewed him as well?

"She asked her fencing teacher to give her a final lesson. They're in the south meadow."

"Thank you." He took Eleanor's hands. "Don't worry, I only want to ask her a few questions."

"I know, only..." She removed her hands from his and

turned away.

"Only what?"

"I wish you'd try to understand Alex." She turned and held his gaze. "She may be impulsive, but what she really wants is a stable life with people who love her in spite of, or perhaps because of, her idiosyncrasies. Is that so different from you and I?"

"Perhaps not, but it's up to me to decide what's best for her future." Declan gave her a small smile. "I'd never hurt her. I doubt if she'd let me."

The ride to the south meadow took forever. In spite of his impatience, Declan slowed Knight to a walk as they entered the trees. Alex should never have gone off on her own. Why didn't she trust him enough to tell him about the fencing lesson? Was she afraid he'd forbid it? Alex valued freedom above all things. Freedom to make choices. Freedom to have a fencing lesson if she wanted one.

He'd never really thought much about women having fewer choices in their lives than men. He supposed they did. Alex didn't want to marry, but then neither did he. In that way they were alike. She would just have to learn, as he had, that life rarely gives you options.

The clearing appeared suddenly. For a moment, he was blinded by the sun and didn't see the figures engaged in a contest at the far corner of the meadow.

He kept to the edge of the trees. Perhaps it was better if he didn't interrupt. This was the perfect time to satisfy his curiosity about Alex's abilities. He worked his way around until he was close enough to have a good view.

Alex wore a silk shirt and breeches with the sleeves rolled up to her elbows. Her opponent was a small wiry man who periodically called out instructions.

Mesmerized, he watched her graceful movement with a

sense of awe. When he'd been on the other end of her blade, he hadn't had the opportunity to admire her technique.

She carried herself well. Her thrusts were clean and concise, with no wasted motion. Small beads of sweat covered her face, causing damp curls to stick to her forehead. The silk shirt clung to her breasts, while her breeches exposed every curve.

His arousal was almost immediate.

It was ironic Alex believed she had no effect on him. But then again, he'd gone to great lengths to make her think that.

For once, Catrina's interference was advantageous. If he'd been left alone with Alex for the next week, could he have resisted her? He doubted it. He was drawn to her like no woman he'd ever known, and for that reason alone, he had to stay away.

Alex lunged at her opponent. They were using button-tipped practice weapons, but injury was still a possibility. He held his breath with each new counterattack. Her opponent was good. His speed and agility forced Alex back across the meadow.

The match seemed to go on forever. He noted Alex no longer tried to press for an advantage. Instead, she simply defended herself. He almost interrupted, but at that moment, Alex's instructor called a halt.

They walked to the edge of the forest and sat on a fallen log. The little man talked intently as he held his weapon out in front of him.

A look of concentration appeared on her face as she tried to imitate his grip. She gave a few tentative thrusts. It was an awkward hold, but after several minutes her skill improved. Declan felt an odd sort of pride in her accomplishment, but immediately squelched the feeling. Fencing would not help her find a husband.

Alex turned toward her teacher and smiled. It was a

smile of love and trust. She hugged the fencing master, and Declan would have given anything to be the recipient.

They stood, and the instructor gave her a bow that would have been envied in King George's Court. She in turn gave him a mock curtsey while holding out the edges of an imaginary skirt. Their laughter rang through the trees as they mounted their horses.

He backed out of sight, expecting them to ride past. He'd join them back at the manor. It wouldn't do for Alex to know he'd been spying on her. She'd accused him of that once already.

The fencing instructor came within ten feet of his hiding place, but Alex wasn't with him. Declan waited until the teacher passed before going to look for her.

When he reached the meadow, he noticed a faint path leading away from the manor. Following it, he expected to see Alex at every turn, but he'd ridden about a mile before the forest gave way to a valley.

It was a beautiful spot. Tiny blue and yellow flowers dotted the banks of a small lake nestled among the hills. He nudged Blade to the water's edge, where the horse could crop the long grass.

Squinting against the sun, Declan searched the area. *Where was she?*

Alex gasped for air as she cleared the water's surface. She hadn't meant to stay under for so long, but after this morning, she was in the mood to nudge boundaries.

The water felt wonderful on her heated skin. It wouldn't be wise to stay in too much longer, but this might be the last time she could swim in her favorite place.

Water plastered the hair to her face. She shoved the thick mass aside and opened her eyes. After a quick glance, she closed them again. Declan stood on the shore about fifteen feet away.

His quiet roar echoed off the water. "Damnation, Alex. What do you think you're doing?"

She opened her eyes and glared at him. "Swimming," she sputtered, as water tried to find its way into her mouth.

"In mid April." Declan crossed to her neatly folded pile of clothes on the rocky shore. "And to whom do these belong?"

Alex shrugged. "I wouldn't know." He knew to whom they belonged. The man was just being difficult.

"Come out of there now. You're going to make yourself sick."

She'd been thinking the same thing before he arrived, but now it was a matter of honor. She couldn't come out with him standing there, and she wasn't going to let him ruin her enjoyment.

"I intend to stay right here. Please feel free to leave if you must." She couldn't see his face clearly, but she'd lay odds the twitch in his jaw was back.

"Stop acting like a child. You're going to come out in the next two minutes or suffer the consequences."

"Just what might those be?" She hated to admit her toes were getting numb.

Declan sat down on a rock and started to remove his boots.

"What are you doing?"

"Coming in after you. I can't very well do that with my boots on now, can I?" Declan finished with his boots and removed his jacket.

"You wouldn't!"

"Wouldn't I?" He started to undo the buttons on his waistcoat.

He was bluffing. The water was cold. Now that her body wasn't so heated, she realized *how cold*. Was she more afraid of her humiliation or Declan's anger?

He removed his shirt. Suddenly the cold didn't matter. As a child she'd often seen him naked to the waist, but he hadn't been so...developed...had he?

In spite of all the water, her mouth went dry. She had to swallow, then remind herself to breathe.

His shoulders were broad and well muscled, as was the rest of his torso. Fine dark hair covered his upper chest and tapered downward.

Her eyes followed the line to where Declan was starting to unbutton the flap on his breeches.

She should stop this and come out of the water. But she felt an overwhelming desire to see him as nature intended. This memory of how he looked, naked at the edge of her lake, would have to last a lifetime.

Declan hesitated, forcing her to look up. "Are you coming out?"

"No." Even from her position, she could see his raised eyebrow.

The cramp hit without warning. She doubled up, tried to straighten, then tried to kick her legs. It was pointless. Nothing worked. Terror engulfed her as she began to sink, the surface a light blur she desperately needed to reach.

Her lungs were bursting. She tried clawing her way upward. God, she didn't want to die like this. She had to breathe. Unable to fight back, she felt herself being drawn toward the bottom.

Declan.

His name still clung to her lips when the lure of the warm, soothing darkness overcame her struggles.

Chapter 9

The ice cold water took his breath away. Declan dived deep, praying this was the spot he'd seen Alex go down. The murky lake allowed for visibility of no more than two feet in each direction.

He stayed down as long as he could. At the last moment, he shot upward, filled his lungs with air, then plunged again.

On the third time, he found her. She floated about ten feet below the surface. Drawing near, he could see small bubbles escaping from her mouth. Her glorious hair did a mesmerizing dance around her face.

He grabbed her waist with both hands, thanking God she wasn't wearing any sodden clothing that would have forced her to the bottom. Straining every muscle, he swam upward toward air and light.

When their heads cleared the water, Declan drew in a quick breath, then faced her. He cleared the water out of her mouth and kept her head above water as he towed her to the shore.

She hadn't moved. The fear that he might be too late gnawed at his gut. With the last of his strength, he put her facedown onto a sun-warmed rock. He turned her head to the side, then rhythmically pressed down on her back, mimicking the motions he'd seen Paddy use on a sailor who'd been fished from the ocean.

That man had died.

Declan prayed long and hard for one of the few times in his life. Making all kinds of promises he wasn't sure he could keep, if God allowed Alex to live.

After what seemed like an eternity, water spurted out of her mouth. She drew in several ragged breaths and started to cough.

He turned her over, cradling her head in his arms. She opened her eyes and tried to speak, her voice low and raspy. He had to lean close to hear what she said.

"You're wet."

"So are you." He gave her a weak smile, trying not to look at her naked body, but his peripheral vision still allowed him a titillating view of her creamy breasts with their puckered nipples. In spite of the cold, his manhood hardened.

"Thank you," Alex whispered. Then her eyes fluttered closed.

She was alive, but they'd both be in big trouble if they couldn't get warm and dry. He grabbed his shirt and settled it over her head. It went to her knees, but he didn't think her silk clothing would offer much warmth or modesty if her moist skin plastered it to her womanly curves.

Knight came at his whistle, and he jerked a leather satchel from the saddle. He stuffed Alex's clothing inside and slipped his jacket on over his wet breeches, then stepped into his boots. With care, he lifted Alex in his arms.

His horse seemed to sense the urgency and stood still as he maneuvered her inert form onto the saddle. With difficulty, he climbed up behind her, then huddled her shivering form against his naked chest. The top of her damp head rested under his chin. He wrapped his coat as far as it would reach around them both, then urged Knight to a gallop toward the manor.

Why hadn't he turned around, or left when he found her? He'd told himself their little game was a good way to teach her a lesson, but to be honest, it had been an excuse. He'd wanted to see her naked. That's why he'd insisted she come out.

He was supposed to be concerned with her safety, not acting like a randy young man watching through the keyhole to get a glimpse of a naked woman.

Alex shouldn't have been swimming at all. Why couldn't she ever do the expected? One moment she'd been taunting him. The next, she'd disappeared from sight.

He hadn't seen any sign of injury. Hopefully she just suffered from the cold. Had she been in the water long? She should have known better than to swim this early in the season.

John peered out of the stable as they galloped into the mews. Declan gave him Knight's reins and asked him to send someone for the doctor and to retrieve Blade. Carrying Alex's slight form, he strode toward the manor, up the steps, and into the hallway.

Morgan saw them first.

"What the..." He rushed over and tried to take Alex from him.

"No. I can carry her. Get Eleanor. Ask Edgar to have the staff bring extra blankets and a warm bath to her room." Declan took the stairs two at a time, rushing past Richards to get to Alex's room.

The valet wore an appalled expression. Declan guessed it had more to do with the state of his clothing than with the shivering girl in his arms. Richards scurried ahead to open the door. "My lord, what happened?"

"A small accident." Declan laid Alex down on the bed. "Help me get this damp shirt off her."

"This is your shirt, my lord. Her hair's soaked it through." Richards appeared to be on the verge of tears. "It's ruined. What was she doing in your shirt?"

"She needed it." For modesty's sake Declan wrapped a blanket around Alex's body, while Richards tugged the shirt over her head.

Declan laid her back on the pillow and started rubbing

her limbs to try and bring warmth back into them. He could hear her teeth chattering in spite of his efforts.

Eleanor burst into the room, followed by servants laden with blankets.

"What happened? Lord Morgan said there'd been an accident." Eleanor rushed over to Alex's bed.

"Alex nearly drowned."

"How?"

"Swimming."

"She was *swimming?*" Eleanor shook her head in resignation. "Where?"

"In the lake, just past the south meadow. I'm not sure what happened. It may have been the cold water."

"Get more blankets on her. Where's the tub?" Two male servants came in bearing a large, wooden bathtub. "I need hot water up here, now." Eleanor turned toward Declan. "You need to get out of those wet clothes."

"I'm fine."

"No, you're not. I'll take care of Alex." Eleanor turned to Richards. "Make sure Lord Worthington gets into some dry clothes."

He gave up. He'd underestimated Eleanor; she could be just as stubborn as Alex. "I'll go, but I want to know the minute the doctor arrives."

"I'll send word." Eleanor turned back to her patient and wrapped a dry towel around her head. He took one more look at Alex's shivering form and left the room.

"Don't be blaming yourself. She'd have drowned if you'd not been there." Morgan poured another brandy, then sat in the wingback chair opposite his friend.

"I wasn't a gentleman, Morgan." Declan ran a hand through the hair on his forehead. "I knew she wouldn't come out with me there, yet I persisted. I even threatened to come in after her."

"And so you did." Morgan leaned forward and raised

his glass in Declan's direction. "To my way of thinking, you're a hero."

Declan started to protest, but Morgan stopped him. "She was swimming before you got there. In water that cold, the doctor pointed out the cramp could have happened at any time. She might have been alone when it hit. Then you'd not be forgiving yourself for her death." Morgan shook his head, his voice cajoling. "The doctor told you she'd be fine."

Declan stuck his booted feet toward the fire and swirled the brandy in his snifter. His life used to be simple. He knew what he wanted, and what he had to do. Alex made chaos of everything. He closed his eyes and sat back.

Morgan broke the silence. "The Countess of Lochsdale is a bit spirited. Beautiful, too."

Declan opened his eyes to find a contemplative look on his friend's face.

Morgan took a large swallow of his brandy. "A man would be looking a long time to find another like her. Perhaps I should be courting her myself."

"No." Declan thought he saw a grin on Morgan's face before he turned to the fire.

"Ah well, I see you'll be wanting some fancy husband for her. Have you any idea who?" He turned back to Declan, his expression serious. "I think it should be a very determined man. Alex will take a bit o' training, but she'd be worth it."

"I don't care who Alex marries." Declan stood up and went to lean against the fireplace, then studied the flames. "Her grandfather trusted me to do right by her, and I shall. Marriage is the only answer." He turned to look at Morgan. "You've been acquainted with her inside a week. Do you think I could leave her to her own devices?"

"Sure as Ireland's green, she'd find herself in trouble. She's not afraid of much." He chuckled. "And, she certainly worked her magic on Catrina. Throws a knife at her one day and gets her to help with finding a husband the next. By the way, I think you should be commending the butler."

"Edgar?"

"Couldn't get over how he handled the knife incident." Morgan shook his head. "The man's not human. He calmly removed the blade from the wall and went back to carving the roast."

"Edgar's been with the family a number of years. I doubt Lady Lochsdale could do anything to surprise him."

"Where might she be learning to throw like that?"

Declan went over and poured himself another drink. "She lived onboard a trading vessel until she was twelve. The sailors thought it prudent to teach her how to defend herself."

"That she can. Did you know her then?"

"I brought her home to her grandfather." Declan sat back down and crossed his legs at the ankles.

"She's a special colleen. How do you think she'll fare in London?"

"We have to get her there first. It's a wonder she's survived till now."

"Did the doctor say she could travel?"

"Yes, but I still want to delay our trip by a day. Just in case she develops a fever. We both know what that could mean." Their eyes met, and Declan knew Morgan understood. On the battlefield, it often wasn't the wound that killed.

"That won't be sitting well with Lady Catrina. I think she might be getting a bit restless."

"She'll have to wait."

Morgan studied him intently. "I thought you might be developing an attachment for Lady Catrina." His brow furrowed. "Though after spending the last week with her, I see why that might not be appealing. Spoiled females are a bit of a trial."

"If I had my way, I wouldn't marry at all." Declan

leaned over and poured the last few drops of his drink on the fire, listening to it hiss. "I need an heir, and Catrina would be as good a wife as any."

"Why her?"

"I could never love her."

Morgan's eyebrows raised. "You'd not be wanting to love your wife?"

"I have my reasons."

"Have you told Alex you intend to marry Catrina?"

"I mentioned it."

"And?"

"She seemed upset. I have no idea why." Declan stood and rubbed the back of his neck. "I can never tell what she's thinking or what she'll do. One thing I am sure of. She needs a husband."

"Do you think she'll be finding a suitable match in London?"

"Let's hope so." Because God knew he couldn't take much more.

Everything hurt. Alex tentatively opened her eyes, only to shut them against the light streaming through her bedroom window.

She tried to take a deep breath, and discovered breathing had become a luxury. What had happened? She'd been at the lake with Declan, then her memory blurred into fragmented glimpses of pain and endless water.

One thing for certain. If it hadn't been for Declan, she would have drowned.

Someone tapped on her door. "Come in." Her voice sounded rough, but at least it worked.

Declan entered and crossed to her bed. He stood there gazing at her until she wondered if he was trying to commit her face to memory.

"How are you feeling?" His light voice seemed at odds with the tortured look that swirled in the dark blue depths of his eyes.

"I've been better, but I'm alive." Alex smiled, but his expression didn't change. She tried a different tact. "You lied to me." At least that comment turned his worried frown into confusion. "You do rescue damsels in distress."

The corners of his mouth twitched upward. "I make an exception for naked fencers."

Her face heated, and she quickly turned away. She'd been trying to forget that she hadn't been wearing anything when he'd saved her. She drew her blanket up under her chin. Her figure had never been something she dwelled on, but now she couldn't help wondering how she'd compared to other women he'd known?

"I'm sorry, Lady Lochsdale. For some reason, you make it difficult for me to be a gentleman." Declan crossed to the window, then stood, staring at something she couldn't see.

He stayed like that for a long moment, his profile stark, and when he faced her, his bitter expression wasn't as hard to take as the self-derision lacing his voice.

"I should have left, or at least turned my back when I discovered you at the lake. I knew the circumstances." He held her gaze. "It was my fault."

"No, it wasn't." Funny, two weeks ago she wouldn't have imagined defending her guardian. Now, well, it wasn't in her nature to let other people take the blame for what she'd done. "I shouldn't have been swimming when the water was so cold. As for the other," Alex said with a shrug, "I guess I was curious about what you'd do."

The vision of Declan, naked to the waist, swam before her eyes. "I knew I should get out. But I wanted..."

Heat warmed his expression, and she had the feeling he knew exactly what she'd wanted. She dropped her gaze to the bracelet on her wrist. One of the small diamonds had fallen out, and she ran a finger over the gap. "It doesn't matter now." She looked up and tried to sound eager. "When do we leave for London?"

"Tomorrow morning, if you're well enough to travel."

"I shall be."

Declan leaned over and gave her a chaste kiss on the forehead. "Good, get some rest. We'll leave at first light."

"Lord Worthington?"

"Yes?"

"Thank you for saving my life."

Declan's smile warmed the blue of his eyes. "You're welcome. Shall we call it even?"

The deafening clatter in the courtyard gave Alex a headache. She was sorely tempted to cover her ears. Between servants calling to each other as they loaded the trunks and horses pawing the cobbles, you couldn't think.

Then again, maybe her head hurt because she knew she'd be traveling in a carriage with Catrina. She felt as if surviving the next few days with that vain, pompous creature would take an incredible amount of patience—not one of her strong points.

Two enclosed carriages stood at the entrance to Oakleigh, the Lochsdale crest clearly emblazoned across the polished black doors. She had personally checked to make sure Blade was attached to the baggage coach. If things got really bad, she'd find a way to ride. Even if she had to do it sidesaddle.

A small group of servants and family had gathered outside to say goodbye. Berta held a coral pink shawl of the finest wool in her hands. She handed it to Alex. "Here, you'll be needing this."

"Berta, it's beautiful." She took the shawl and gave the old woman a peck on the cheek. "I'll think of you whenever I wear it."

"See that you do. And remember what I told you. I don't want to hear about any more foolishness like yesterday.

London's a dangerous place. You don't need to go looking for trouble."

"I'll be careful. I promise."

Tears stood in Berta's eyes. "Good luck to you, Lady Lochsdale." She leaned over to give her a hug and whispered in her ear, "Hurry home, and bring a husband with you."

Alex stepped back and gave the older woman what she hoped was an encouraging smile. She didn't want to be reminded about the reason for this expedition. Especially as she had one immediate concern. Catrina.

Edgar spoke up. "Don't worry about things around here, my lady." He was fiddling with his neck cloth as though he suddenly found it too tight. "We'll do just fine till you come back."

"I have every confidence in you, Edgar." She smiled at him and a dark red blush spread across his cheeks. He turned away, making a big display of checking one of the straps on the carriages.

Eleanor stepped around the piles of trunks still strewn across the courtyard and came over to her. "It's a good thing you don't have much of a wardrobe. Lady Catrina's things are liable to take up all the space."

Alex lowered her voice so only Eleanor could hear. "If I'm really lucky, there won't be any room for me in the carriages, and I'll have to ride."

Eleanor smiled. "Now how would that further your growing relationship with Lady Catrina?"

Alex sighed. "I don't know if I can do this." She gave her cousin her best imploring look. "Are you sure you won't come with me?"

"Who would take care of the estate?" Eleanor gave her a hug. "You'll do fine. Do you have your list?"

Alex patted the pocket of her skirt. "It's right here. I hope it helps. I don't remember discovering any good husband material last time. What if they're all the same?"

"You're looking at them in a different way now. Just try to act like a lady." Eleanor pinned her with a knowing gaze. "No breeches or knives."

Alex hoped her expression didn't give her away. Had Eleanor guessed she'd tucked a shirt and breeches in the corner of one of her trunks? There might come a time when she needed freedom of movement. Men were lucky. They never had to worry about skirts weighing them down, let alone panniers, corsets, and stays.

Catrina came out of the manor wearing a ruffled dress of pale blue. Lace frothed at the elbows and neckline. Her only concession to travel seemed to be the wearing of hip pads instead of panniers.

"How is she going to travel in that?" Alex stared at the outfit in disbelief, then down at her serviceable grey gown. The dress was a favorite when she traveled because all it required was an underpetticoat and no stays. If Catrina was miserable on this trip, it was her own fault.

"Some people are more concerned with appearances." Eleanor gave Alex a searching look. "I know you despise Catrina, but following her example will help you fit in. It's only until you marry."

"If I marry the right man."

"You will. Go on now. Lord Worthington looks like he wants to leave. Lady Catrina and Lord Morgan are already in the carriage."

Alex gave Eleanor a hug. "Take care of yourself."

Eleanor laughed. "I'm not the one who's had two accidents in the last fortnight. Things are going to be very dull around here without you."

"Think of it as a much needed rest after the last eight years." Alex grinned at her, then headed for the carriage.

Declan stood waiting to hand her up through the door. He'd already informed them he'd be riding Knight. Alex wished she could ride Blade, but due to her recent injuries

Declan had expressly forbidden it. Still, she had to try. "There'd be extra room in the carriage if I rode."

"No."

The tone left no room for argument. Alex took comfort in the replacement knife she'd placed in her boot, squared her shoulders, and allowed him to help her into the lion's den.

Chapter 10

In order to get a better view of the street, Alex drew back the dust-laden curtain and repressed a sneeze. She'd forgotten how many people seemed to inhabit London.

"Alex, come away from the window this instant. It's vulgar to stare." Catrina began to straighten her clothing in preparation for their arrival.

If she had to listen to one more "do this," or "Alex wear that," she'd scream. Why couldn't she have been blessed with the ability to sleep most anywhere like Morgan? With as much sleep as he'd had in the last three days, he shouldn't need to rest for a week.

She stole another glance out the window. London fascinated her. In spite of the suffocating smell from the sewage in the streets and the ill-kept appearance of many buildings, she liked the city.

The carriage passed Hyde Park, veered onto a tree-lined side street, then stopped in front of a massive home made of yellow stone. The color reminded her of the buildings she'd seen in the Cotswald region with her grandfather. The weathered structure gave the impression it had always graced that spot and always would.

Several steps led up to the entrance. Carved, brass knockers adorned imposing looking wooden doors, which Alex suspected were heavy enough to need two men to open them. Flanking the steps were stone platforms, upon which crouched mythical lions, their feathered wings unfurled. The sculptures enhanced the power and beauty of the mansion, yet added a touch of whimsy. It was an impressive building, but why were they stopping here?

She'd assumed they would be occupying her grandfather's home near Westminster. They'd stayed there three years ago, during her first Season. Perhaps this belonged to Morgan.

Two women and a bevy of servants poured out of the front doors. The older woman bore a striking resemblance to Declan. *Was she his mother?*

Morgan let out a low whistle. "I wondered who was going to play chaperone." He winked at Alex. "You don't know what you've accomplished, Wee One. Worthington never asks his family for anything."

"Is the auburn-haired woman his mother?"

"His aunt. The girl is his cousin."

"You're mistaken, Lord Worthington would never let Lady Lochsdale stay at his residence." Catrina appeared flushed under her powder. "It's unheard of."

"I suspect his family will be staying for the duration of her visit." Morgan couldn't keep the amusement out of his voice. "Lady Lochsdale will be well chaperoned."

Catrina huffed and shoved past them when the footman opened the door. "We'll see." Her voice floated back to them, sickening in its sweetness. "Lady Bradford, how nice to see you again."

"Lady Catrina, I didn't know you were coming, and Lord Morgan."

Morgan helped Alex out of the carriage. Before she could take a step, the black-haired woman came over, took her hands, and stood back to look at her.

"You must be the Countess of Lochsdale. I'm Lady Bradford, Declan's aunt." Her eyes were kind. Alex liked her immediately. "I'm sorry about the loss of your grandfather. Lord Lochsdale was a special man."

"You knew him?"

"We had mutual acquaintances. He was always spoken

of with the highest regard."

"I see you've met my aunt," Declan said.

Alex hadn't heard him come up behind her, but she could feel his presence. It was oddly comforting in these new surroundings.

"She's a beauty, Declan." Lady Bradford dropped her hands and turned to Declan's cousin. "May I present my daughter, Lady Anna."

"Lady Lochsdale." Anna giggled and bobbed a slight curtsey.

"It's a pleasure." Alex could see Catrina's coldly polite smile over Anna's shoulder. It was a strange contrast to Anna's enthusiastic grin.

"Let's all go inside." Lady Bradford led the way. "I'm sure the journey was fatiguing."

That was an understatement. Lady Bradford couldn't begin to imagine what she'd been through the last three days.

Catrina had seen herself as an instructor of social etiquette. Alex had been subjected to hours of how to eat, what to wear, and whom to socialize with. Thank God it was over, and she hadn't drawn her knife once.

Perhaps her hand *had* drifted toward her boot a couple of times, but in each instance Morgan's look stopped her. How he knew what she was going to do when he appeared to be asleep, she couldn't guess.

They followed Lady Bradford. The hallway appeared as awe-inspiring as the outside.

Light green marble covered the floor, a perfect contrast to the mahogany wainscoting. Deep green silk decorated the upper section of each wall, along with the gilt-framed portraits of the Devereaux family.

It was a decidedly masculine décor, right down to the staircase, which wound up the right side of the hall. The stairs were wide enough for two women in court gowns to descend side by side. Ornately carved spindles led upward toward two landings, but what drew her eye was the winged lion at the base.

Unlike the lions out front, this one was far from benevolent. It appeared to be made of some kind of oak, the body carved as though ready to spring, its face menacing. Amber eyes seemed to follow her every move. She hoped she never had to come downstairs after everyone else had gone to bed.

The group made their way past the lion to a drawing room on the left. A woman's touch could be seen here; the fabrics were light and cheery. A small fire burned in the fireplace, taking the chill off the late spring afternoon.

She gratefully sank onto a chair without arms. The hip pads Catrina had insisted she wear would never fit in an armed chair. At least this seat didn't rock and sway with each bump in the road.

"Williams, will you bring tea, and let Cook know there will be two more joining us." Lady Bradford sat next to her daughter on the rose brocade settee.

"I didn't know you were visiting Lord Worthington." Catrina's low voice held polite interest. "Was it a sudden decision?"

Lady Bradford glanced at Declan, who leaned against the fireplace. "We'd been staying at our townhouse for the Season, but then we got Declan's note asking us to visit. We see so little of him. This seemed like the perfect opportunity."

"Will you be staying long?"

Lady Bradford gave Declan a look Alex didn't understand. "As long as he'll let us."

Declan turned away.

"Lady Anna, how might you be finding your first Season?" Morgan asked as Williams returned with the teacart and Lady Bradford began to pour tea. "Are the young bucks keeping you busy?"

Anna blushed to the roots of her sandy colored hair.

"It's been wonderful. There are parties every night, and the entertainments are astounding." Her eyes sparkled. "We went to Vauxhall Gardens, the theatre, and in two weeks there's going to be a masquerade ball." Anna turned toward Alex. "You're going to attend, aren't you, Lady Lochsdale?"

"I—"

"Of course she will." Declan's eyes met Alex's across the room. "As a matter of fact, Anna, I'd appreciate it if you took her to all the parties. Lady Lochsdale doesn't know many people in town yet."

"I'm sure I could secure invitations to any event you'd like," Catrina offered. "Make up a list of what you want to attend, and I'll send it around."

"I appreciate the offer, but I'm afraid my wardrobe is limited at the moment." Alex was glad to have an excuse not to attend too many parties. They'd always bored her.

"Nonsense." Lady Bradford paused in the middle of pouring tea. "We can go to the drapers tomorrow. You could have several new gowns by the end of the week."

"I appreciate the offer, but the funds—"

"Are at your disposal whenever you need them." Declan raised an eyebrow in her direction. "You do remember the reason for your visit?"

"That's right, I wouldn't want all my education to go to waste." Catrina preened like she'd just married a Duke, although in this case she was settling for an Earl. "In fact, if you'd like, I'd be happy to go with you to the drapers tomorrow."

"No." Alex hadn't meant it to come out quite so sharp, but if Catrina went with them, there was no telling what kind of clothing torture she could devise. "I don't want to bother you. Besides, I'd like to do a little sightseeing."

Lady Bradford passed her a plate of biscuits. "Why don't Anna and I go with you in the morning and show you the sights in the afternoon?"

"I'd like that." Alex let out a small sigh. She must be more tired than she thought.

"It's settled then," Lady Bradford said. "Right now I think I should show you to your room so you can freshen up." She and her daughter both stood.

"If you'll excuse me," Anna said. "I have a previous engagement."

Alex almost laughed when Anna left the room at a very unladylike pace. Declan's cousin was going to be a joy to have around.

"Morgan, could you escort Lady Catrina home?" Declan asked. "I have a few things I need to catch up on here."

"Be glad to. Might I be seeing you at White's later?"

"I'll be there." Declan took Catrina's arm and escorted her from the room. Morgan followed behind.

"Will you attend Lady Renlow's soirée as well?" Catrina's throaty question carried back to Alex. "I'd really like to see you."

Alex couldn't hear his reply. Why should it bother her if he wanted to spend time with Catrina? He intended to marry her, didn't he? She stared after them until Lady Bradford gave her a thoughtful look.

"I really am rather tired." Alex didn't relish the chance to rest as much as she wanted to be alone.

Lady Bradford led her to a room at the top of the stairs. It was beautiful, with blue brocade bed curtains, chairs, and pillows. Fresh spring flowers stood on the carved table by the bed. Instead of a window seat, she had a bench that allowed for storage underneath. Her trunks stood open, and most of her things were already unpacked.

"I'll leave you alone." Lady Bradford smiled and patted her arm. "I've assigned a maid. If you need anything, just ring for her. Dinner's at eight."

"Lady Bradford?"

"Yes?"

"Is Lord Worthington's mother living?"

"No, my sister died bearing him." Lady Bradford's eyes filled with regret. "He's so like her."

"I take it he hasn't remained close with the family."

"No, in part I blame myself. He must have felt isolated as a boy and now...Well, he's developed into a very private man. I'm hoping your being here will give us all a second chance."

"How?"

"We'll finally get to know him."

There was a crush at White's. Declan searched the dimly lit club, stopping occasionally to greet an old acquaintance. The hour was late, so Morgan may have left.

Declan was about to turn around, when he spotted him at an alcove table seated with a large, blond gentleman.

"Morgan, I thought you'd gone." Declan greeted his friend as he approached the table.

"Almost did, but then I ran into Lord Bradford. It's a strange thing Worthington, seeing all your family in one day."

Declan nodded to the other man. "Bradford, I didn't know you were in London." He never ceased to feel amazement at the difference between his cousins. Anna was high spirited and fun loving, while Adrian Leighton bordered on serious. With his white-blond hair and unusual light grey eyes most people thought him older than his years.

"I just got back. There were some problems with one of our estates up north."

Declan sat down. "Anything serious?"

"Not really, but I would like your opinion on a couple of things. Mind if I drop by tomorrow?"

"As you wish." He felt satisfaction in the arrangement

he shared with his cousin. In all actuality, he enjoyed helping Bradford with estate problems, and Bradford reciprocated by keeping him advised of commercial opportunities. They'd furthered both their fortunes. "It will give you a chance to see your mother and sister."

Bradford's glass paused halfway to his mouth. "They're staying with you?"

"Did I neglect to tell you?" Morgan lifted his glass in Declan's direction. "Your cousin has just been named guardian to a twenty-year-old beauty. He's asked your mother to chaperone." He raised the glass high. "Here's hoping he survives the experience." In one swallow he downed what was left of his drink.

"I'm glad you're here, Bradford." Declan leaned back in his chair as a footman came by with another round of drinks. After the man left, Declan continued. "Have you ever heard of a Lord Addington?"

"The name's not familiar."

"I wonder if you'd ask around?" Declan had every confidence that if there was something to learn, Bradford would uncover it. He'd developed an information network most of Society did not even know existed.

Bradford inclined his head. "Might I know why you're interested?"

"The man tried to put a bullet in him," Morgan said.

"I believe he hired someone to make it look like a hunting accident." Declan swirled the amber colored contents of his glass. "The assassin just wasn't prepared for the Countess of Lochsdale."

"Countess?"

"My ward, she took the bullet for me."

The minute raise of Bradford's eyebrow was all that indicated his surprise. Unlike Anna, Bradford didn't believe in displaying excess emotion. "Exemplary girl, but why was someone shooting at you in the first place?"

"To get me out of the way. He wants to marry her, and I was making it difficult. From what I gather, he came into his title without an estate."

"Would your ward have him?"

"Even if she agreed, I wouldn't let her. My gut tells me there's more to all this. I don't trust him."

"Consider your questions asked, but it might take a couple of weeks."

"I doubt Addington will make his move before then. As I brought the Countess of Lochsdale here, I suspect he'll show up in a day or two. It should make things easier. I'll let you know when he arrives."

Bradford leveled his steel-gray gaze at Declan. "How long are my mother and sister staying with you?"

"Only until I get Lady Lochsdale safely married."

"Mother must be pleased."

"I wouldn't know." Declan's relationship with his family was tenuous. He'd only associated with them since his father's death. Asking for help had been, difficult, especially from his aunt.

If only he could trust Alex to stay out of trouble, he'd put her up in her grandfather's townhouse, but he knew better. This was the only solution.

"I take it you attended Lady Renlow's soiree." Morgan gave a shudder. "It's a trial, the things a woman will be putting a man through. I stay away from the marriage mart myself. What about you, Bradford?"

"I would find marriage *inconvenient* at the moment, but I imagine I'll get around to it eventually."

"You should meet the Countess of Lochsdale. I'm thinking you'd make time."

"Morgan." Declan's voice held a warning.

"Well, isn't that what you'd be wanting? To get her married off as soon as possible."

"Bradford's not interested." Declan glared at his cousin, and Bradford was wise enough to keep quiet. "He's too old for her."

That wasn't true. His cousin was his junior by a year, but Bradford wasn't the right man for Alex.

Morgan smirked. "I'll be curious to see whom you consider the perfect man for her."

"I'll know him when the time comes."

"I'm guessing you know him quite well already." Morgan swallowed down his drink and winked at his friend.

Declan ignored him. Morgan never made sense when he was drunk.

Nothing had changed since Declan last visited Madame Colette. The chair he sat in, the décor, the service. Everything spoke of the finest quality. No wonder the Ton considered the shop the most elite draper establishment in London.

Alex stood on a platform surrounded by his aunt, cousin, and several seamstresses. She wore a fitted garment that accentuated her curves. He remembered how those curves felt, and his fingers itched to trace their path once again. He clenched his fists and rested them on his knees.

"Mademoiselle, could you raise your arm a little higher?" A sharp-faced woman began to measure around the top of Alex's breasts.

He refused to watch.

Two of the women in the shop were whispering and casting suggestive glances his way. He acknowledged them, which made them titter. God, he hated that reaction in a female. With a shake of his head, he returned his attention to his ward's face.

"Will it be much longer?" Alex's voice held a tinge of impatience.

"It is almost finished." Madame Colette stepped back

from the platform. "There, now the gowns will fit and make you look like a princess."

He hoped the woman didn't see Alex cast her gaze toward heaven. A smile curved his lips. One more item to add to the list of things his ward didn't like—being fitted for gowns. Judging from the sparse number of trunks she'd brought with her, she'd aptly managed to avoid that activity.

He'd come along to make sure she didn't order a shirt or a pair of breeches, but now that they were here, he had the strangest urge to dress her in finery. It almost felt as if she belonged to him. Fear shivered up his spine, and he concentrated on tapping his gloves against his thigh. She *wasn't* his. He needed to remember that.

"I realize pastels are all the rage, but mademoiselle would look much better in jewel tones." Madame Colette was a tall, attractive woman, with yellow blond hair and laugh lines at the corners of her eyes. Part of her success was due to the way she treated each of her customers, making them look their best, instead of outfitting them in the most current fashion.

He'd used her in the past, whenever he needed a gift for a mistress. Experience had taught him he could trust her judgment.

"Mama, how about this one?" Anna slid a brilliant turquoise silk from amongst the bolts of material.

Alex's eyes lit up. "Oh Lady Anna, it's beautiful."

"Yes, it would make a nice gown for the theatre." Colette brought it over for Alex to examine. "You will be needing several gowns, no? I would also suggest the dark green brocade shot with black and the coral silk. Done *a l'Anglaise*."

"What about the masquerade? Have you decided what you'll go as?" Anna's eyes were filled with mischief. "I'm going to be the goddess Athena. I've had my costume for weeks."

Alex glanced over at him and grinned. He wished she'd stop doing that. It made him want to kiss her.

"I know just what costume I'd like, but it's a secret." Alex turned to Madame Colette, leaned down, and whispered in her ear.

"Perfect. I could not have made a better selection. Leave the materials to me."

The seamstresses finished Alex's measurements. She scrambled from the platform, left the room, and returned a short time later in her normal attire. He mourned the close fitting gown.

She turned toward his chair and gave him an inquiring stare. "I've ordered a new habit, morning dresses, and ball gowns. I think I now own a piece of clothing for every occasion. Have I missed any, my lord?"

"A wedding gown?"

A hush fell over the small group until Lady Bradford spoke up. "Declan, don't you think she should find a groom first? It just isn't done."

"Call me an optimist. I want her to have one."

Alex's cool voice came to him from the platform. "Any particular type, my lord?"

He had to commend her. She was learning to control her temper. Someone who didn't know her would never guess she was furious.

He steepled his long fingers and studied her over them. "I'm not sure. What would you suggest Madame Colette?"

"I would do the gown in pale peach organdy with pearls and lace. And, of course, we would give mademoiselle the necessary undergarments." She moved to a table and started thumbing through the books containing current styles. "Her figure is perfect. I would chose a gown with a fitted bodice in front and back with a separate attached train."

"Your sense of style is perfect,"—Declan rose and gave her a small bow—"as always. When do you think the wedding gown and others can be completed?"

"It will take at least three weeks." Colette appeared to figure the time in her head. "I can have the habit, two of the gowns, and the costume done by Friday."

"That would be acceptable. Send them around to my address." He tugged on his gloves. "Ladies, shall we go?" He offered his arm to Alex and saw the hesitation in her eyes as courtesy warred with anger. Courtesy won.

The sound of a slamming door at the top of the stairs reverberated through the hallway. Declan glanced toward Alex's room and shook his head. What was so wrong about insisting she order a wedding gown? From the silence in the carriage on the return trip, he'd have thought he killed someone.

Anna gave him a timid look and rushed upstairs, but his aunt remained in the hallway. "The Countess of Lochsdale doesn't want to marry, does she?" Lady Bradford removed her hat and pinned him with a knowing look.

"She must. That's why we're here."

"Was there someone she fancied at home?"

"No, she's just stubborn. If I said she didn't need a wedding gown, she'd want one." Declan ran his hand through his hair. "She knows she has to marry. Why should it matter if I try to expedite things?"

"Perhaps Lady Lochsdale wanted to marry for love."

He scoffed. "She's better off marrying to protect her title and estates."

"Declan, sometimes love matters more than anything else in the world."

"Yes, it can matter more than anything—or anyone." Hurt curled around his heart, squeezing till he thought he couldn't breathe. "And we're well aware of the results of a love match, aren't we, Aunt?"

Lady Bradford tried to take his arm, but he brushed her hand off and shut himself in the library.

I'm in love with him. Alex stood with her back to the door wishing she had somewhere to run, but she couldn't run from herself. All this time she had thought she hadn't found the right man, when the truth was she'd never find anyone to compare to Declan. Even as a child, she'd secretly looked up to him.

She respected him. Yes, he made her angry, but she had to admit his requests had never been unreasonable. And though he discouraged her unconventional pursuits, he'd never ridiculed her or disparaged her abilities.

He'd slipped in under her guard, just as he'd done in their fencing match, only this time she'd sustained permanent injury. She'd fallen in love with him, while he felt nothing for her. If only he'd ordered the gown for her to wear at their wedding. Instead, he expected her to marry another man, while he married his spoiled beauty.

Could you marry one man, while loving another? She supposed you could. She picked up her list off the carved table by her bed and read the first item. Declan would never let her do as she pleased, but he fit the second requirement admirably. He didn't love her.

Someone tapped on her door. If it was Declan, she couldn't face him yet.

"Lady Lochsdale, may I come in?" Lady Bradford's voice carried through the door.

"Yes."

She entered and closed the door behind her, then turned with a concerned look on her face. "My nephew can be difficult."

Alex shoved the list in the writing table drawer. "I would agree."

Declan's aunt crossed to the padded bench and sat down, motioning for Alex to join her. "There are things you don't understand."

"Such as?"

"Such as why Lord Worthington is..." Lady Bradford chewed on her bottom lip, then gave a weak smile. "I suppose I should start with my sister. Maura was such a beautiful, wild young woman. Everyone she met loved her, including Edward Devereaux.

"He'd come to Ireland to visit friends. He was supposed to stay two weeks. He stayed two months. At the end of that time he asked Maura to be his wife."

Lady Bradford clutched the cameo at her neck, rubbing her thumb over the figure. "I came to visit shortly after they moved to England. During my stay, Maura discovered she was with child. I remember how excited they were." Her face wore a sad, wistful smile. "They spent hours trying to decide what to name the baby. Edward made the cradle himself and placed it in the nursery.

"Ten months later, I received a letter telling me my sister had died in childbirth." The older woman's eyes filled with tears.

"I'm sorry." To have a sister, only to loose her, Alex couldn't imagine the pain. She reached over and squeezed Lady Bradford's hand.

Declan's aunt rose, keeping her back to Alex. "At first I was so caught up in my own grief, I didn't even think about Maura's son. A year passed before I visited England again and went to see my brother-in-law."

Lady Bradford turned and raised her hands in a helpless gesture. "Initially he refused to see me, but I persisted. I couldn't believe the change in him." Her slender white fingers plucked at a pearl button on her gown as she stared vacantly over Alex's head. "He told me he never wanted to see me or my family again. I'll never forget his eyes. They were wild, crazed."

"Surely he didn't mean it." She rose and grasped the other woman's arm. "People often say cruel things when they're hurting."

Lady Bradford placed her hand on top of Alex's, then closed her eyes. "When I asked to see my nephew, Edward went berserk and started throwing things. He screamed, 'I'll take care of the murderer in my own way. Now get out.'" Suddenly, all the energy appeared to leave Lady Bradford's body and her hand dropped to her side. She stared at Alex, remorse and pain etched into her features. "I was a coward. I left. It occurred to me to go to the magistrate, but what could he do? Declan was Edward's son." She crossed to the window, then grasped the edge of a damask curtain and peered out.

"I stayed in England and finally married my husband. Lord Bradford had some influence. We were able to get reports on Declan, but I never saw him." She turned toward Alex, a tremulous smile lifting the corners of her mouth.

"That's one of the reasons I knew of your grandfather. Our reports went into great detail on how he'd taken my nephew under his wing. Because of Lord Lochsdale's kindness, I slept easier at night."

She joined Lady Bradford. Pride for her grandfather mixed with the horror of what Declan's life must have been like. "I suspect they helped each other. It wasn't easy for grandfather after my mother left. Lord Worthington acted as a replacement. They needed each other."

The distraught woman wrapped her arms around her slight form. "It wasn't until Edward died that I found the courage to approach Lord Worthington. By then my husband had passed away, but I wanted my nephew to know he had family." Her voice became rough. "It was a shock when I saw him for the first time. He looks so like Maura. I felt as if she'd returned."

She sighed. "Unfortunately, physical appearance is where the resemblance stopped. All those years with his father have done something to him. He's learned to keep everyone at a distance."

No wonder her guardian found it hard to trust in love. His aunt had left him in the hands of a madman. What must it have been like, growing up, thinking no one cared? "Surely he's forgiven you?"

"I'm afraid not."

"But you had no choice."

"Perhaps. Is there something else I could have done?" She pursed her lips and shook her head. "I don't know."

"Why are you telling me all this?"

"Because you need to understand. Lord Worthington hasn't experienced love, only what the loss of it can do." Lady Bradford studied her until she blushed and looked down. "You do care for him." She sounded relieved. "I'm hoping, that in time, you can teach him love is not something to be afraid of."

"But I don't have time. I need to marry quickly." There was no point in denying her feelings.

"Then we'll just have to make him realize he loves you."

She raised her head. "But what if he doesn't?"

Lady Bradford gave her a conspiratorial smile and patted her cheek. "I've never seen a man so anxious to marry a woman off. He loves you, and we're going to make him admit it."

Chapter 11

Alex had forgotten how badly her feet could hurt after dancing till the early morning hours. This was her fourth ball in the last two days. Her physical pain couldn't compare to the torture of constant suitors vying for her attention.

In spite of her discomfort, she was nicer than normal to her current dance partner. The poor man had a very bad habit of batting his eyes.

She'd inquired if he had something in them, but he'd blushed, creating a strange contrast to his lavender-colored wig, and stammered an incoherent reply. Thank God dancing the Quadrille only required polite conversation, as you weren't with your partner for very long.

"Lady Lochsdale,"—blink, blink—"are you staying in London for the season?"

"I believe so, yes."

"Splendid, perhaps I'll see you again." Blink, blink.

The dance ended, and they parted. She realized she hadn't paid much attention to his last comments, but he'd batted his eyes thirty-one times. Had she agreed to see him again? She hoped not.

Before he spoke, she felt Declan's presence. To be honest, she'd been watching him off and on all evening. It hadn't been difficult. Wherever Catrina was, she'd be sure to find him.

"Are you enjoying yourself?" He reached down and took her dance card, eyeing each entry.

Her next dance partner approached, and Declan coolly raised an eyebrow in his direction. The man couldn't turn around fast enough.

"Better now, thank you," she said. "I think I'm just tired." In spite of her fatigue, she could still appreciate Declan in full evening attire. He wore the elegant black and white formal garb with his usual nonchalance. Still, the way it fit to his body nudged her imagination, and she felt her face grow warm. She lowered her gaze.

"Tired?" Declan returned her dance card. "I thought all young women were thrilled with entertainments such as this. I know my cousin is."

She glanced across to where Anna held court. At least eight young men were gathered around her, laughing at something she said. At one point, she stopped speaking and gave a particularly handsome young man a coy look from behind her fan. This was Anna's element. Alex felt washed out by comparison. "She likes all the bustle."

"And you don't?"

"This isn't my kind of excitement."

"Oh really, and what excites you?" He reached out and brushed a loose curl out of her eyes.

She wanted to tell him he did, but fear of his response kept her silent. His touch kindled such yearning that it was a wonder he couldn't feel the heat.

Her mind searched for a safe response. "I like the thrill of testing my abilities."

He gave her a devilish smile. "Poor Lady Lochsdale, you haven't had much opportunity to stretch your wings, have you? Would you like to go riding with me tomorrow? Sidesaddle, of course."

"I'd love to." It was one of the few times he'd wanted to be alone with her since they got here. Perhaps they were making progress.

"We can discuss how you're coming along in your search."

Declan didn't have to say what search. He wanted to

see if she'd found a husband yet, so he could be rid of her. She opened her mouth to tell him to forget the ride, when a strong sense of unease prompted her to turn around. Luther stood across the room. The minute their gazes locked, he crossed to them.

"Isn't this a pleasant coincidence?" Luther gave her a graceful bow and nodded curtly in Declan's direction. "I've been looking for you, cousin." He touched one of the diamond-studded patches at the corner of his mouth, as if to reassure himself of its presence. "I went to your grandfather's townhouse, but you weren't in residence."

"Lord Worthington deemed it necessary for me to stay with him." She made a conscious effort to stop worrying at her dance card.

"I'm sure Lord Worthington had his reasons"—Luther's eyebrows raised—"but surely you aren't staying there alone?"

Declan moved closer to her. She could see the tension in his jaw as his gaze narrowed on Luther.

"My mother and sister are staying with me." His voice held thinly veiled anger. "You needn't worry. She's well chaperoned. I'll take good care of her until she's married."

"I'm sure you will." Luther plucked at the lace around his sleeve. "Well, little cousin, perhaps Lord Worthington will allow us to dance. You can tell me what you've been doing since you arrived."

"Another time, Lord Addington." Her guardian became politely formal. "Lady Lochsdale just told me she's tired. I'm taking her home."

Declan put his hand at the small of her back and propelled her toward the door. They stopped long enough to say goodnight to his aunt and cousin, but she knew Luther watched every movement from across the room. Relief swept over her when they stepped outside, away from the malice in his eyes.

Declan didn't want to be in an enclosed carriage with Alex, alone, at night. He sighed. There really hadn't been a choice. Either he took her with him, or he left her there for Addington to play his games.

"I really wasn't that tired," Alex commented as Declan handed her up into the carriage. "Isn't Catrina going to miss you?"

"Morgan will take her home." He'd already made arrangements for him to do so. Catrina was beginning to annoy him. Two nights of being constantly at her side could try anyone's patience. He got in and sat across from Alex, making sure their knees didn't touch.

It was warm for the beginning of June. Alex removed her cloak and set it beside her on the seat. He wished she'd put it back on.

She wore her mother's dark green gown. Damn, he'd been right about how she'd look in that dress. The simplicity of the lines, as well as her upswept hair with two fat curls trailing over her shoulder helped accentuate her fragile beauty.

Why couldn't the fabric have come to her neck? Instead, it dipped down, exposing the tops of her creamy breasts. He closed his eyes. Maybe he could feign sleep.

"Lord Worthington, tell me about yourself. I know so little about you, but you know a great deal about me."

He stared at her not-so-innocent expression dimly visible in the carriage. Why the sudden curiosity? Wary, he wished he had the slightest inkling what she was up to. "What do you want to know?"

"Do you have any brothers or sisters?"

"No."

"Are your father or mother alive?"

"No."

"Are you going to answer any of my questions with more than one syllable?"

"No."

"A man of mystery. I bet everything I read about you in those newssheets is true. Did you really challenge the Duke of York to a horse race on Derby Day?"

"Yes."

"I'd love to go." She absently brushed at one of the curls that had worked its way into her cleavage.

He had difficulty taking his eyes away from the spot. When he did, he realized Alex gazed at him expectantly. "What?"

"Could we go to Derby Day?"

He shook his head, feeling somewhat bemused. "Of course. I'll see to the arrangements. It's three weeks from Saturday." He hadn't been there in years. Unlike most females, he suspected Alex would enjoy it.

"What if I'm betrothed by then?"

He found it incomprehensible that in three short weeks she could belong to someone else. Surely it would take longer than that.

Without warning, the coach lurched around a corner, feeling as if it rode on only two of its four wheels. The waxed leather seat gave Declan little purchase. He grabbed for the loop near the door, missed, and found himself tossed to the floor. Alex soon followed, landing on top of him in a tangle of limbs. He tried to straighten in the cramped space, grunting slightly as his back struck one of the warming bricks.

The horses snorted, and frantic curses filled the air as the carriage lurched hard to the left, then righted itself before coming to a stop. Quiet descended.

Alex had landed so that her chin came even with his forehead, and her attempts to right herself brought about a different kind of pain.

"Please stop wiggling." He managed to get the words out between gritted teeth. "Are you hurt?" His question created a puff of warm air that reflected back at him from the alabaster perfection of her throat.

"No."

His breathing quickened. Her welcoming curves pressed along his entire length. He shifted, the slight friction rubbing his now throbbing manhood against her. His brain refused to work.

Unable to resist, he nuzzled forward until his lips traced the soft skin exposed to him. He inhaled her fragrance. The smell of vanilla, mixed with her unique scent, was driving him wild.

With his tongue, he traced a small circle on her neck. She tasted salty. He licked the spot, moistening it for his kiss.

Just as he was about to press his lips to the tender area, Alex shimmied down his body and gave him access to her mouth. She couldn't have been aware how erotic her movements were. Dazed, he drew her to him. His demanding kiss went far beyond all rational thought. A groan escaped him as he cupped her face, then moved his hands further back to remove the pins from her hair and twine his fingers in her glorious mane.

"My lord, my lady, you all right?" The driver's voice came from somewhere above them. He stiffened.

With his hands on her shoulders, Declan lifted Alex off of him and settled her onto the seat before the driver's torch could illuminate the inside of the carriage. "We're fine." He scrambled back onto his seat and picked up Alex's cloak from the floor.

The coachman opened the door and peered inside. "Sorry about the turn. Didn't ken I had that much speed. Saw the street at the last minute. These flambeaux aren't much help."

While attempting to straighten his cravat, Declan peered at the driver in the flickering light. "How much farther?"

"It's just ahead. A few hundred yards."

"Good, we'll walk the rest of the way." He handed

Alex down from the carriage, paid the driver, then placed the cloak around her shoulders. They started down the street, and after several minutes, Alex broke the silence.

"You never answered my question. Will you still take me to Derby Day if I'm betrothed?"

Thank God she was going to ignore his indiscretion in the carriage. "That will be up to your future husband to decide. Once you're married, we won't be seeing much of each other."

"I see." She stopped, and he joined her, even though he had no desire to halt their progress. With her hand on his arm, she studied his face. "Will that make you happy?"

What did she want from him? He understood the rapier-wielding hoyden in breeches better than this woman. "Alex, you aren't making sense. Three weeks ago you couldn't wait to be rid of me."

"I've gotten rather used to having you around." She wrapped her cloak tighter about her body. "I thought you might miss me."

"Let's see, what might I miss about you? Trying to keep you from danger? No, I prefer my life quiet. Stepping in every time you use that knife of yours? I rather enjoy my skin intact."

"How about stolen kisses?"

So, she wasn't going to ignore what happened in the carriage after all. He lifted her chin so the light from the nearby torch played across her features. She didn't look real. "I'll not deny my attraction to you. But that's all it is." Hope seemed to die in her eyes. "Dammit, Alex, I have my life planned, and you're not a part of it."

She jerked out of his grasp. "You'd rather be lonely. So be it." She turned and ran the last few feet, up the steps, and into the house.

Lonely? Just because he'd learned to depend on himself

didn't make him lonely, did it? He enjoyed her company, but when she was gone, would he miss her? That tiny part of him he'd considered dead answered.

Yes.

Alex threw herself on her bed, her skirts flying in every direction. She reached up under them and yanked out the rump and hip pads, tearing off one of the ties in the process. She struggled with the lacings up the back of the gown and finally took out her knife. With a feeling of satisfaction, she cut the satin strips.

Dressed only in her chemise, she sat down at the end of her poster bed and laid a cheek against the cool, polished wood. Lady Bradford had been wrong. She'd been through all the balls and suitors for nothing. How could she make Declan jealous if he didn't love her? Her throat constricted, and she swallowed several times, trying to ease the tension. She'd made a fool of herself, but no more.

Tomorrow she would give Declan her list. There were only four names she would even consider. All four were out to increase their wealth with her holdings. She hoped their greed would make them manageable.

Lord Duprey was the only one on the list she worried about when it came to the marriage bed. He had a look in his eye she didn't like, but he would be preferable to Luther.

She lay back, staring at the ceiling. If only the driver hadn't opened the door. There was no doubt Declan desired her, but if she made love to him, would it make a difference? She'd broken with convention all her life, but this time she was afraid of the consequences.

"Milady, there's a Lord Addington here to see you. I left him in the drawing room."

Alex looked up from the letter she'd been writing to Eleanor. Her maid seemed a bit anxious. Luther had that effect on people.

"Thank you, Mary. Do you know where Lord Worthington is?"

"He left early this morning."

"When is he expected back?"

"He didn't say."

"Are Lady Bradford or Lady Anna in?"

"They've gone on their afternoon calls. No one's in residence, milady." Mary studied the floor, as if tying to find a spot she'd missed in cleaning. "Besides, Lord Addington seemed very anxious to see you alone. He said to tell you he had some information about Lord Worthington."

What trouble was Luther trying to stir up? She sighed and put her ink and quill away. She might as well face him. He'd keep coming back until she did. "That will be all, Mary. I'll see him."

The maid left. Alex dusted her letter and slipped it in the drawer of her writing desk, then took Berta's shawl out of the window bench and wrapped it around her shoulders. It wasn't cold this morning, but she needed its reassuring feel.

She entered the brightly lit drawing room and stopped a few feet from the gold brocade settee. Luther sat in a high-backed chair beside the fire, snuffbox in hand. He rose. His cream colored breeches were a perfect match for his velvet coat. Pale lace spilled from his cravat and draped at his wrists.

The man had the appearance of an angel. Then why did she have the feeling he was going to put her through hell? "Lord Addington, this is a surprise."

"Lady Lochsdale, cousin,"—he crossed to her and gave a slight bow—"I just wanted to see you. Worthington spirited you away before I had the chance to make sure you were well." His face wore a mask of concern.

"Why wouldn't I be?" She drew her shawl tight around her shoulders.

Luther returned his snuffbox in his pocket and studied her, as if gauging what to say. "How well do you know Worthington?"

"Not well. Why?"

"Please, sit." He motioned toward the settee.

She hesitated before taking the seat. It was silly to be afraid. What could he do with a servant within calling distance? She sat, and he settled himself next to her.

"After you left, I made some inquiries. It seemed odd to me that your grandfather made Worthington your guardian."

"He had his reasons."

"I'm sure he did, but were you aware Worthington was the only man with your father when he died?" Luther made this pronouncement with a flourish. His eyes narrowed, as if watching her every reaction.

She tried to remember the particulars of that awful day. Declan had returned to *The Merry Elizabeth* with her father's body, and later she'd learned they'd been set upon by thieves near the pier.

A picture of her father's face, as he'd looked in death, played across her memory. At the time, she'd resented Declan. He still lived, while her father lay dead.

Luther appeared to be waiting for her reply. She spoke softly. "I knew he was with Father. They were both attacked."

"Isn't it amazing that they allowed Worthington to live? Was anything taken?"

"No, Lord Worthington carried the proceeds from the sales, but he managed to return with them intact."

"How convenient." Luther raised an eyebrow and took Alex's hands, extracting them from the warmth of the shawl.

His skin felt cool to the touch, as though no blood ran in his veins. As her cousin, she couldn't berate him for being too forward, but the intimacy made her stomach churn.

"Did you know your grandfather and I discussed making you my ward?"

"No." Her grandfather had hated Luther. They may have discussed it, but he would never have agreed.

"Lord Lochsdale was an excellent horseman. Yet his horse threw him? Didn't you ever wonder about that?"

With a firm tug, she removed her hands from Luther's grasp and sidled away from him. "It was an accident." She clutched the shawl to her chest, her breathing rapid.

"Was it?" Luther gave her a chilling smile. "It appears to me, Worthington had much to gain through their deaths. Has he asked you to marry him yet?"

She wouldn't listen to any more perversions of the truth. With a practiced motion, she reached down and swept her blade from her boot. The weapon lay along Luther's throat before she even thought about it. He went pale under his powder, pressing his back against the settee to keep away from the point.

"For your information, Lord Worthington has no interest in me." Saying the words out loud hurt, but she wanted Luther to know how ridiculous his claim was. Declan had made it plain he didn't want her, but even if he had been interested, she knew he would never have hurt her family. "Now, I want you to take your lies and pompous attitude out of this house." She let the blade slide over his throat as she removed it and stood, holding her weapon at the ready.

Luther scurried for the door, showing himself to be the coward she'd always suspected. "Luther." Her voice betrayed none of the rage she felt toward the snake.

He turned and glared at her.

"If we happen to meet at any social events, you don't know me."

Luther exited the study, grabbed his hat from the footman, and strode to his carriage.

"Where to, my lord?"

"The docks, and make it quick."

He climbed in and sat back against the seat. *The bitch, draw a knife on him, would she?* She must be fonder of Worthington than he had suspected.

If she wouldn't come with him willingly, he'd have to have her abducted, and he knew just the men for the job.

Once he had her as his wife, he'd make her pay. Luther felt himself harden just thinking about it.

Chapter 12

Alex's quiet unnerved him. Declan couldn't be sure if it was due to last night, or Luther's visit this morning. Williams had informed him about the unwelcome guest, but perversely he wanted to hear it from her.

They rode their horses side by side through Hyde Park. He glanced at her, noting her new riding habit with approval. The vivid blue was a perfect foil for her hair. The sun warmed the red highlights in her curls, giving them a life of their own. Even the hat enhanced her allure. The elaborate creation sat at a jaunty angle, which allowed the ribbons to billow out behind her as she took Blade to a canter.

He wished his hands could travel the velvety curves the outfit emphasized. His jaw clenched. That line of thinking would only get him in trouble.

With a slight pressure on the reins, he urged Knight to catch up with her. "Slow down, there'll be a crush ahead. I wouldn't want anything to happen."

For once, Alex complied. She reined Blade to a walk and studied Declan, as if looking for something. "Luther came to see me today. He said he needed to speak with me privately."

"Oh?" He didn't like Alex being alone with her cousin. It wasn't safe. He'd advised Bradford that Luther had returned to London. But until the man made some overt threat, all they could do was watch.

"Luther wanted to warn me about you." Alex fiddled with her bracelet, turning it around and around on her wrist. "He seems to think you murdered my father and grandfather so you could marry me."

"What?" He jerked on Knight's reins, causing the horse to sidestep. "Did he have any evidence?"

"Not really. He simply pointed out that when my father died, the thieves let you live without taking anything."

He'd wondered about that at the time. But as there were only a few attackers left standing, he'd finally decided they were cowards. "And how does he think I killed Lord Lochsdale?"

"I'm not sure. He didn't mention it, just insinuated grandfather was too good a horseman to die in a riding accident." Alex met Declan's gaze.

"And what did you say?"

"I drew my knife and told him to get out."

He didn't know how to react. She should never have done anything so dangerous, and yet knowing she'd defended him made him want to hug her and shake her at the same time. If she hadn't been on horseback, he might have done both. "That was a foolish thing to do."

"Perhaps. But I won't listen to his lies."

"In future, I don't think you should speak with him alone."

"Don't worry, I doubt he'll return. I explained to him that he was wrong. You didn't kill my family, and you certainly don't have any interest in me as a...wife." She reached into the pocket of her habit and brought out a slip of paper. "I thought about what you said last night, and you're right. I shouldn't expect you to change what you want in life because of me." She handed him the list. "Here are the men I would find suitable as husbands."

Her choices were numbered in her neat handwriting. He should be glad his name didn't appear on the tiny slip of paper, but instead he had the irrational impulse to crumple it up and throw it away. "Only four names?" With deliberate movements, he folded the small sheet and slipped it in his pocket. "What if they don't ask for your hand?"

"They will."

He raised an eyebrow at the certainty in her voice. "I'll have to check them out thoroughly."

"As you wish."

"Might I ask what they all have in common?"

Alex gave him a defiant look. "They'll all allow me to return to my old way of life. They're only interested in my possessions. As long as the estates make a profit under my supervision, they'll leave me alone."

"Are you so sure?" His fingers ached with wanting to touch her. In a low whisper he added, "I would never let you go."

"Then it's a good thing I'm not marrying you."

Alex preferred the quiet path they'd been riding to this bustling thoroughfare, but at least now she had an excuse to look at everything but Declan. Not that it mattered. He'd seemed distracted since she'd given him her list.

A highly polished curricle, drawn by two matched horses, sped by, the occupant's crest emblazoned on the door. Small groupings of well-dressed men and women sat atop blooded horseflesh at every turn.

At least she now understood why the women of the Ton rode sidesaddle. They perched on their horses as if on display. It would never do to gallop and have a curl blow out of place. How staid their lives must be.

"Isn't this a surprise?" A silky low voice rose above the sound of horses and people. Alex would know Catrina's breathy tones anywhere. She turned to see Declan's intended riding toward them on an intersecting path, her grey mare a wonderful backdrop for her habit, a work of art in shades of coral. An older, bald gentleman accompanied her atop a docile looking bay.

With a steady hand, Declan reined Knight up beside Catrina. How Alex wished she could ignore them, but she halted Blade next to Knight.

Declan wore the expression of a boy who'd been caught stealing biscuits. "Lady Catrina, I didn't know you were riding this morning."

"I'm sure you didn't. This is my cousin, Lord Danby." Catrina gave Alex a coldly polite smile. "Lord Danby, may I introduce the Countess of Lochsdale and Lord Worthington."

The little man bobbed his head in Alex's direction as he twisted his horse's reins. "Nice to meet you."

"I've seen very little of you, Lady Lochsdale." Catrina didn't even glance her way. Instead, she gave Declan a seductive look, making Alex feel like an interloper. "Lord Worthington and I have been making up for lost time."

At least Declan didn't return her warm regard. In fact, judging from his clenched jaw, her insinuations annoyed him.

"Are you enjoying the Season, Lady Lochsdale?" Catrina asked.

"Yes." She could have replied the moon was blue, and Declan's intended would never have noticed.

"Lord Worthington, I wonder if I might see you at Lady Ashton's this evening?" Catrina moved her horse closer to Declan's mount.

"If you'll excuse me." Alex turned to Declan. "I think I'll go and allow Blade to graze under that little grove of trees." She indicated a spot several hundred feet further up the path to the right. "I'm sure you and Lady Catrina have much to discuss."

She didn't give Declan a chance to say no. With a tug on Blade's reins, she cantered away. There wasn't any reason to stay. It hurt too much, watching the two of them together, knowing Catrina would someday be his wife.

Several laughing couples dotted the main path. To

avoid them, she veered off and entered a cluster of trees. To her delight, someone had put a bench under one of the massive oaks. She dismounted, wandered over to the bench, and sat down.

The branches created a canopy overhead, as if she were in the middle of a forest. She couldn't see the path or hear the bustle of Society beyond her haven. It felt good to have some time in the woods. Alone. Problems had always seemed smaller to her when surrounded by nature. It put things in perspective.

She leaned back and shut her eyes, letting the pleasant sounds of the small creatures she heard in the underbrush soothe her. A nearby branch snapped. She opened her eyes, and a prickle of awareness spread across the surface of her skin.

She wasn't alone.

Without warning, she was shoved forward and a cloth sack dropped over her head from behind, blocking out daylight. She clawed at the hands gripping the material, until another person yanked her to her feet. The bag fell below her waist, and her attackers wrapped it tight against her body, pinning her hands and arms. They wound a rope from her elbows to below her waist, cinching it tight.

She couldn't breath. Her mouth opened to scream. Dust filled her lungs, choking her.

Think. She stood still, trying to make out the muffled voices of her captors.

"Ye got her? That's a good girl. Don't struggle. Won't do no good anyways, will it, Spider?" The man seemed to find that funny and started to laugh.

"Quiet, you fool. An' don't go usin' my name again. Can ye carry her?"

"A mite o' a thing like this?" One of the men hefted her up on his beefy shoulder, effectively cutting off even more of her air. "Just like a sack o' potatoes."

"Good, let's go."

"Wot about the horse?"

"Leave it. Don't want nobody wonderin' where we got it."

She couldn't tell how far they had traveled before they dumped her onto something hard. From the jerking and bumping motion, she assumed she was in some sort of cart.

She tried to work her hands down to reach her knife, but the sack had been tied tight. No room to maneuver.

Who were these men? The vision of Luther's face as he'd left that morning came back to her. He had to be behind this, but what did he want? Did he think he could force her to marry him?

The cart lurched to a halt. One of her captors picked her up and threw her over his shoulder, then took her up a flight of stairs. They must have been somewhat narrow because he kept banging her into something, probably the wall. He carried her for a short time before dropping her onto a bed of some sort.

"She's a pretty little thing. Ye sure we can't hav' some fun for he gets here?"

She heard lust in the beefy man's voice and started to pray. In her current position, all she could do was kick, and that wasn't going to stop them.

"The bloke wat hired us were right particular 'bout that. You'd be sorry tangling with the likes o' him."

"Too bad. Ye gonna leave her tied in the sack? Don't know as she can breathe."

"Just loosen the rope. She'll get out soon enough. Don't want her glimpsin' that ugly face o' yours. Probably scare her to death. Besides, ain't no way she's gonna escape."

Hands started an exploration of her body through the layers of cloth, beginning with her breasts. Swallowing the nausea bubbling in her throat, she edged away, but he pressed down on her stomach until she stopped struggling.

Spider spoke from a distance. "Stop that. You'll be sorry if the man with the dead eyes hears about it."

The hands stopped, and relief surged through her. The man fumbled with the rope, and the pressure on her arms and hands eased. As the blood flowed back into the area, she bit her lip against the pain. She would not give them the satisfaction of knowing they'd hurt her. After a moment, she managed to move her arms, though she still didn't feel like she could control them.

"Come on, I got a cold ale downstairs. We'll wait there till he comes."

The door opened, then closed. The click of the key in the lock told her there would be no escaping that way.

Inch by inch, she worked her hand down under the loosened ropes to her boot. At last she grasped the familiar hilt of her knife, then maneuvered the blade up and under the ropes. They cut easily. She wiggled down, until she'd cleared the sack.

Daylight streamed through a crack in the shutters of the lone window, marking a spot on the plank floor. It must be late afternoon. If so, only a few hours had passed. She took a deep breath and gagged. The stench of fish and God only knew what else seemed to wrap itself around her. Only shallow breaths kept her from losing the contents of her stomach.

She sat up. Pieces of straw stuck out through the worn cloth cover on her mattress, and a grimy grey blanket lay across one end. She scrambled from the bed, uneasy with what might be living in the bedding. Only a crude wooden chair, shoved in a corner, decorated the room.

She tried the door. Locked, as she'd suspected. Muffled male voices came to her through the wood, but how far away the men were, or how many, she couldn't tell. That left the window.

Of course, they'd nailed the shutters closed. Thank God the metal had begun to rust. She retrieved her knife, using the flat of the blade to pry the nails out.

How fortunate they hadn't checked for weapons. A strangled laugh escaped her. Men assumed you weren't armed, one of the advantages of being a woman.

How much time did she have before Luther arrived? She didn't doubt he was the man with the dead eyes. Fear increased her efforts.

The last nail came loose with reluctance. She unfastened the latch and yanked. With a squeak of hinges, the shutter broke free.

She held her breath, expecting her captors to come through the door any minute. When they didn't appear, she coaxed the other shutter open.

The windows were filthy from years of neglect. She brushed away the cobwebs, turned the latch, and shoved. Nothing happened.

She leaned all her body weight against it, hoping she wouldn't break the glass. At last, it swung outward, the smell outside even more intense.

Her prison appeared to be in the rear corner of the building, on the second floor. Another stone structure backed up to it, perhaps sixty feet away. A porch roof sloped below her, extending the full length of the building. A tree grew at one end, a little further away from the roof than she liked, but it was her only chance.

She glanced down at her riding habit. What she wouldn't give for her shirt and breeches. It took a moment to reach up under her skirt and remove the false rump. Without the enhancer, her habit had an exceptionally long train. She bunched up the excess material and stuck it into her waistband.

She brought the chair over to the window, scrambled out, then dropped with a thud to the roof a couple of yards below. There was no turning back now. At the edge, near the tree, she looked down at the thirty-foot fall. At least she'd worn her jumps today instead of her regular corset, and the light boning allowed for some movement. *Just pretend this is rigging.*

Taking a deep breath, she launched herself into the air and caught a branch, praying it would support her weight. For a moment, she hung precariously by her hands, then dragged herself up onto the rough barked limb.

She tried to crawl toward the trunk, but something held her back. Damn, she'd managed to catch the train of her habit in some of the smaller twigs. She yanked on her skirt. Somewhere below her, a door opened. An old man with shaggy gray hair stepped off the porch.

If he happened to look up, her blue habit would be clearly visible against the tree's greenery. Heart pounding, she froze.

Chapter 13

"Bloody hell, Morgan." Declan paced in front of the library's marble fireplace, wishing he could hit something, anything. "Alex couldn't have disappeared into thin air."

"No."

Morgan's short response caused him to glance at the man who'd been unflappable in battle, and now wore lines of worry on his face. Fear crept around Declan's heart. Could he really lose Alex?

Lady Bradford and her son entered the library. "Is there any word?" She turned to face him, stretched out her hand, her eyes reflecting concern.

He ignored her hand and crossed to his cousin. "No, she's still missing. It's good of you to come, Bradford."

His cousin's impassive face belied the keen interest in his eyes. "When was the countess abducted?"

"In Hyde Park, a couple of hours ago. Addington had to be behind this."

Bradford shook his head. "Someone in my employ has been watching him, and they've reported nothing. Were there witnesses?"

"No."

"Where was she—exactly?"

Declan leaned one hand against the fireplace and stared at the empty grate. "We were on the edge of the park, near Nottingham House. She entered a clump of trees near the path, but when I arrived, only her horse remained."

"Are you sure she didn't run off on her own?" Morgan came to stand beside him. "You didn't do anything that might be getting her riled, did you? Our Lady Lochsdale is a bit headstrong."

Declan ran a hand through the hair on his forehead and straightened. "Lady Lochsdale would never leave that horse willingly."

I thought you might miss me. Alex's words echoed in his head. He would give anything to have her safe with him again.

He continued to pace in front of the fireplace. If she'd just stayed with him.

Exasperation tinged Morgan's voice. "You and your men have scoured the area. You can't be telling me no one saw anything."

"My men said she wasn't seen after she'd veered off the path." He pounded his hand against the mantel's cool surface. "Hell, *I* saw that." In the mirror above the fireplace, Declan saw an assessing look cross his cousin's face.

"How long was she alone?"

"Perhaps ten minutes." He wanted to be furious with Catrina, but he knew the blame to be his. Alex should never have been allowed to go off on her own. It was one thing to ride unattended on her estates, but something else in London.

Bradford rubbed his index finger along the edge of his jaw. "There are a series of smaller paths in that area. They could have used a cart. It would be too obvious to carry her out, even on horseback." He walked to the desk, took out a quill and ink, and started to write. "What does she look like?"

"She's small, with auburn hair." He could picture how she'd appeared that morning, her ribbons flying. His gut clenched. "When I last saw her, she wore a blue velvet riding habit."

"Right." Bradford set down the quill and folded the missive in half. "We'll send this round to my contacts. I suggest we go and see if there is anything to report concerning

Addington." The three men prepared to leave. "Mother, please stay here. Notify us immediately if she turns up."

"I shall." Lady Bradford fingered the brooch at her throat. "Do you think you'll find her?"

"We have to." Declan turned and led the way out the door.

Alex watched from her perch in the tree as the man shuffled toward a huge mound of refuse and dumped his bucket of fish heads on the pile. He wore rough clothing, covered by a leather apron spattered with blood. He must be a fishmonger.

Could she be in Cheapside? She'd only visited London's commercial center once when she'd stolen out of the house with Cook. It had seemed like a fascinating place. People buying all sorts of wares, but Cook had warned her it could also be dangerous.

The old man rinsed his bucket in a trough nearby, and every time he turned her direction, she expected him to look up. After several minutes, he went back inside and closed the door. Relief surged through her.

She yanked on her skirt with all her might. A loud ripping sound filled the air, but the train broke free. With hurried movements, she gathered the excess material and inched toward the trunk, then searched for limbs that would support her descent. Climbing rigging was much easier. At least there you had even hand and foot holds.

When she reached the bottom, she leaned against the tree for a moment to get her bearings and catch her breath.

The bells of a church rent the air. The bright, happy sound was a definite contrast to the dingy buildings surrounding her. Excitement warred with fear. Wasn't St. Mary-le-Bow supposed to be in Cheapside? The nuns would give her sanctuary. Perhaps they could get a message to

Declan.

Keeping to the sides of the buildings, she headed toward the sound of the bells, thankful to be in an alley. She doubted her attackers knew she'd escaped, but she held her knife in the folds of her riding habit, just in case. Any man could be her enemy, until she heard him speak. Both her captor's voices were branded into her memory.

She'd gone perhaps a quarter of a mile before her taut senses caused the hair on the back of her neck to stand on end. Someone was following her. With a quick side step, she ducked into a doorway and waited. No one passed, but she still couldn't shake her apprehension.

After several minutes, she continued on, glancing behind her every few steps. When the ancient church reared into view, she increased her pace. Trying to avoid being seen, she skirted the open square in front of the building, as there were still several hawkers near the steps trying to sell their wares.

A woman's voice filled the air, her worn face as craggy as the greystone used to construct St. Mary's. Her Cockney accent was evident as she shouted a familiar rhyme. "Hot Cross Buns! One a Penny, two a Penny, all hot Cross Buns!"

Alex's stomach rumbled. She longed to purchase the treat, but the fewer people who saw her the better. Besides, she hadn't any coin.

Staying in the shadows, she made her way to the church's side entrance, inched open the heavy wooden door, and stepped inside. Coolness swept over her, and not a sound echoed from the welcoming blackness. She put her knife back in her boot and waited a moment for her eyes to adjust, then closed the door and scanned the interior.

Lit candles cast a warm glow over a magnificent wooden altar at the far end of the church. It gleamed in the dim light, dwarfing the short, pudgy man in a priest's robe who knelt, head bowed, at its base. The man began to pray, his words incomprehensible.

This cathedral was no different than most she'd visited. The vaulted space and grand design conspired to make people feel small, insignificant, when they entered the building. That philosophy had never made sense to her. She felt a greater awe at God's creation when she stood on a ship's deck, the wind blowing her hair and a brilliant sunset skimming the water's edge.

Without making a sound she crossed to the corner and sat on the floor, her back propped against a bench. If she were being followed, they'd be here in the next few minutes. She remained alert, her muscles aching from the strain. The drone of the priest's prayer echoed off the stone walls, his deep voice enhanced, as if he spoke into a barrel. If someone came for her, could he prevent a second abduction? Would he?

After about half an hour, she stood. If she *was* being followed, the perpetrator didn't seem inclined to come into a church. Using her skirt, she wiped as much grime off her face and hands as possible, then she headed down the aisle toward the front of the church. "Father?"

The man jumped. She hadn't meant to startle him, but the look on his face when he turned around was so comical she almost laughed. She'd forgotten how she must look.

She'd lost her hat long ago and, as usual, when not restrained, her hair billowed about her shoulders and down her back. The skirt of her riding habit was in tatters, and she suspected her face had collected as much dirt as her hands.

"May I help you, my child?" The priest approached her. His round face had an overly large mouth, but his eyes were kind. "If you're looking for food, I'm afraid we are unable to..."

"I'm looking for sanctuary, Father, not food."

"Have you done anything for which you should repent?"

She could imagine the members of polite Society

telling her she had a whole lifetime of sins to repent. Laughter bubbled up and she let out a chuckle. "I think that may depend on who you ask." If she were lucky, the good Lord would be a little more tolerant than the Ton. The priest seemed somewhat disconcerted by her behavior and tried to direct her back outside.

"Father, I know how I must look, but my appearance is unavoidable. My name is Alexandra Kendrick, the Countess of Lochsdale, and I need your help." She wasn't sure he believed her, but at least he stopped encouraging her toward the door. "I was abducted earlier today from Hyde Park."

"Who abducted you?"

"I have no idea. They never let me see their faces." No sense going into her suspicions about Luther. She gave the priest her best helpless female look. "I'm sorry to be such a bother, but if you would just contact Lord Worthington at Castleton House, I'm sure he would clear things up."

The front door to the church slammed against the wall. Alex jumped, and the priest crossed himself. The hollow sound reverberated through the vast interior. A man stood in the entrance, outlined in the doorway by the sunlight at his back. He paused a moment as if to get his bearings, then strode directly toward them. Alex reached for her knife, then stopped. She'd know Declan's stride anywhere.

When he reached them, he grabbed her by the shoulders and shook her. She thought her teeth would come loose with the force. "Lady Lochsdale, don't you *ever* do that to me again."

Then he kissed her. His kiss wasn't sensual. In fact, it seemed almost desperate. He kissed her lips and face, then crushed her to him so tightly she couldn't breathe.

It didn't matter. For the first time in hours, she felt safe.

"Uh, uhum."

She heard the priest, but Declan didn't seem inclined to release her. Before the good Father lost his patience, she nudged them apart and stepped back to break the contact.

"I don't mean to interrupt,"—The priest glanced heavenward and gave a slight shrug—"but your wife seems to have had a very trying day. Perhaps you should take her home?"

"But I'm not his—"

"I agree, Father." Declan took her by the arm and propelled her down the aisle. She could hear the holy man following behind.

Before they left, her guardian tossed the priest a bag of coins that he caught with both hands. The man's large mouth formed a perfect circle, like a singer intent on Christmas carols.

Declan inclined his head. "Thank you for keeping her safe." Then he guided her from the church.

An enclosed carriage waited in the open square. Morgan and a stranger were inside. She and Declan entered, then took the seat across from them.

"It's glad I am to see you again, Wee One. You gave us quite a merry chase." Morgan gestured toward the man next to him. "May I introduce Adrian Leighton, the Earl of Bradford, and Worthington's cousin."

"I'm pleased to make your acquaintance." Bradford took her hand and raised it to his lips. "Morgan didn't lie when he told me about your charms."

"That's enough, Bradford." Declan glowered at his cousin from the corner of the carriage.

"What happened, Wee One? Are you all right?" Morgan reached forward and offered his handkerchief, indicating she should use it on a spot near her cheekbone. Obviously, she needed a bath.

Heat rose in her cheeks. She must look a sight. "Two men put a sack over my head while I was sitting in the park." She rubbed her face with the cloth, but without a mirror she couldn't tell if she accomplished anything. "They locked me in a room and left." She had never seen Morgan angry, but the look in his eyes made her happy he counted her amongst his friends.

"Did they hurt you?"

"No. I think they were waiting for Lord Addington."

Morgan's low voice carried over the sounds of man and animal outside the carriage. "How did you escape?"

"I used my knife on the nails in the shutters and climbed down a tree."

"They left you a knife?" Bradford's incredulous voice contrasted with his politely surprised expression.

She grinned at Morgan. "I don't think they expected me to carry one."

Morgan broke into laughter, and Lord Bradford smiled. Declan didn't appear to find it amusing. He sat forward and gave her the reproving look he'd used with her as a child. "You could have been killed."

"Well, I would have been killed, or worse, if I had remained there." Where was the desperate man from the church? Ever since she'd been handed up into the carriage, Declan had cast her sullen looks. Rather like a little boy who had been denied something he wanted. None of this was her fault, but he acted as if she'd planned it.

She crossed her arms and held his gaze. "What was I supposed to do, wait until you came to rescue me?"

Declan's face became more grim, and a muscle in his jaw twitched as he sat back on the seat. She could almost feel the barrier he erected between them. His withdrawal hurt more than his harsh words.

What had she expected, that he'd tell her he loved her? Disgusted that she'd allowed herself to hope, she stared out the window. An uneasy silence ensued.

He should be gratified she'd returned without his help. At least he didn't have to rescue her again. She cast a furtive glance in his direction. A lock of sable hair caressed his forehead. How she longed to brush back the wayward curl and run her hands through his hair. No doubt he'd evade her grasp. With a sigh, she turned her attention to removing the dirt from the hem of her tattered skirt.

"Did your abductors use any names?" Lord Bradford asked.

"One of the men did call the other Spider. Does that help?"

"Yes."

Lord Bradford tapped his fingertips against his thigh for several moments. "Would you be able to show me where you were being held?"

"I'm not sure. It was a two-story building, with a fishmonger's shop below my room." She stuck the handkerchief up her sleeve. "I followed the bells to get to the church. I'm afraid I didn't try to memorize my surroundings."

"No matter. Based on what you and Lord Worthington have told me, Lord Addington is behind this. He visited the docks today, but then returned to his establishment. He could have hired henchmen to do his bidding."

"How did you find me?"

"One of the boys in my employ spotted you from the description we gave him."

"So that's who was following me."

Lord Bradford smiled. "Yes. He sent someone to get us after you entered the church. You've won his respect. It seems you nearly outran him." Declan's cousin tilted his head and gave her an assessing look. "I don't think that's ever happened."

She could feel her face grow warm. "I've had practice."

"Outrunning kidnappers?" Lord Bradford raised an eyebrow, a look of admiration in his eyes.

"No."

"Lady Lochsdale has a number of interesting pastimes."

Declan gave her a disapproving look.

"You carry a knife and outrun kidnappers." Lord Bradford shook his head. "Anything else?"

Thank God the carriage lurched to a stop in front of Castelton House, and she didn't have to answer. Who knew what else her guardian would disapprove of next? Declan got out first, helping her down. He made it a point to touch her as little as possible.

Lady Bradford came out the front entrance, followed by Anna. "Oh my dear child, come in. We were so worried about you." Declan's aunt directed her into the house and bustled her upstairs, leaving the men in the entrance hall.

Alex wanted to be alone, but the women followed her into the bedroom. Lady Bradford asked Williams to have a bath drawn and a fire started. In the meantime, they washed her face, combed out the worst of the tangles in her hair, and settled her on the window seat with a blanket thrown over her shoulders. They acted as if she were family, fussing over her more than a captain watched over his charts, and it made her happy. She hadn't expected to care for Declan's family. It was nice to know they'd missed her, even though Declan hadn't.

Alex glanced around her bedroom and wrapped the covering close to her body. Nothing had changed. Was it only this morning she'd thrown Luther out?

The maid who'd started the fire left the room, and Lady Bradford shut the door behind her, then turned. Alex thought there were new lines at the corners of her eyes. She must have noticed Alex's concern, because she took a deep breath and pasted on a smile. "So, what happened?"

"I was abducted in the park."

"Oh my." The older woman's hand flew to her throat.

"Were your captors handsome?" Anna asked in a dreamy voice from her perch on Alex's bed.

"No. Well, actually, I couldn't tell. They'd put a sack

over my head. But they didn't sound handsome."

"I bet they were." Anna gave a long sigh. "I'd love to have an adventure like that some day."

Lady Bradford and Alex both answered, "No, you wouldn't." They looked at each other and laughed. It felt good to be able to find amusement in her abduction, now that she was home safe.

Home?

When had she started to think of this as home? Initially, the thought of residing at Declan's residence had been daunting, but she liked it here. She had to admit a great deal of that desire to remain was due to the possibility of seeing Declan.

Williams entered, followed by two servants bearing a wooden tub. They set it in the middle of the floor and began to make the necessary trips back and forth to fill it with hot water. When they'd finished, she watched the steam coming from the bath and longed to soak away the grime of her little prison. She stood and crossed to the bed to deposit the blanket.

Lady Bradford must have guessed her thoughts. "Why don't we let you bathe. You can tell us what happened when you're rested. Would you like Mary to attend you?"

"No, thank you. I need a little time to myself."

Everyone left, but Lady Bradford paused a moment before exiting. "I've never seen Lord Worthington so upset."

"He's angry with me."

"No, he's not. He's angry with himself. Give him a little more time."

Alex shook her head. "I've decided to make my choice after the masquerade ball this weekend. I suspect my attackers were hired by my cousin, Lord Addington." She sat down on the edge of her bed and tried to run her fingers through her matted curls. "I can't wait any longer to marry. He could try this again."

"But the Season isn't over. Lord Worthington will protect you, now that he knows what could happen."

"I can't depend on that. There's too much at stake. I've given Lord Worthington my choices. All four will be there on Saturday night. If he has any feelings for me, he'll have to speak up then."

"I hope you know what you're doing."

"So do I."

Water pummeled the windows outside the library. Declan hadn't seen a storm like this in several years. Lightning streaked across the sky, brightening the room considerably.

He hadn't bothered with an oil lamp, preferring the meager light from the fireplace and the show nature provided. The storm matched the turmoil in his soul.

His ward had been kidnapped, when he should have protected her. That was the only reason for his panic. She was his responsibility, and he'd failed to keep her safe.

It didn't have anything to do with love.

Alex's grandfather had given her to him, and he'd let someone abduct her, almost under his very nose. He took another long drink of brandy from a snifter that had rarely been empty that evening. Hell, she'd rescued herself as well.

Crack. The loudest burst of thunder he'd heard caused the windows to vibrate. He stood, amazed to find he was still steady after the amount of alcohol he'd consumed.

He found his way over to the lamp, adjusted the wick, and lit it with a stick from the fire. Then he withdrew a crumpled piece of paper from his pocket. Alex's list. He knew every name, and her assessment was correct. They'd marry her quickly when they discovered her holdings.

Lord Holford was too old. Alex knew nothing about procreation, and he had to assume she didn't know older men were rarely prolific when it came to fathering children. He'd point out her intended could die first, then she'd be right back where she had started.

It might be a little more difficult to come up with something for Lord Avery and Lord Brighton. They were ideal. At least in Alex's eyes. They'd leave her alone, provided she supplied much needed capital. Then again, he'd heard rumors that Brighton preferred boys, but that wouldn't change much for Alex. The man still needed an heir.

Lord Duprey appeared last. He didn't trust him. Alex didn't need a ladies man with a reputation of flitting from one affair to the next. He doubted she would tolerate a parade of woman constantly connected to Duprey's name. He'd end up with her knife hilt sticking from his chest.

Of course, she'd have to love him to care. From what she'd said, she didn't love any of these men. Not that it should matter to him. Whom she loved was her own business.

He found some solace in knowing she was safe in her bed upstairs. He'd been lucky. The whole affair might have had a different ending. Perhaps he should check on her? He picked up the lamp and left the library. As he crossed the hallway, the light caught the amber eyes of the winged lion at the foot of the stairs, causing them to glow.

Some people were startled by the piece, but he'd always liked it. For him, the large cat's fierceness represented strength and the ability to take on the world alone. Those were qualities he admired. It was dangerous to depend on someone else.

When he reached the top of the stairs, he thought he heard moans. It wasn't the wind. These sounds were gaining in intensity and seemed to be coming from Alex's room. A large clap of thunder rumbled through the house, then he heard a cry. Without knocking, he opened Alex's door.

She was naked to the waist. That in itself was enough to cause him to go hard instantly, even in his somewhat inebriated condition. But the look on her face overrode any feelings of lust. She was in anguish. Her unfocused eyes were wide open, and tears streamed down her face.

She shook her head back and forth. "Mother, I'm here. Can't you see me? Don't die, Mother. What will we do without you?" She started to tremble and reached her arms out to her imaginary mother. "You're burning up. Father says I should keep you cool. Please don't go. I'll be good. I'm afraid, Mother, the storm ..."

Declan put his lamp on the table by the bed, then took her by the shoulders and gave her a slight shake. When she didn't respond, he tried harder. "Lady Lochsdale, Alex, wake up. You're dreaming." She started to cry in earnest now, and he cradled her head to his shoulder.

"Shh, it's all right. You're safe." He patted her back, rocking her like a child. After a time, the sobbing stopped. He could tell the moment she knew he was there. She jerked backward, only to grab the blankets and lift them to her chin.

He regretted the short view he'd received of her magnificent breasts. They were just as he remembered them, shell colored nipples against pale smooth skin.

"What are you doing in my room?"

"You were having a nightmare. I heard your cries and came in." He smiled at her. "You really should lock your door if you persist in sleeping nude."

"How I sleep is my own affair." Alex wrapped the covers tighter around her body.

"Do you have these nightmares often?" He wasn't going to argue with her. She'd been under a great deal of strain. He'd heard that could often cause sleep disturbances.

"Not since the early days with my grandfather." She fluffed up the pillows behind her, still retaining her death grip on her blankets, and laid back. Her hair billowed over the pillows, making her look like some sort of sad fairy that had lost her wings.

"What do you dream about?" He was curious what could reduce a woman as strong as Alex to tears. From her comments, she had dreamed about her mother's death, but that had occurred years ago.

She turned away and stayed still for so long he didn't think she would answer. "I dreamt about my mother. We're on *The Merry Elizabeth*, in the middle of a hurricane." As if to give her tale life, thunder rent the silence, battering more rain on the windowpanes. "She's so sick. I'm trying to help her, but I can barely stand with the sway of the ship. I'm helpless. One moment she's clasping my hand and then ..." She turned her tear-streaked face to him. "There wasn't anything I could do."

He reached down and gathered her against him. "It wasn't your fault. She was sick. Nothing could have been done." He kissed the top of her head. "Be happy for the years you had together." She leaned back, and he gazed down into her face, then used his thumb to wipe away a lone tear that was about to enter her mouth.

"I'm sorry." She appeared calmer. Only her haunted eyes told him the memory lingered. "I shouldn't go on so. You never even knew your mother."

He laid her back against the pillows, then maneuvered to the edge of the bed, facing the lamp. The flame danced on its wick, as he tried to ignore the portrait of his mother that flickered in his memory. "Who told you I never knew my mother?"

"Your aunt." Alex reached out a hand and placed it on his arm. "If it helps, from what little I've discovered, she sounded like a wonderful woman."

"I wouldn't know. My father never talked about her. At least to me."

"You weren't close?"

"Hardly." He thought back to those years of loneliness and isolation. His father had chosen his employees well; not one dared show any concern for their employer's son. "My father spent his days in the drawing room, pondering the painting of his beloved through a stupor of alcohol."

"I don't recall a painting of your mother in there."

"I had it taken down after he died. It's in the attic." He turned toward her. Perhaps now she'd understand why it was impossible for him to love her. He would never be like his father. His son would not have to endure bitterness and hate.

Alex studied him intently, golden specks swirling in her green eyes. "If you gave your aunt a chance, I think she'd relish talking about her sister. Lady Bradford loved her, just as she loves you."

"Does she?" As a child, he'd had hopes his mother's family would rescue him from his father. He remembered the despair he'd felt the day he realized they'd deserted him. "Is that why she didn't come to see me all those years?"

"She didn't come to see you because she was threatened with physical force if she refused to keep away." Alex reached out, her palm warming his cheek. "Not everyone is brave. She did what she could, and she has regrets. Lord Worthington, you keep yourself apart from everyone and everything. If you live your life without learning to forgive, you'll never know real joy."

"You'd have me forget?"

Alex dropped her hand. The storm outside couldn't begin to compare with the look on her face. He stood, then crossed to the end of the bed and turned. He couldn't forgive, but if it would make Alex happy. "All right, all right, I'll speak with her."

She relaxed back against her pillow. "Good. I'm sure she'll enjoy sharing wonderful memories about your mother. From what she tells me, you look like her."

"Growing up, I didn't consider that a benefit. My father would take one look at my face and burst into a rage, but now ..." He'd been a fool to blame his mother for what had happened. All these years, and he knew so little about her.

"Did my aunt mention that my mother named me

Declan before she died?" He supposed he was fortunate his father had let the name stand.

"No, but I've always liked your name."

Even with her tear-streaked face, Alex tugged at his soul. "Then why don't I ever hear it cross your lips?"

She adjusted her blankets, as if they were the finest ball-gown. "I don't think it's proper for me to call you by your Christian name."

He leaned against the bedpost, his arms crossed. "Why not? I've used yours often enough."

Alex grinned at him. "Only in anger."

"Then I think I should rectify that situation." He straightened and faced her, then crooked his finger. "Come here, Alexandra." He was afraid she wouldn't come, but she awkwardly maneuvered herself up on her knees and crossed the short distance, still clutching the blanket.

She stopped in front of him. "Yes?"

He swallowed. "I want you to call me Declan. Let me hear you say it."

"Declan."

"Again."

"Declan." She touched his forehead. "Declan." She touched his nose. "Declan." She left her finger in the dimple on his chin. "There, is that enough?"

"It'll never be enough." He took her hand and kissed the center of her palm. When she didn't draw away, he lightly nibbled at the inside of her wrist, feeling her quiver under his lips. God, he'd never wanted a woman so much before.

He trailed small kisses up her arm, until he got to her face. Tasting the saltiness of her tears, he kissed her everywhere except the mouth, until finally her lips sought his. Even then, he didn't linger. His mouth trailed down her neck, making the unconscious journey to her breasts.

When he lowered the blanket down to capture a taut little peak, he thought he would die from the joy of it. She was his. *No, she wasn't.* The thought was like receiving a gift, only to be told you would never be allowed to open it. He leaned back. Alex's hurt and confused expression didn't help.

He let go of her. "Alex, I can't. It wouldn't be right. You're going to belong to someone else in a short period of time." He straightened his attire, refusing to look at her.

"I'd forgotten." Alex's bitter voice drew his attention. "How silly of me. You're right, of course." She brought the blankets up over her drooping shoulders and looked away.

"Alex, Lady Lochsdale, I'm sorry."

"So am I. I think you'd better leave."

He picked up the lamp, then hesitated. "Are you sure you'll be all right? The storm seems to have abated."

"I'll survive." She waited till he got to the door before adding, "I'm going to make my choice on Saturday, after the masquerade. You'll soon be rid of me."

He exited, shut the door softly, then leaned back against it. He honestly couldn't remember what filled his days before Alex came into his life, but he'd damned well better find out.

Chapter 14

"Lady Lochsdale, may I come in?" The tap on Alex's door was soft, but there was nothing quiet about the visitor. Anna was entirely too cheerful for this early in the morning.

"Of course." She sat up in bed, surprised that full daylight streamed through the windows. "What time is it?"

"One o'clock. Mama said I should let you sleep as you'd been through a terrible ordeal."

Not nearly as terrible as the ordeal she'd been through last night with Declan. He must be the most stubborn man alive.

Anna's everyday chatter soothed her taut nerves. Who cared if marriage to a man she didn't love loomed in her future? She'd cross that bridge when she had to on Saturday night.

Until then, she was going to make an all out assault on Declan. "Lady Anna, if you wanted to entice a man, how would you do it?"

"What?" Anna stopped in the middle of her description of last night's ball.

"If you'd decided who it was you wanted to marry, how would you get him to do so?"

"I'm not totally certain, as I've not met anyone I'd marry, but I can tell you what men seem to like." Anna crossed the room, sat on her bed, then leaned forward, her voice a whisper. "Brush against them often, and make sure you wear low-cut gowns."

"But how can you do that in a public place?"

"You don't. Get them in private. But don't let them

think it was your idea. They're funny about that. They want to do the pursuing."

Alex thought for a moment. Where might they have the chance to be alone? She couldn't count on Declan visiting her room again. There was a place called The New Spring Garden located across the Westminster Bridge. Cook had told her about dark walkways where all sorts of alliances were supposed to occur.

"Lady Anna, are you familiar with The New Spring Garden?"

"Of course. They're calling it Vauxhall Gardens now. Some in the Ton don't approve but—"

"I'd like Lord Worthington to take me there." Alex could pinpoint the moment Anna realized what she was about.

"Oh, that's perfect." Anna clasped her hands and brought them to her chest. "This is so exciting." Her bright smile turned to a frown. "Are you sure you want to get involved with him? My cousin has a reputation of going from one lady to the next."

"I'm already involved. I'm trying to make sure he is."

She dropped her hands and leaned forward. "What do you want me to do?"

"Are there any entertainments being held there before Saturday?"

"I believe they're holding a concert of Handel's music on Thursday. Would that do?"

"Perfect. Tell him that the three of us simply must go and ask him to chaperone. At the last minute, you and your mother remember a previous engagement. I'll tell him how much I was looking forward to the concert. If I'm lucky, he'll still take me."

"What will you wear?"

She wasn't at all sure what you wore for a seduction. "How about my new coral silk gown?"

"Wonderful. It's the lowest of your new gowns. You can keep the lace buffon in until you're alone." Anna clapped her hands with enthusiasm. "I must go tell Mama. It's so romantic, and just think if it works, we could be cousins."

Alex smiled at her. "I'd like that."

"Me, too. I'll go and make sure the concert is set for Thursday, then Mama can ask Lord Worthington to take us." Anna practically skipped out of the room.

Alex ran her index finger over her bottom lip. Any time Declan had kissed her, they'd been in a situation Fate prescribed. Maybe this time she could give Fate a little help.

Declan watched the matrons as they sat on their small gilt chairs along the ballroom wall. A number of them had their gazes fixed on him, assessing, no doubt, the chances of their daughters catching his eye. He gave a slight bow and raised his drink in a salute, acknowledging the game. He was thankful for any distraction at the moment.

Alex was driving him mad. She'd been coldly polite the last two days, yet he had a nagging suspicion she was up to something.

After her kidnapping, he didn't dare leave her to her own devices, but he'd made sure the two of them were never alone.

For two nights now, he'd had to stand by and watch as she traded polite conversation with the men on her list. Alex appeared to be the perfect lady, laughing at all the right places, using her fan to flirt, her glorious eyes just peeping over the top of the feathers.

He'd come close to calling Lord Duprey out after he had overheard some of the cad's suggestive remarks to Alex. She'd just laughed and hit the blackguard with her fan. He'd wanted to hit him with much more.

As he worked his way through the crowd toward Morgan, he searched the ballroom for the men on Alex's list. All four of them had approached him about her hand in marriage. He had stalled them thus far by telling them it was her choice, and he'd assured them she would be making it soon.

Even Lord Holden, the oldest of the group, had wanted to know what she was worth. The white-haired buzzard would be lucky to find any woman to marry. Alex was so much more than her title and wealth. Didn't they see that? If only he didn't like her, he'd marry her and to hell with the inheritance. Alex could do with it as she pleased.

Catrina, on the other hand, was spoiled, self-centered, vain, and ambitious. All things he could never love. She would be a much better choice.

She'd never be faithful, but what did it matter as long as she wandered after producing a couple of heirs? It would be a perfect arrangement. Then why couldn't he bring himself to ask her?

He joined Morgan and two men he didn't know. They were having an animated conversation about horseflesh. He'd learned long ago that Morgan could go on for hours when discussing horses or women. Rather than get sucked into the conversation, he surveyed the room.

His gaze came to rest on Catrina, faultless in a blue gown, as she stood near one of the giant candelabra used to light the room. She chatted with Lady Asbury, touted to be one of the elite within the Ton. Catrina liked power. Thank God he'd diffused her threat to Alex. If Catrina had thought of her as competition, she would have made sure Alex wasn't accepted by Society.

Morgan finished his conversation, moved closer to him, then lowered his voice. "It's tired I am of all these balls. When do you think the ladies might be wanting to go home?" Morgan looked done in. Even the laugh lines around his eyes drooped.

Declan laughed. "I thought you liked balls."

"I do, but I find every night till the wee hours of the

morning excessive. Wouldn't be here if I didn't think you might be needing my help when Addington shows up. Have you seen him?"

"No, and that worries me."

"Have you heard from Bradford?"

"Not a word, but it hasn't been two weeks. I'm sure my cousin's finding it difficult to uncover all the unsavory details. Addington's good at covering his tracks."

He caught his aunt's eye and gave her a small nod. He'd attempted, as of late, to be nicer to her. It really wasn't that difficult, but he had to remind himself not to slip into familiar patterns. They'd even had a pleasant conversation yesterday. She'd asked him about taking them to...Damn!

"Morgan, could I get you to take Catrina to Lord and Lady Ellington's tomorrow night?"

His friend groaned. "Not another ball. What is it you need to be doing instead?"

"I just remembered, my aunt asked me to escort the three of them to Vauxhall Gardens for a Handel concert. It seems he's one of Lady Lochsdale's favorite composers, and my aunt's setting it up as a surprise."

"If it's for the Wee One, I imagine I can be putting up with Lady Catrina for a night. I'd not be doing it for anyone else."

"You like Lady Lochsdale, don't you?"

Morgan shrugged. "What's not to like? Her temperament, beauty, and intelligence combine to make a chord of music that's easy on the soul."

"You, my old friend, are a romantic."

"And might I be asking you what Irishman worth his salt isn't. It wouldn't be hurting you to look at the world through my eyes for a time."

"The good Lord spare me, I'd want to fight every man and love every woman."

"It's happy I'd be if you'd love one woman, but since

you're so pigheaded, it looks like I'll just have to keep trying to talk sense into you."

"If I ever fall in love, just run me through and put me out of my misery."

"It's comments like that which make me want to bash you over your fool head."

He gave his friend a little bow. "All the ladies would be very unhappy with you."

"Speaking of which,"—Morgan's eyes gleamed with mischief,—"they were asking me about you at Madam Rose's. Seems you've not been to see the dear ladies. They miss you."

"I've been busy."

Morgan raised his eyebrows. "It's been several weeks. I might be thinking you're a reformed man."

"No." He didn't want to talk about it. The truth was there were no petite women with chestnut hair and free spirits at Madam Rose's. Even if there were, his body wouldn't stop yearning for one in particular. This self-imposed celibacy was ludicrous, but he couldn't help the way he felt.

Once Alex was married, he'd go back to normal. Then she'd be out of his reach for good. He glanced over at his ward, resplendent in a turquoise gown. He needed some air.

"Keep an eye on her for me." Fighting the urge to bolt from the room, he strode out the French doors into the cool, still night.

"I'm sorry, Lord Worthington,"—Lady Bradford's voice carried up the stairs from the entrance hall below,—"but I didn't realize it was the same night."

Alex stopped on the stairwell landing, just out of sight, and waited for Declan's reply.

"If it's a party you and Lady Anna are helping to host, how could you forget it?"

"There's been so much going on the last few days." Lady Bradford sounded very convincing. "I thought the concert seemed like such a good idea, but I didn't double-check the date. I'm sorry, dear, but couldn't you take Lady Lochsdale? It's a public place. You needn't have a chaperone."

"I don't think that would be wise."

"Why not? Lady Lochsdale was so looking forward to it. You don't want to disappoint her."

She held her breath, waiting for his reply.

There was a long moment of silence, then a sigh filled the air. "I suppose I have to take her."

He obviously didn't like the idea, but at least he'd agreed. Alex continued her descent, gratified that Declan seemed unable to look away once she came into view.

"You look lovely, dear." His aunt came forward and gave her a peck on the cheek.

"Thank you, Lady Bradford. I'm looking forward to this evening." She studied Declan from under her lashes. His evening clothes molded to his form. Somehow they didn't look stiff and formal on him, but seemed to be a natural extension of his body.

"There's been a slight change in plans." Declan's aunt came forward and took Alex's hands. "Lady Anna and I have to host a party for Lord Darnby. I'd promised him months ago, but it completely slipped my mind."

"Oh." She didn't dare look at Declan. If she did, he'd know something was amiss.

"Don't worry, Lord Worthington has agreed to escort you anyway. I'm sure you'll have a lovely time."

He held his arm out for her and escorted her to the carriage. Neither one spoke. She didn't know how to make conversation easy between them after their harsh words the other night. What if Lady Bradford was wrong? Maybe he didn't feel anything for her.

The silence continued throughout the ride. She concentrated on looking out the window and tried to avoid the almost overwhelming urge to twist the bracelet on her wrist.

They crossed over the Westminster Bridge, which seemed to be alive with carriages. It amazed her at how skillfully their driver maneuvered. He stopped in front of the gardens in a very short time, considering the throng.

Declan helped her out of the carriage and into the middle of a fairy tale. She'd left the London she knew behind, and entered a magical land filled with color and gaiety. She hadn't really thought much about the gardens when she'd chosen them as a place to get Declan alone. Now she was glad she had come.

They pressed forward until they passed through one of the many arches leading to an ornate building that housed the footman's waiting and cloakroom. The structure appeared ancient, its worn stone held together with crumbling mortar. It was most assuredly one of the original buildings.

A footman took her cloak as she entered, and they were directed to a supper box. The opulent room boasted intricate paintings on all three walls. Candelabras stood in the corners of the room, casting warm glows on the intricately carved furniture.

Declan motioned toward the closest landscape. "I'm told they were done by Francis Hayman."

Could it be that she was getting an art lesson because he also didn't know what to say? "They're beautiful."

She didn't know much about art, so she wandered toward the balcony, which covered the length of the room, allowing the occupants an unobstructed view. The beauty of the design lay in the ability see the gardens, without being seen, unless you stood at the railing.

The panorama before her eyes held something for everyone. A cascade, ruins, and statues mingled with trees and flowers. The main areas and paths were well lit, which allowed her to see the colorful dress of the guests as they milled about on the walkways below.

She started when Declan took her elbow.

"Dinner's being served."

"Oh."

He guided her to the middle of the room where a table had been draped with a pristine white cloth. China and silver glistened in the candlelight. Red roses adorned the center, their heady fragrance floating on the air around her. It was the perfect setting for a seduction. She hoped.

The footman served the meal promptly, appearing like a ghost out of the shadows whenever they needed something. She didn't want the elaborate dinner to go to waste, but her rebellious stomach wouldn't accept anything more than a little wine.

She should have planned the seduction, instead of assuming it would happen naturally. This didn't feel natural at all.

Declan seemed so sure of himself. She watched him take a bite of quail. The juice moistened his lips, and she couldn't tear her eyes away from his mouth.

Distracted, she bumped her fragile crystal goblet and watched in horror as it toppled over. She attempted to stand so her dress wouldn't be spotted with water, but instead, sent her fork skipping across the floor.

The footman appeared, as if by magic, to clean up the mess. She refused to look at Declan. At least he didn't say anything.

Why couldn't she just challenge him to a fencing match to win his love? It would be so much easier than this.

The footman cleared away the main courses, and left them with wine, cheese, and fruit. If she didn't make her move soon, the concert would be starting. She took a deep breath and thought about keeping her voice low and seductive.

"Do you mind if I remove my scarf?" Good, it didn't sound like her at all. "It feels quite warm in here."

"I'd rather you didn't."

"Why? It's impolite for you to object."

Declan turned his attention to slicing a piece of cheese. "I have my reasons."

"Will you tell me what they are?"

"No."

She got up and went to sit on a settee against one wall. How was Declan supposed to notice her breasts if she had them covered? She defied his wishes and tried to seductively remove the scarf. The fine lace caught on her amber brooch. With a nonchalance she didn't feel, she worked to free the material, but it refused to come free. Giving up all pretext of being casual, she yanked on one end. Still, nothing. At last, she grabbed it from both sides and with a loud rip, extricated the fabric.

She tried to hide the tattered remnants of the fichu in her lap. When she glanced up, Declan *was* watching her, but she couldn't read his expression. His eyes certainly didn't seem clouded with passion. What did Catrina do to get his attention?

Of course. She leaned down and gave him a clear view of the tops of her breasts. "See, there's nothing wrong with this, is there?"

Declan stood, looking at her as if she were a naughty child. "Alexandra, what are you doing?"

He'd never be able to appreciate her charms from this far away. She straightened and crossed to him. Tracing her finger down the side of his face, she stopped at the depression in his chin. "I thought we might pick up where we left off in my bedroom."

Declan closed his hand around her wrist and redirected her finger away from his face. "Stop this." His voice had a funny, strangled sound to it.

"But I don't want to stop." She put her other hand around the back of his neck, stood on her tiptoes, then kissed him full on the mouth. She waited for him to respond. It was difficult keeping her lips locked on his because of a rumble in his chest. Was she doing this correctly?

Suspicious, she leaned back and studied his face. Amusement danced in his gaze, etching fine lines at the corners of his eyes. Declan was laughing at her! No matter that he hadn't made a sound, she knew laughter when she saw it.

Her face grew warm. Lady Bradford was wrong. He didn't love her. Bloody hell, now he could add her name to the list of women who always seemed to be throwing themselves at him. Mortified, she yanked her wrist free, picked up her skirts and raced through the door.

"Alexandra, come back here!"

She rushed through the cloakroom where several footmen gaped at her. With as much dignity as she could muster, she elbowed past them and entered the gardens, then broke into a run. Where she went didn't matter, as long as it was away from Declan.

When she glanced back, she couldn't see him, but the sounds of pursuit were clear. Tears streamed down her face. She'd made a fool of herself. Again. She couldn't face him.

The running feet behind her were closer now. She didn't dare go any faster. These secondary paths were pitch black.

The opening strains of the orchestra's first selection surrounded her. It was a fast piece, which seemed to be keeping time with her pounding heart.

She no longer felt the path beneath her slippers. Had she missed a turn in the dark? She slowed her speed, but not in time. Her momentum sent her tumbling over the stone barrier, which rose like a jagged obstacle from the earth.

With a low cry, she clutched at the uneven sides of the

steep incline. For once she was grateful for the layers of skirt protecting her, although the tangled silk kept her from getting a foothold.

When she reached the bottom, her legs buckled from the force of the impact. Shaken, she drew a tentative breath and let it out with a soft hiss. Where was she? The air felt damp on her skin, and there appeared to be a stone wall to her left. The floor felt smooth, but she couldn't see more than a couple of feet in any direction.

When she attempted to stand, a sharp pain in her right ankle forced her to sit again. Tears of frustration pricked the back of her eyes. Did she dare try to crawl out and take the chance there might be a deeper hole to fall into?

"Alexandra, Alex, where are you?" Declan's frantic voice came to her from somewhere close by.

"I'm here." Her voice sounded faint in the darkness, and she was afraid it wouldn't carry up and out of the pit. She took a deep breath and called again, louder this time.

Declan's voice sounded at the edge of her prison. "Are you all right?"

"What do *you* think?" With rescue imminent, she felt caught between needing his help, and never wanting to see him again. She sighed, then responded in a more reasonable tone. "I think I've injured my ankle. I'm not sure I can walk."

"Don't move. I'm coming down." Declan appeared at her side within a couple of minutes.

"How did you get here? I didn't hear you approach."

Declan crouched beside her. "There are steps on the other side. Which ankle is it?"

She lifted her skirt and rubbed the injured area. "What is this place?"

"The old orchestra pit. It's been abandoned for years. Normally, the stone barriers are enough to keep anyone from falling in."

On top of laughing at her, he must think she was an

idiot. Declan removed her hand and examined the ankle. She winced once, when his fingers brushed over a tender spot.

"It doesn't appear to be broken, but I still think I should carry you." He reached down and picked her up.

She buried her face in his cravat, and inhaled the smell of damp night air and soap. At any other time she would be thrilled with the close contact. Not now. More than anything, she wanted to go back to her old life, and a time when she didn't love Declan Devereaux.

Chapter 15

The entire household seemed to be all a flutter with anticipation about tonight's masquerade ball. Alex could hear excited voices and hurrying feet, as servants bustled around with last minute details.

She went through the motions of getting ready, as if in a dream. Unlike most days, she hardly felt the bristles as she brushed her hair the required hundred strokes.

Her costume lay on the bed. Yards of forest green diaphanous material with gold accents. Even the cleverness of Madam Colette hadn't made her smile.

What had Declan been doing the last two days? After their fateful dinner, he'd carried her up to her bedroom and left her in the care of Lady Bradford. His poor aunt had stammered and stuttered something about leaving her ball early. Declan just raised an eyebrow in her direction and left.

The doctor had insisted she stay in bed. Unlike previous occasions, Declan chose not to visit. It was just as well. She wasn't sure what she would say to him. Her ankle seemed to have recovered nicely. Too bad her heart hadn't.

Anna and Lady Bradford visited often, trying to cheer her up. She'd told them what had happened and admitted her stupidity in running away. Why couldn't she have made a cool, dignified exit when Declan made it plain he wasn't interested? She hoped someday she'd be able to look back at that moment in her life and it wouldn't seem so awful.

Tonight she had to face him. He and Morgan were escorting them to the party.

She was going to be gay and carefree if it killed her.

When the evening ended, she'd make her decision, and the direction of her life would change forever. Until then, she still had a few hours.

She put her brush on her dressing table and walked over to the bed. At least she could dispense with hip and rump pads. The costume may not be quite as comfortable as breeches, but it was close. She couldn't wait to see Morgan's reaction.

Alex turned as Anna burst through the door with her usual enthusiasm. She was dressed as the Goddess Athena. Her gown was white, shot with gold. The flowers woven in her hair had small golden petals with jeweled centers, not that you really noticed them over the large, fluffy, white feathers. She'd accented the gown with bracelets on her upper arms and a heavy jewel encrusted necklace at her throat. She looked lovely. Her eyes grew wide when she saw Alex's costume.

"Oh, Lady Lochsdale, it's perfect."

"Ah, but tonight, I am not the Countess of Lochsdale. I am a river fairy of Norse mythology, waiting to charm mortal man."

"I know many men who won't be able to take their eyes off you." Anna seemed perplexed for a moment. "Are you sure you can't see through that material?"

"Colette's design gives that illusion. See, she's put skin tone material under the sheer."

"How clever." Anna walked behind her, studying every aspect of the costume. "I wish I'd thought of wings. I doubt anyone else will have a costume like yours. How did Colette get them to stay on?"

"It's a narrow metal framework that ties around my waist. I hardly feel them at all, unless of course I wanted to stand against a wall." She attempted to do so, then raised her hands in mock resignation when the wings refused to cooperate. "I guess I'll not be a wall flower this evening." They both laughed.

"I just want you to have a good time." Anna grabbed her hands. "Maybe there will be someone new at the masquerade who catches your eye. I can just imagine him, a man of mystery. He sweeps you out to the garden and kisses you madly."

She wished Anna's eternal optimism was catching, but the only man she wanted to kiss her madly was Declan. She sighed. That wasn't likely to happen.

"We'd better go. They'll be waiting downstairs." Anna started for the door, but turned to look at her before they crossed the threshold. "Don't worry, things will work out for the best. They always do."

Best for whom? Alex followed Anna out and closed the door.

He should never have let Richards tie his cravat. Declan adjusted it for the tenth time in as many minutes. Where were they?

He was just about to send a footman to inquire, when all three ladies came down the stairs. Lady Bradford was dressed as Lady Macbeth. Her costume was all black with irregular pieces of material draped off the arms and shoulders. It was an interesting contrast to her daughter, dressed as Athena. They were clever, but the choices weren't unusual.

He couldn't see Alex. Intentional or not, she was keeping behind the other two. When he got his first good look at her, he wanted to send her right back upstairs to change.

She looked like some mythological siren. The dark green gown's filmy fabric gave the impression you could see right through it, even with several uneven layers in the skirt. The bodice was the same material, but its fullness was gathered with a golden cord. It started at her waist, crisscrossing under and over her breasts, leaving no part of her form to the imagination.

Her arms were bare, except for the tendrils of her glorious hair that hung in curls to her waist. She'd crowned her head with a ring of coral pink roses and ivy. The overall effect was breathtaking.

Morgan started chuckling when he saw her. "Turn around Wee One, and let Worthington see the back."

He watched as Alex slowly turned around, her gilt edged wings coming into view.

When she'd finished displaying her costume, Alex gave Morgan a small curtsy. Quite an accomplishment, considering there was very little skirt. Then again, Declan had seen her curtsey with an imaginary skirt.

"Kind minstrel, would you spare a song for a river fairy?"

Morgan appeared properly downtrodden. "Alas, beautiful fairy. You'd be looking at a bard whose lute doesn't work," Morgan said, holding up the stringless instrument he'd borrowed for the occasion, "and who knows nary a song."

"Fie on you. Then I must teach you one." Alex began to sing, her voice soft and melodic. A look of mischief crossed her beautiful face.

> *There is a tavern in the town*
> *And there my dear love sits him down*
> *And drinks his wine 'mid laughter free,*
> *And never, never thinks of me*

Alex concluded with a little pout, as if she were unhappy at being forgotten.

"I'd be doubting any man could forget you." Morgan

took Alex's hand and gallantly bowed over it. After he straightened, he grabbed his imaginary lute and proceeded to try and imitate Alex's song. It was so bad, the ladies covered their ears and burst into gales of laughter.

"Enough of this." Declan hadn't meant to sound harsh. When had he become the outsider? "We can't stand around here all night."

Obviously, staying away from Alex the last two days hadn't lessened her effect on him. He'd reached a point where just thinking about her aroused him, and he couldn't *stop* thinking of her.

They gathered their cloaks and filed out to the carriage. He caught Alex's gaze once, but she turned away.

She was probably still hurt and embarrassed, but she shouldn't be. Every woman he'd ever known had tried the same ploy. Still, he'd never laughed at them.

Even now he could picture her. She'd been so uncomfortable with her role as seductress. He wished he could explain to her that she didn't need smoldering looks, or a breathy voice.

Her sensuality was natural, not some learned art that was boring in its repetitiveness. When she'd tried to mimic other women, it was wrong somehow. Like a pink rose trying to be red, all because the other roses were.

Isn't that what he'd been asking her to do? Conform. He sat back in the cushioned seat, barely aware of the voices around him. He didn't want her to be something she wasn't, but what he wanted didn't matter. After all, she wasn't his wife, and never would be.

The carriage slowed, caught up in the long line of vehicles waiting to deposit their patrons.

"It's time for us to put on our dominos." Anna could barely sit still.

Her excitement made everything seem like fun. It helped Alex hold to her resolve to enjoy the evening. She glanced around the carriage, amazed at the various dominos her friends had chosen to cover their faces.

Anna wore a white feather concoction that almost came to her mouth. Lady Bradford preferred red velvet, a startling contrast to her black attire. Morgan chose a geometric diamond pattern, the same on that appeared on one leg of his hose and doublet.

Declan was the only one who hadn't joined into the fun. He wore his normal black and white evening attire, his only concession a black silk domino. She found the mask boldly seductive. Even in the half-light of the flambeaux, she could see the startling blue of his eyes.

When his gaze turned to her, she fidgeted with the layers of her gown. It was difficult enough to sit on the edge of the seat so she didn't crush her wings. She didn't need Declan's disconcerting looks.

She breathed a sigh of relief when it was finally their turn. They descended from the carriage into a mass of humanity.

Touted as the highlight of the Season, the masquerade was hosted by the Duke and Duchess of Westerham. As they were close friends of King George, rumor spread that he might make an appearance, although he hadn't attended public affairs as of late.

She rather hoped he'd come. She'd only seen him once, just before the start of her first Season. At the time, she'd been so concerned with following all the rules for presentation to royalty, she couldn't even remember what the king looked like.

Their small group struggled up the stairs of the greystone mansion. She kept her gaze on Declan. Taller than most of the men, she spotted him easily, as did the woman nearby who cast him appreciative stares.

She arrived on the second floor without crushing her wings. Quite an accomplishment, considering the press of revelers.

When they reached the recessed ballroom, she peered down from her vantage point at the top of the stairs. The floor seethed with costumes and swirling color. With everyone wearing a domino, you couldn't recognize individuals. Instead, she felt as if she were entering an enchanted land of beasts and magical folk.

A long queue of guests waited to be presented to the host and hostess. Declan avoided them and led their little group along the chair-lined walls to an area near the orchestra.

The dexterity of each dancing couple amazed her as they vied for their spot on the marble dance floor. She thought she recognized Lord Avery, and was sure of it when he headed toward them.

"Countess, how lovely you look!" Lord Avery acknowledged her companions and made an elegant bow to her. "Your costume is beyond compare." His appreciative gaze gleamed behind his domino of black and silver.

Smaller than Declan, Lord Avery was rather plain, although not unattractive. He wore his brown hair powdered, unlike Declan's raven locks. *Stop that!* She felt foolish for comparing her suitor to a man she couldn't have. After a quick glance at Declan's impassive face, she turned her attention to her admirer. "Lord Avery, how nice to see you." Her voice was warmer than usual, to make up for her uncharitable thoughts.

"Ah, so I'm found out. And I thought my costume a good one." Dressed as a knight of old, with chainmail and a surcoat, he did appear more dashing than normal. He gave her a tentative smile. "I was hoping to speak with you later. Perhaps you would save a dance for me?"

"I'd be delighted." She wished her words were true. Lord Avery would be a very uninspiring husband, but he appeared to be the best of her choices.

She focused on his departure, so the low sultry voice to her right took her by surprise.

"Lord Worthington, I've been looking for you." Catrina wore a costume fit for a princess. Her low-cut, frothy pink creation came complete with a matching domino comprised of feathers and pearls.

Alex felt underdressed.

Catrina crossed to Declan, took his arm, and rubbed herself against him. "I've missed you."

Declan didn't appear pleased by Catrina's announcement. In fact, he seemed rather annoyed. "I've had matters to attend to." He stepped away.

Catrina kept her hold on him. "There's someone I'd like you to meet. Do you think I could pry you away from your friends for a few moments?"

Declan didn't look like he wanted to go, but he nodded and followed her through the crowd. Alex watched until he was swallowed up by the swirl of costumes.

Morgan leaned over and spoke to her quietly. "She'd not be letting him go easily."

"I'm not asking her to."

"Aren't you?"

"No, Lord Worthington doesn't want me."

"Doesn't he now? And what might you be basing that bit of nonsense on?"

She couldn't tell him Declan had practically laughed at her attempt to seduce him. "He's made it clear he's not interested, and at this point I need to find a husband."

"You're not thinking of doing something foolish, are you?" Morgan looked concerned. "You still have the rest of the Season. There's no rush."

"My cousin isn't giving me the luxury of time. I told Lord Worthington I'd select a husband tonight." She turned away. "It's the only thing I can do."

"Is it, now?" Morgan's voice sounded thoughtful.

Lord Brighton saved her from any further conversation by spiriting her away to the dance floor.

Alex needed to escape. The crush of people and Declan's apparent indifference wore away at her resolve to have a good time. Thank God she'd been able to bow out of the dancing, using her costume as an excuse, but that meant she was stuck carrying on light banter with her suitors.

At the earliest opportunity, she sent the young men on various tasks and went in search of Declan's cousin. Anna was ensconced amidst her normal group of admirers. A dark-haired man, dressed as a pirate, hovered over her hand as if he never intended to give it up.

"Lady Anna," Alex said. "I'm going out for a breath of air. I'll be back in a few minutes."

"Lady Lochsdale, do you really think that's a good idea? Perhaps I should go with you." Anna's voice lacked enthusiasm.

"No, I'll only be gone a few minutes. You stay." She turned and left before her friend's conscience could get the better of her. She wanted be alone to think about what to tell Declan.

It wasn't nearly as crowded on the stairwell, and she could walk easily by the time she'd reached the doors that led out back to the gardens.

For the first time, she appreciated the elegance of her surroundings. Formal gardens descended off a paved terrace. Flambeaux lit several walkways, inviting her to explore their depths. She chose a path to the left and wandered down the stone steps.

Several minutes later, she came upon a hidden water garden enclosed by hedgerows. At the center of the small pool stood a whimsical fountain. Several winged cherubs poured water from an urn, while white marble dolphins frolicked below.

She crossed to the pool and knelt down, trailing her fingers through the cool water. On impulse, she removed her slippers and placed them at the edge, then lifted her skirt, and waded out to the center. It wasn't very deep, coming just below her knees, but it felt wonderful.

"Aren't you taking the costume of a water fairy a bit too seriously?" A smooth dark voice sounded above the tinkling fountain. "Though I do admire the view it affords me."

Startled, she searched for who had spoken. She recognized Lord Duprey by the hooded monk's robe he'd been wearing earlier. In the flickering firelight, the costume did nothing to dispel her unease, especially as he was standing in the only exit to her secluded garden.

She felt for the reassuring heaviness of her knife. Thank God she'd sewn a sheath for her blade into a pocket, after discovering she wouldn't be able to wear her customary boots.

With as much speed as possible, she got out of the pool and put her slippers on while he watched. "What are you doing here?"

"I followed you, of course." He crossed over to the pool, standing closer than she'd like. "Lord Worthington tells me you're going to decide whom you'll marry this evening. I wanted to make it very clear that I'm interested."

He'd removed his domino. She could see the silver glitter of his eyes, in spite of the shadow cast by the hood. She moved out of his reach. "I'm flattered, but I'm afraid I've chosen another."

"That would be a shame." He stepped closer. Before she realized what was happening, he'd reached up and untied the ribbons to her domino. The green and gold creation fluttered to earth. "There, now I can see your beautiful face."

She started to bend down to retrieve it, but he grabbed her shoulders and forced her to look at him. With her right hand, she reached for the blade in her pocket.

"You don't know what you'd be missing. I kissed you once long ago," Lord Duprey said, lowering his head to hers, "but my passion wasn't fueled as it is now."

The demanding kiss made her feel ill. Even when Declan kissed her in anger, it had never been like this. She worked feverishly at the knife in its secret compartment. Her hand closed over her weapon as she brought her knee up to Duprey's groin. She didn't hit her mark, but managed to break free and back away.

He laughed, his teeth shining white in the dimness of his hood. "A fighter. I like that in a woman."

Lord Duprey started toward her, but she held her blade out between them. "If I were you, I wouldn't come any closer."

The man had the audacity to smile as he continued to advance. "Do you think that little thing will stop me?"

"I'm betting it would." Declan's voice came from the shadows. "But then again, if it didn't, I'd have to."

Her guardian stood in the shadows, with his shoulder resting against one of the solitary pillars scattered throughout the gardens. With his arms crossed over his chest, he looked as if he didn't have a care in the world. Relief flooded her, not that she couldn't have handled the situation.

"This is a private conversation." Lord Duprey no longer sounded quite so cocky. "It doesn't concern you, Worthington."

"Doesn't it? Last I knew, Lady Lochsdale was still my ward." Declan moved a few steps closer.

"Consider carefully, Lady Lochsdale," Lord Duprey said. "I could ruin you. A woman who carries a knife is scandalous," he said, taking another step toward her, "but add a few well-placed rumors about you and your guardian, and you'd never be accepted in polite society again."

"The Countess of Lochsdale has been well chaperoned." At the control she heard in Declan's voice, she backed up. "As for the knife, it was a part of her costume." He gave a slight shrug as he stepped away from the pillar.

Her attacker recognized his danger too late. In an instant he found himself dangling up against the shrubbery, Declan's hands around his throat. The smug look on his face changed to desperation as he attempted to breathe.

"Now, we're going to have a little chat," Declan said. "You will not be spreading unfounded lies about Lady Lochsdale, will you?" Judging from Lord Duprey's bulging eyes, Declan had increased the pressure. The man could barely shake his head from side to side.

Declan released him suddenly. Duprey fell to the ground, his dark monk's robes pooling around him. "If I hear even the slightest whisper of scandal, I'll come looking for you. Do we understand one another?"

Lord Duprey nodded and stood. At the entrance to the path, he turned and struggled to speak. At last a hoarse whisper rattled from his chest. "You haven't heard the last of this. I'm going to enjoy seeing you brought to your knees, Worthington."

"If you think *you're* going to do it, you'll be waiting forever." Declan adjusted his cuffs and straightened his coat.

Lord Duprey gave them a venomous look and left.

"You shouldn't have come out here alone." Declan came to stand beside her. "Are you all right?"

"I'm fine." She slipped her knife back into the sheath in her pocket and bent down to retrieve her domino. "I think I can safely remove Lord Duprey from my list." She smiled up at his darkly masked face. "I didn't like the way he kissed, anyway."

"Are you such an authority?"

"I know what I like."

Declan reached out and traced her lips with his index finger. "And what do you like?"

"I don't think I should tell you."

"Why not? I could help. You need to consider everything when you chose a husband. For instance, I doubt you'd get much kissing from Lord Holdon."

"What makes you say that?" She thought of kissing the balding older man and felt slightly repulsed.

"He's too old for you, Lady Lochsdale."

"Perhaps, but what about Lord Brighton? He's young and pleasing to look at."

Declan shrugged. "I've heard it said he prefers boys."

Her face grew warm. Long ago she'd overheard Paddy talking to one of the boys who wanted to hire on the *White Falcon*. Paddy advised against it, telling him the captain used his cabin boys as he would a woman.

"And what's wrong with Lord Avery?"

"Nothing yet. Except he needs your money."

"They all need my estates. That's why I chose them."

"I'm not letting you marry someone who can't provide for you."

"I can provide for myself."

"What about love?"

"You are the last person to talk about love. I'm surprised you even know the emotion exists."

"My decision stands, Alex. I'm not going to let you marry any of the four." He reached out and took her arm, his voice softening. "I'm just asking you to wait until someone more appropriate comes along."

She jerked out of his grasp. "And who's going to tell Luther to wait?" This was pointless. She turned away and headed toward the path.

"Alexandra, come back here."

She ignored him and started to run back toward the

manor, favoring her aching ankle. If Declan thought he could protect her, he didn't know Luther.

"What might you have done to upset all the women?" Morgan's voice was muffled as he faced the library bookshelves.

"Nothing." Declan grabbed the crystal decanter of cognac and a glass, then fell into a chair across from the fireplace. He filled his snifter, and set the decanter on a table nearby. "Lady Lochsdale is just being unreasonable."

He raised the glass to his lips and let the fiery liquid poor down his throat. It seemed like a soothing balm compared to the last few hours.

He attempted to swirl the remaining spirits in the snifter, but the contents refused to stay in the glass. The amber liquid sprayed in all directions. Was he foxed? Not bloody likely. He must just be more tired than he realized.

After all, Morgan was still sober, and he had matched him drink for drink. Or did Morgan just *appear* sober?

They'd left the masquerade shortly after the interlude in the garden. No one spoke on the return trip, which was fine with Declan. The women acted like he was an ingrate and immediately retired to their chambers, so he and Morgan had sequestered themselves in the library with his favorite cognac.

How had his life become such a muddle? Why couldn't Alex just do as she was told?

He'd complained about the foolishness of women until Morgan reached over and took the drink out of his hand. "I'm thinking you've had enough."

He reached for his glass. "Had enough for what?"

Morgan kept it away from him and poured the last of its contents on the fire. The flames flared briefly, sending sparks up the chimney. Morgan put their glasses on a marble-topped table, then leaned against the mantle, studying his friend. "Lady Lochsdale looked beautiful tonight."

"I noticed." Hell, he couldn't help but notice. Every man in the room had watched her. By the look on their faces, they were mentally trying to remove the transparent layers of her costume. He should never have let her go out looking like that.

Morgan crossed to a chair next to his, and sat down. "Lady Lochsdale told me you were having a bit of trouble with Lord Duprey."

Declan sank back into the leather cushion of his chair. "Nothing I couldn't handle." He closed his eyes, but the sight of Alex in that pool was indelibly etched on his eyelids. He opened them again and tried to focus on Morgan.

"She also mentioned you'd not been pleased with her choice of a husband, and, in fact, turned down all of her possible suitors." Morgan raised an eyebrow at him. "Do you think that's wise?"

"I can protect her until she finds someone suitable. None of them deserve her. She'll eventually come to see that."

"You'd not be in love with her, would you?"

"Of course not." Declan gazed into the fire. He had never loved any woman, and he wasn't about to start now. Alex said he didn't know love existed. She was wrong. He knew it existed. That was the problem.

"Might there be a possibility you *could* fall in love with her?"

"Never." He tried to give Morgan a look of assurance.

"Well then, I'm thinking I've solved your problem." Morgan had the look of a man who'd come up with the best idea since the invention of the carriage. "It's you who should be marrying Lady Lochsdale."

"What!" He shook his head. His friend had gone mad. "That's the most ridiculous idea you've come up with yet."

"Why?"

"Because, because..." He couldn't tell Morgan that he was afraid he'd come to love Alex. He'd just admitted he wouldn't. And he did have a choice, didn't he? Just because he wanted her desperately didn't mean he couldn't keep her at an emotional distance. As a matter-of-fact, once his body got what it craved, he could treat her like any other woman.

"Exactly," Morgan said, as if reading his mind. "I'm thinking it's the perfect solution. You get your heir with no strings, and Lady Lochsdale would be out Addington's reach for good." He studied him for a moment, then added, "She might be wanting to go back to her estates, once she's given you a son."

"After that," Declan said with a shrug, "she can do as she pleases." It made sense, and best of all, she'd be his wife. His body fairly sang for joy. He got to his feet, not wanting to waste one more minute.

"Where might you be going?"

"I've got to tell her."

"I'll be letting myself out."

He couldn't be sure, but he thought he heard Morgan chuckling as he left.

Chapter 16

"We're getting married."

Alex's sleep-shrouded brain could have sworn she heard Declan's voice. She opened her eyes. It *was* Declan. He sat on the edge of her bed. "What did you say?"

He leaned toward her. "I said we're getting married."

"That's what I thought." The smell of strong spirits assailed her nose. "What are you doing in my room, and what makes you think I'd marry you?"

"You certainly wanted me the other night."

"Yes, but as I recall, you didn't want me."

"Things have changed." He leaned down and started nibbling on her neck.

"How?" It took momentous effort to get out that one syllable with all her attention focused on that little spot under her ear.

Declan drew back, his hands on her shoulders. "I realized, since I don't love you, it's not a problem for us to marry."

"That doesn't make sense." She broke free and wrapped the sheet around her naked body, then backed out of his reach. "What about Catrina?"

"She'll find someone else. You're the one who needs to marry quickly."

How could she marry him when he didn't love her? She would come to resent his indifference. But what if, once they were married, he returned her feelings? Should she take the chance?

Declan's hair had come free of its queue and hung

down around his face. She wanted to reach out, entwine her fingers in his black locks, and pull his mouth to hers. Sanity prevailed. "My lord, I—"

"Declan."

"Fine, Declan, we can't marry."

He stood and ran his hand through his hair, pulling it away from his face. "Why not?"

Any of her suitors would be preferable to him. With them it would be strictly a business arrangement. Love wouldn't be involved. Before she could say anything, he answered his own question.

"You needn't feel restricted by me, Alex. All I ask is you supply me with an heir. Something we both want. After that, I don't care where you go."

Stung, she got off the bed and awkwardly walked to the window, her sheet dragging behind her like a train.

"You're welcome to return to your grandfather's estate." Declan sounded like he was offering her a much-awaited treat.

She turned to look at him. "How nice." Her voice reflected hurt and disappointment, but he didn't seem to notice.

"I'll stay in London and let you take care of things on your estates." He grinned at her. "Of course, I'll expect quarterly reports."

"Of course, and our son? Would you expect me to leave him behind?"

"He'll stay with you until he needs to learn about his responsibilities."

"You have it all worked out, don't you?" She felt caught between a marriage she desperately wanted, and the knowledge that he would destroy her if he didn't eventually return her love. "All I have to do is agree to a loveless marriage."

"As I recall, you were going to marry without love

anyway. You don't feel anything for your other suitors, do you?" He seemed concerned about her answer.

"No." She might as well answer truthfully. "But why should I marry you?"

"Because I can give you the freedom you crave. What better reason? I'll let you do as you please, after you produce an heir."

"What if you change your mind?"

"I won't. I honor my contracts." Declan walked over and captured a curl that lay on her bare shoulder. He appeared fascinated by it, twining the strands around his index finger. "It won't be so bad, Alex. This may surprise you, but most women find me attractive." He smiled at her, humor and warmth in his eyes.

The smile was her undoing. She wanted to see his smile, every day, for the rest of her life. She reached up and traced his mouth with her fingertip. He captured her hand and pressed a kiss in the center of her palm.

"All right, I'll marry you." This moment should be filled with joy, but all she felt was foreboding. What if she couldn't make him love her?

A scraping noise in the hallway drew their attention to her bedroom door. Declan had left it ajar.

He motioned for her to be silent, picked up the lamp, and went out into the hall, then returned a few moments later. "No one's there. It must have been a tree branch on the hall window."

Declan closed the door and turned to look at her. "You're beautiful in the lamplight."

His devilish grin made her quiver inside.

"I think you should always wear a sheet."

She wanted to be beautiful. Every female they'd met had flirted with him, but now he was going to be hers. He may not love her, but at least she'd be part of his life.

He was still dressed for the masquerade, but his

cravat hung loose and slightly off center. His hair brushed his shoulders, giving him a slightly wicked look. Even in disarray, he'd never been more handsome.

Somehow, she had to find a way to unlock the love he guarded so jealously.

He placed the lamp on the table and slowly walked toward her. His blue eyes seemed to be lit from within by an intensity she didn't understand. "I've wanted you since that first day you challenged me in the library."

Without breaking eye contact, he advanced. She toyed with the idea of asking him to leave, but she knew he wouldn't. She wasn't even sure she wanted him to.

With some difficulty, she tucked her sheet into a makeshift knot above her breasts, keeping one hand on the tenuous closure. She'd meant to back away, but her feet stayed anchored to the floor, waiting for what her heart told her was inevitable.

When he stopped in front of her, he stood so close she could see the rise and fall of his chest. She lifted her head. The cleft in his chin added character and strengthened what would otherwise have been a beautiful face. She watched in fascination as he lowered his head.

His lips brushed against hers, causing her whole body to tingle. "Please don't deny me," he whispered into her mouth before claiming it in a kiss that made her long for... something. She lifted her arms to his shoulders, wishing she could feel the warmth of his skin instead of velvet.

As if he knew her thoughts, he backed away. His hungry gaze never left hers as he removed his coat, then untied his cravat and leisurely lifted the white shirt up over his head.

She felt as if she'd been turned to stone. She couldn't move, could barely breathe. He moved close to her, and she was amazed to find her arms worked. Of their own accord, they reached out to him. Her hands glided up his chest, feeling the individual muscle ridges.

He groaned and drew her against the length of him. Finding her mouth again, he kissed her. His tongue teased her lips, demanding entry. She let him have his way and was startled by the feelings he evoked as his tongue explored her mouth. He tasted of spirits, the warmth of him settling into her soul.

Tangling his hands in her hair, he leaned his forehead against hers. "God, Alex, you taste wonderful."

Declan released her hair and backed away. She wanted to cry out in frustration, until she realized he intended to remove his breeches.

His hand on the buttons, he gazed at her, a challenge in his gaze. She could tell him to stop now, or suffer the consequences.

She'd lived her life acting first and thinking later. This was most assuredly not the time to think.

"Go on." She crossed her arms and waited. Declan undid the buttons and bent down to remove his breeches. He was moving too slowly. She didn't realize she'd been holding her breath until he stood up. When she got her first good look at him, the breath left her body.

As a child, she'd caught glimpses of naked men on *The Merry Elizabeth*, so it wasn't that she didn't know how a man was formed. But Declan was beautiful. Her hands dropped to her sides, and she couldn't look away, even if she'd wanted to.

The lamplight cast highlights and shadows over Declan's muscular body. Long wavy black hair drew her attention downward, past broad shoulders to his chest. His skin glistened in the lamp's soft glow, as if inviting her touch. Her hands wanted to take the same path as her eyes, following over each muscle, until they reached slim hips. Her inspection stopped at his manhood. The thick column sprang from its nest of dark curls, fully erect.

Raw power emanated from his lithe movements as he

started toward her. He stopped a couple of feet away.

"I want to look at you." He fumbled with the makeshift knot. The sheet fell to the floor with a whisper of sound, exposing her to his view.

"I'm glad you didn't take my advice about sleeping in the nude." Declan ached at the sight of her. She was petite and perfectly formed, with high creamy breasts tipped by seashell pink nipples. Constant exercise had smoothed the skin over muscle, but she was well rounded at hips and breasts, her curves emphasized by a tiny waist.

It took all his control to keep from grabbing her and making love to her quickly. He'd spent years learning to pleasure women, but this was different. She was a virgin, and he'd avoided virgins.

Alex returned his gaze, as if daring him to find her wanting.

"You're perfect," he whispered. "I knew you would be." He moved closer and leaned down, then kissed the tip of her breast. He drew the softness of her into his mouth, wanting never to let go.

"Declan, stop. No. Ohhh." Alex grabbed his hair, keeping his mouth at her breast. He tormented first one, then the other, rolling his tongue over the hardening nubs. "Please," Alex moaned.

He removed her hands from his hair and kissed a trail upward, between her breasts, to the delicate skin on her neck. He'd waited so long to hold her like this. It felt like a dream. He hugged her closer and roamed her silken back with his hands. Her soft body yielded to his. She fit as though she belonged in his arms.

He breathed deeply, his face buried in the vibrant hair that held him spellbound. She smelled of vanilla, a fragrance he would never associate with anyone else.

His Alex. She *was* his. For tonight at least, and until he

had to let her go.

His hands continued their exploration, one finally finding its way to the soft nest of curls between her legs. Warm moisture met his touch. He listened to her breathing. Small gasps mixed with tiny whimpering sounds fueled his passion. She clung to him as if she'd never be able to stand on her own.

Alex felt as if she was coming apart. Declan's hands seemed to be everywhere. She cupped his buttocks and leaned back, relishing the firm muscles beneath her fingers. His hand was between their bodies, teasing that sensitive spot between her legs.

He stopped. Before she knew what was happening, an arm slid under her thighs. Declan picked her up and carried her to the bed. Their mouths still joined, he gently lowered her to the soft mattress. He lay beside her, kissing her eyes and nose, finally returning to her lips.

Feeling a bit unsure, she leaned back and began an exploration of her own. She wanted to really look at him, so she sat up. Using her hands as her eyes, she started with his face.

She loved his face. She could feel the strong bone structure that made him look like a sculpture of Apollo she'd seen once. Declan's eyes followed her movements from under thick-lashed eyelids as she continued downward.

Marveling at the strong column of his neck, her hands continued caressing until they smoothed over his chest, her splayed fingers not covering half the expanse. She felt the muscles in his belly tighten as her hands moved in small circular motions, relishing the feel of the springy hairs under her palms. Her exploration went lower, until she came to his silken shaft. When she took him in her hand, he sat up quickly, and drew her into an embrace. He groaned into her mouth as she continued to caress the smooth flesh.

The feel of him built the tension in her. She was just

starting to satisfy her curiosity, when he leaned back and looked at her. "Alex, I can't wait much longer."

She wasn't sure what to do, but she wanted to experience everything. Nothing mattered except the new and exciting feelings he evoked. They stared at each other for a long moment, desire pulsing between them. "I want you, Declan," Alex whispered as she slanted her lips over his.

Those few little words let loose passions she hadn't realized he'd kept in check. She tried to shove him back down on the bed, but he resisted. Instead, he turned her over on her back and moved on top of her, bracing most of his weight on his arms. He rubbed the lower part of his body against hers as she arched up, trying to meet him.

He entered her carefully at first. Capturing her mouth, he stifled her cry as he pushed all the way in. The pain momentarily dimmed her feeling of euphoria.

Declan stilled, his whole body tense. "Are you hurt? I promise I'll not go on until you're ready. But God, don't ask me to stop."

His voice sounded strained. What did he mean, go on? He started to kiss her again and, with one hand, rubbed a tender nipple.

Sensation engulfed her again, stronger than before. She wasn't even aware when he began to move. Slowly at first, then faster, until she felt as if she was on the brink of some great discovery. The intensity became so great, it teetered on the edge between pain and pleasure.

She wanted to stay here forever. Joined in this amazing act to the man she loved.

Then her world exploded. Spasms radiated from where they were joined. She felt her body clench around him. Emotion and physical sensation blended as one. She clung to him, not really knowing where she stopped and he began.

He was still moving inside her when she felt him stiffen, small shudders coursing through his body.

"Alexandra."

Somehow he captured all the wonder of what they'd shared in her name. He collapsed on top of her, but she didn't mind. She relished the weight of him, wanting to keep him close.

Slowly their breathing quieted, and Declan rolled to one side. He propped himself up on an elbow, studying her. "What am I going to do with you?"

"I thought you intended to marry me."

"Have no doubts." He brushed a damp curl off her forehead. "My lionhearted Alex. Most women are terrified their first time."

Should she have been hesitant? She wasn't going to pretend. She liked what they'd just done. If he wanted some simpering miss, then he should have found another woman to marry. "I guess I'll never be like most women."

Declan laughed. "Thank God for that."

"Have you been with many women like this?"

Declan's finger had started to blaze a path between the valley of her breasts, but he leaned back at her question and tapped her on the nose. "One of us needed experience."

"But were those other women... Was it the same with them?"

He kissed her lightly on the lips. "You ask too many questions."

"How else am I going to get answers?"

Declan raised an eyebrow. "All right, you may ask any question." He held up a hand when she opened her mouth. "As long as it doesn't concern other women. Now, what do you want to know?"

She really wanted to ask if he could ever love her, but didn't dare. Until he dealt with his father's memory, she doubted he could love anyone. If only he'd talk about his past. Then maybe...

"What do you remember about your father?" The

question was out of her mouth before she thought about it. She doubted Declan would answer, but it was worth a try.

For a moment, he studied her intently, then turned onto his back. With his hands clasped behind his head, he stared at the ceiling.

"He was a hard man," Declan said quietly.

"Perhaps, but he must have had some goodness in him. He loved your mother."

"Yes. Although I never saw it myself." Declan turned to look at her, a rueful smile on his lips. "He certainly never loved me. I can count on one hand the number of times my father and I were in the same room. My governess and the servants were under strict orders to keep me out of his sight."

He stood and turned out the lamp, then crossed to the fireplace. The small glow from the fire illuminated his beautiful body. She wished she could capture his image as he rested one hand on the mantle and studied the fire.

"Did you know you can see into the drawing room from the first landing on the stairs? I used to watch my father whenever the door was open. He'd sit there for hours, a brandy snifter in his hand, staring at that damned portrait of my mother."

"Surely you had others you cared about. What about friends?"

Declan turned toward her, his face a handsome mask. "The highlight of my life was being sent to our country house. The servants at Eberly didn't really care what I did as long as I stayed out of their way.

"Meeting your grandfather saved my life. Without him, I had nothing. That's why I went to *The Merry Elizabeth* to watch out for you and your family."

"I'm sorry I was so difficult." She wanted to say she was sorry for the lonely little boy who'd needed someone so desperately, but she knew he'd never accept her pity.

Declan gave her a slight smile. "You didn't want to

be taken away from your home. I understand that now. You were lucky, you had twelve years with your parents."

She rose and crossed to where he stood, then reached up and brushed back the wayward hair on his forehead. "I'm sure your mother loved you."

"I wish I'd known her. My life could have been so different if only..." Declan gave a little laugh. "It doesn't matter now."

In spite of the fact that he towered over her, all she could see was a broken little boy. "What your father did was wrong. Instead of cherishing the gift your mother left him, he let bitterness rule his life. Not everyone reacts the same way."

"I wouldn't know." He turned away and studied the fire, his voice reflecting all the lonely years.

She turned him to face her. "Declan, listen to me. You're not like your father. Love won't destroy you." She stood on tiptoes and ran her hands through his hair, then tugged his head down, forcing him to look at her. How could she make him understand he was no longer on the outside looking in?

"I love you, Declan."

He stiffened. The muscle in his jaw started jumping furiously before he drew her to him, kissing her as though she would disappear at any moment. He lowered her to the rug in front of the fireplace, making love to her with an urgency that left her breathless.

Filling her senses, he seemed to be everywhere. She clung to him, her body responding like a harp in the hands of a master. His music echoed in her, even after they lay back, sated, on the thick carpet.

Declan spread her discarded sheet over them, warding off the chill of the predawn hours. She snuggled close and rested her head on his chest. Swirling a fingertip through the silken hair near one of his nipples, she marveled at the small intimacy.

She closed her eyes and drifted, half asleep. In her mind's eye she saw a lonely little boy sitting on the stairs. Unaware, she murmured, "You're not alone now, you'll never be alone."

Not alone. Declan took a deep breath and let it out slowly. It was a seductive thought.

He gazed down at Alex's sleeping form. Smoothing the hair away from her face, he pressed a kiss to her forehead.

She'd said she loved him. Sighing, he lay back. He shouldn't be pleased, but he was. Why was it no other woman made him feel the things she did? Drawing her closer, he shut his eyes.

Unbidden, the memory of his father's drink-ravaged face intruded on his thoughts, a firm reminder that love could destroy everything he'd worked for. He didn't love her, did he? Maybe not yet, his inner voice warned, but this desire to keep her with him was dangerous.

Once they had a son, she had to leave. It would be best for them both. In the last hazy moments before sleep, he wondered if, even now, he had the strength to let her go.

Chapter 17

With her eyes closed, Alex stretched, enjoying a rare sense of well-being. She reached beneath her blanket and searched for her sheet. Could she have kicked it to the bottom of the bed? Odd, she was sure there was one last night when she... Her eyes flew open.

What had she done?

She sat up and attempted to search the room, but the bright sunlight momentarily blinded her. When she became accustomed to the light, she saw her sheet crumpled before the fireplace, but the room was empty. Declan was gone. He must have carried her to the bed during the night, then left.

An irrational part of her wished he'd stayed. Doubts flitted at the edge of her consciousness. What was he thinking? Did he regret his offer?

She could almost hear Eleanor telling her this was not the time for regrets. The damage was done, and Alex had to live with the consequences of her actions.

With a sigh, she pushed back the covers and swung her legs around, then put her feet on the cold floor. Eleanor would be right, of course. She'd agreed to this marriage, now she had to make the best of it. The cold seeped up her legs, seeming to invade her soul.

If only she hadn't fallen in love with him! Declan could give her everything she'd ever wanted, including her freedom, but she'd trade it all to hear him say he loved her.

She angrily brushed her tangled curls away from her face and shoved the heavy mass back with one hand. Hell and damnation, she wasn't accomplishing anything just sitting here. She got up, strode over to the dressing table, and snatched a comb from the tray. Pain radiated from her scalp as she tugged on her curls.

So Declan hadn't said he loved her. What difference did that make? She had a lifetime to convince him love could bring great joy. A lifetime of doing what they did last night.

Heat rushed into her face as she gazed in the mirror. Had she changed? No, the reflection was the same, but if she closed her eyes, she could still feel the touch of his hands, his tongue, his body joined with hers. Never had a memory been so vivid.

Without a doubt he'd been with many women, but surely last night was special? Fear, swift and strong, enveloped her. What if last night hadn't changed anything? She needed to see him, if only to be reassured he wasn't totally unaffected.

She rushed to her wardrobe and chose a day gown of coral silk. The color gave her complexion a translucent quality. It wouldn't hurt to look her best when she saw him again.

In the midst of trying to lace her corset, Anna came flying into the room without knocking. "Oh, Lady Lochsdale, I just heard the news. Isn't it wonderful! You're going to be my cousin."

"Who told you?"

"Mama. She and Lord Worthington had a talk this morning. He's planning an engagement ball for next Saturday."

Typical Declan, he didn't wait to consult her. Surprised, she found she didn't mind. It was rather nice to have someone do things for her.

"Was it terribly romantic?" Anna was practically jumping up and down. "How did he ask you?"

"Actually, he didn't ask me."

"No, but I thought..."

"He told me."

"Oh." From the look on Anna's face, she couldn't seem to decide if that was romantic or not.

"I've agreed to the arrangement. At least I'll be his wife." She held up her laces. "Would you help me with these? I'd like to get downstairs as soon as possible, and I haven't a clue where Mary's gone off to."

In less than twenty minutes, they were headed down the stairs. At the bottom, she patted the winged lion's head. Funny, how things could change in just one night.

Yesterday, she'd felt threatened by the carving. Today, she felt as if he was protecting her. Anna's romantic fancies must be rubbing off.

As they entered the dining room, Alex took a deep breath and tried to organize her jumbled thoughts. She supposed she'd have to answer their questions, but what to say?

Lady Bradford glanced up as they came through the door. "There you are, Lady Lochsdale, I'm so pleased. I spoke with Lord Worthington this morning. Please, sit and have some breakfast."

She took the chair across from Lady Bradford.

Anna kissed her mother on the cheek and dropped into a chair at the head of the table. She promptly started to fidget with her silverware, all the while glancing at Alex.

Sometimes Anna seemed so much younger, even though they were only separated by two years. She reminded her of a new colt, terribly curious and full of boundless energy.

"I was pleasantly surprised at this turn of events." Lady Bradford nodded to Williams to serve their breakfast. Once he and the footman departed, she continued. "I thought after last night you were through with my nephew. When did you change your mind?"

"I couldn't sleep, so I thought I'd find something to

read in the library." Her face grew warm. She didn't like to lie, but she couldn't very well admit he'd come to her room. "I spoke with Lord Worthington, and we agreed that marriage to each other would be the best solution to both our problems."

They didn't need to know he wanted nothing to do with her after she'd provided him with an heir. God willing, he'd come to care for her before then.

"I see." Lady Bradford gave her a searching look. "Did you tell him you love him?"

"Yes."

"And."

"It didn't matter." She glanced down at the eggs and sausages on her plate. Though they'd smelled heavenly a few moments before, she'd lost her appetite.

"My cousin is an ingrate. He doesn't deserve to marry you." Anna viciously stabbed at a tomato on her plate. "I wish he was here this very minute."

She grinned at the mental picture of Anna brandishing her fork at Declan. It was fortunate no one had ever taught Anna to use a weapon. Someone would have gotten hurt.

Lady Bradford shook her head. "I had hoped..." She sighed. "Lord Worthington seemed so changed this morning. He wanted the engagement ball to be held right away. I assumed he'd finally come to terms with his feelings."

With dignified grace, Lady Bradford rose. "No matter, at least you'll be his wife, and my niece." She circled the table, then reached down to give her a hug. "Welcome to the family." She tipped Alex's face up, and gave her an encouraging smile. "Don't worry, he'll come around."

"He'd better," Anna muttered as she attacked yet another defenseless piece of food.

Alex smiled at her soon-to-be cousin. Warmth spread through her at the thought of how readily Lady Bradford and Anna had accepted her as part of the family. She wanted to belong. If only Declan could come to love her.

The door opened, and Williams interrupted, "Lady Bradford, you asked me to tell you as soon as it was done."

"Thank you, Williams."

With a slight bow, the butler left, and Lady Bradford turned to her. "Lady Lochsdale, I'd like you to see something. Would you come into the parlor?"

She followed Lady Bradford, with Anna bringing up the rear. The massive double doors were closed, but Declan's aunt swung them open and stepped to the side.

Bright sunlight lit the room. Alex had always thought the furnishings in this part of the house subdued, but now she understood why. Her gaze was drawn immediately to a painting above the fireplace. The woman in the portrait gave the room the vibrancy it lacked.

Declan's mother.

The resemblance was unmistakable. She'd chosen to be painted in the entranceway of Castelton House, one hand lightly resting on the amber-eyed lion at the foot of the stairs.

Her gown was a deep claret, with flounces on the sleeves and lace at the neck. A bouquet of what appeared to be forget-me-nots trailed from her other hand. The artist gave the impression Declan's mother was only now coming down the stairs. No rigid poses for her. It was an unconventional portrait of an extraordinary woman. She could almost pity Edward Devereaux.

Lady Bradford's unsteady voice sounded beside her. "This is why I thought Lord Worthington had changed. I haven't seen Maura's portrait in years."

Anna crossed from the doorway to get a closer look. "This was Aunt Maura? She's beautiful. You're right, Mama, Lord Worthington does favor her."

When she glanced over at Lady Bradford, Alex observed tears threatening to mar the older woman's powdered cheeks. She searched her pocket and brought out a handkerchief, handing it to the distraught woman.

"Thank you, dear." Lady Bradford wiped her eyes and looked back at the portrait. "Lord Worthington asked me to have it brought down when I saw him this morning. It was the first time he ..." Lady Bradford turned to look at Alex. "He actually talked to me, asked me about his mother. It wasn't a long conversation, but it's a start. I'm not sure how you did it Lady Lochsdale, but I want to thank you."

A glow started in Alex's stomach, warming her whole body. So, he'd listened after all. She clung to this slight hope, like a brand burning amongst the ashes. Maybe he could change.

She stared up at the portrait of the free-spirited woman who'd loved with such boundless joy. This is what Declan would have been like if his mother had lived. So many wasted years. Even now, he was a prisoner of the past, unable to move on.

She made a vow to the woman in the portrait. Regardless of the cost, she would do her utmost to teach Declan not to fear love.

Declan strode into the solid expanse of Bradford Hall, and wondered who trained Bradford's servants. He hadn't knocked, yet the door was opened to admit him. An impeccably liveried butler led the way to the breakfast room, showing no surprise at the earliness of the hour.

When he glanced around the sunny room, he discovered it was empty. Blasted, where was his cousin? Bradford's note had arrived at daybreak this morning and had said to come immediately. He welcomed the diversion. Anything was better than thinking about last night, and Alex.

Unable to sit still, he circled the room, noting Lady Bradford had been allowed to decorate the space. Even the table chairs had cushions. Bradford wouldn't have concerned himself with the amenities.

At last he sat on one of the chairs, its high wooden back

carved with Celtic designs. He shut his eyes and rested his head back against the woodwork.

The Celtic knots dug into his scalp. The pain added to the pounding in his head. He deserved it for getting foxed last night. The result had been a disastrous proposal.

Perhaps it would be better if he avoided Alex. It wasn't that he was afraid. That would be ludicrous. He didn't love her, so what was there to be afraid of?

Last night was only... what? He could vividly recall Alex's hands in his hair, her warm soft lips inches from his own. The way her eyes flashed when she'd told him she loved him.

Love.

He hoped to hell she didn't mean it. Nevertheless, he couldn't stop thinking about what she'd said. If she did love him, it would be cruel to encourage her.

Once they were married, and they would marry, he'd get her with child as quickly as possible and try to rid her of this notion that she loved him. That's what he should do. He didn't want her love. Did he?

Either way, the less time spent with her, the better. He might not have to deal with her at all. After last night, she might already be carrying his heir.

Now he just had to come up with some way to break the news to Catrina. His head began to pound in earnest.

He opened his eyes to find his cousin studying him from the doorway. *How long had he been there?*

"I understand congratulations are in order."

"How in the hell did you know that?" He sat forward, giving his head a slight shake, which increased the throbbing behind his eyes. His cousin's talents had come in handy on several occasions, but they were still a mystery to him.

"You underestimate the value of servant's gossip." Bradford, dressed only in his breeches and a shirt, crossed the room and took the chair opposite him. "Cook heard the news at the market this morning. My steward informed me.

"As with all gossip, there are only elements of truth. But based on your apparent distraction, I take it you have asked the Countess of Lochsdale to be your bride."

"Yes."

"I was under the impression Lady Catrina would be your choice."

"She was, but Lady Lochsdale needs the protection of marriage."

Bradford raised an eyebrow. "And you have to be the one to give it to her?"

"It seemed like a good idea at the time." Declan stood, walked over to the window, and peered out on the meticulous gardens that were Lady Bradford's passion. "As long as I get my heir, it doesn't really matter whom I marry."

"Well, you're correct about one thing. The Countess of Lochsdale does need protection."

The tone of Bradford's voice made Declan uneasy. He turned to see a slight frown on his cousin's face. "What have you found out?"

"If you'll come to my study, I have something to show you." Bradford left without a backward glance.

He followed his cousin through the labyrinth of elegantly appointed hallways. Thank God Castleton was laid out in a simpler design than the twisting passageways of Bradford Hall. The place was a nuisance, but it suited his cousin.

As they crossed the threshold of the study, he was struck anew by the clutter. He'd forgotten Bradford's unique method of organization. No servants were allowed to clean this holy sanctum. Books and papers lay scattered in piles atop of every flat surface.

The irony was, his cousin never lost anything.

As if confirming his thoughts, Bradford went to a table

in front of the fireplace. It sat next to the only chair in the room that was devoid of papers. After glancing through several in the stack, he handed a slightly grimy sheet to Declan. "I received this yesterday afternoon."

He took the paper and perused its contents. "A registry for The Swan dated February, 1775?"

"Look toward the bottom."

Two names were very familiar. "Luther Addington and his mother. Staying at The Swan? Not a typical haunt of the Ton, I admit, but nothing nefarious."

Bradford shook his head. "Because it was so close to the time you and Alex's father were attacked, I did some checking. Seems the arrogant boy didn't make a favorable impression with the landlord. The man was more than willing to talk. On two separate occasions, Lord Addington and his mother met with a man known in those parts as 'Spider.' Later, Spider bragged about coming into extra cash. Said he did a little work for them."

"Wasn't one of the men who kidnapped Lady Lochsdale named Spider?"

"Indeed."

"A rather large coincidence, don't you think?" He needed proof. "Could you get me a description? I'll lay odds this 'Spider' was one of the men on the docks that day. The bastards hadn't been after the money at all." He gave a low whistle. "No wonder they let me walk away."

He began to pace the small distance between a cluttered table and his cousin's mounded desk. Tapping the list slowly on his other hand, he considered the likelihood of "Spider" being a killer and Alex's kidnapper. If they *were* one and the same, then she was in more danger than he'd thought. Unease clenched his spine. He handed the list back to his cousin, fighting the impulse to rush home.

Bradford set it back on its pile, then crossed to his desk. "I'm still working on 'Spider's' identity. He hasn't been seen in the area for a couple of years."

"I'd appreciate anything you can get."

Bradford studied at his cousin, uncharacteristic concern in his cool gray eyes. "Lord Worthington, do you think this is a good time to announce your betrothal? I believe Addington has killed at least once to get Lady Lochsdale's estates. What's to keep him from adding to his list?"

"I'll have to take the chance. Besides, this might force him to do something rash. Do you still have someone watching him?"

"Constantly."

"Might you also watch my future bride? If I'm otherwise occupied, I want to be sure she's safe."

His cousin raised an eyebrow. "As you wish."

Before last night, Declan would have balked at the idea of someone else protecting her. But how could you protect someone you were avoiding? "Thank you."

Bradford nodded. "I'll send you any information I receive, but be careful. I can assure you, nothing this man does will be in the open."

Declan crossed to the threshold and tugged on his doeskin gloves. "Addington cloaks his machinations with a fair façade, but the fox isn't able to hide from the hunter forever."

Taking his leave of Bradford, he waited in the front hall while his carriage was brought around. He half hoped Alex wasn't in residence when he returned.

It was bad enough he hadn't been able to stop thinking about her most of the morning. How was his treacherous body going to react to being in the same room?

He didn't have an answer, but he was about to find out.

Alex felt a prickle of awareness. Someone was behind her. Lady Bradford and Anna didn't seem to notice. They were both engrossed in the portrait of Declan's mother above the mantel.

She took a deep, steadying breath, then turned around. Declan stood in the doorway to the parlor.

He was staring at the portrait, one expression after another crossing his face. What was he feeling? Longing, pain, hatred? By the time his gaze met hers, he was in control, his demeanor one of polite distance.

He kept looking at her, yet spoke to his aunt, disapproval in his voice. "I see you wasted no time bringing the portrait down."

Lady Bradford's tentative reply came over Alex's shoulder. "I assumed you meant right away. When we spoke this morning, I thought...never mind what I thought. Would you like me to have it returned to the attic?"

"No."

Declan kept watching her, his face unreadable. The silence echoing in the room intensified the heaviness in her heart. The old Declan was back, more of a stranger than before. Even Anna didn't try to fill the stillness with her chatter.

"We'll leave you alone." Lady Bradford sounded as if she didn't want to go. "Lady Anna, come help me decide on the invitations for the ball. We are still having an engagement ball, are we not?" It was the closest thing to a challenge she had ever heard from Declan's aunt.

"Of course," he replied.

He still intended to marry her. She hadn't realized she'd been holding her breath until she felt the air leave her body.

Lady Bradford swept by them, with Anna trailing behind, casting worried glances over her shoulder. Declan's aunt gave Alex a nod of encouragement, before she closed the double doors with a soft click. They were alone, but she didn't have the slightest idea what she should say.

When she glanced back, she discovered Declan was still watching her, the small muscle near his mouth jumping erratically. She wanted to throw herself in his arms and end this awkwardness. Instead, she turned to look at the portrait. "She was beautiful."

"My father seemed to think so. Perhaps if she'd been less comely, things would have been different."

The bitterness in his reply left her feeling cold. "It's not just appearance that causes one person to love another."

"I suppose not." Declan crossed to the brandy decanter that sat on a table near the fireplace.

Instead of coming within inches of her, he chose to go around the outside of the room, placing a marble-topped table between them. He poured a brandy and took a small sip, then swirled the contents of the glass, watching in fascination as the amber liquid climbed the smooth sides.

"I apologize for last night," Declan said. "It should never have happened."

"I'm glad it did."

Did he regret asking her to marry him, or did he feel he'd taken advantage of her? Either way, she didn't want him to be sorry.

She swallowed with difficulty and glanced down. She'd been twisting her bracelet. Her chaffed skin appeared raw from the repetitive motion. Funny, she didn't feel any pain. At least, not in her wrist. She forced her hands to her sides and looked up into his eyes.

For just an instant, she fancied she saw passion and longing swirling in their dark-edged blue depths. Then, like the end of a piece of music, it was gone. The intensity still thrummed through her soul.

He placed his glass on the table. "Be that as it may, we have to move on from here. We'll announce our betrothal a week from this Saturday. Allowing time for the banns to be posted, we can be married a fortnight after that."

"So quickly?"

"I thought you needed to marry posthaste."

"I do, but what about the preparations?"

"They won't be a concern." Declan gave her a small smile. "After all, you already have your wedding gown."

Her wedding gown, the one he'd designed for her. Now she was glad he'd forced her to get it.

He started to move around the table toward her, then stopped. "Alex, I don't want you to leave the house in the next few weeks without my aunt or myself at your side."

"Why?"

"Never mind why. I'm asking you to obey me in this."

Had he learned something new? The threat her cousin posed was the same as before. What was going on? "Lord Worthington, I'm not going to be confined to the house without good reason."

"Declan."

"What?"

"I want you to use my Christian name when we're alone."

"All right, *Declan*, I'll not be a prisoner. Until you can give me a good reason why I need lock myself away, I won't do it."

"Yes. You will."

"No. I won't."

Declan raked the hair off his forehead and strode toward her, then stopped several inches away. She was forced to look at his broad chest. He wasn't wearing his waistcoat, as was his wont this early in the day.

She could see the well-defined muscles still faintly visible through the fine lawn shirt. Her gaze crept upward to the thick column of his neck, swathed in its intricate cravat. By the time she reached his face, her breathing was shallow and fast. Fighting the urge to reach up and loosen the ribbon binding his shiny black hair, she tried to collect her thoughts.

"Yes, you will," Declan said. The words were disjointed, as if he were struggling to get them out. With each syllable he uttered, his lips drew closer to hers, until the word "will" vibrated between their mouths.

He crushed her to him, pressing the breath from her body. His kiss made promises. Promises of long conversations, nights of passion and love.

Suddenly, he jerked away, his eyes filled with panic. The sound of his labored breathing filled the air. Sweat sheened his brow.

She didn't know what she could do to help him. He was trapped in a well of his own making. His terror at loving a palpable thing.

"Declan, do you..."

"No, Alex, I can't. I just can't." He turned and bolted from the room.

"I can't" lingered on the still air, but she hugged her arms to her body and closed her eyes. Declan loved her. She was sure of that now.

It was just a matter of time before he realized he was running from himself. When she opened her eyes, Declan's mother seemed to be smiling her approval. If it took years, she would wait. She wanted to be there the moment Declan admitted he'd loved her all along.

Chapter 18

"It's not going to be getting any better."

"What isn't?" Declan knew what his friend was referring to, but wished he'd keep out of it.

"Your wanting to see her." Morgan raised his glass, acknowledging the Earl of Cholmondeley with a tip of his head. The old man was a fixture at White's, and it was a habit of Morgan's to acknowledge the old guard. They seemed to love him for it.

"I don't know what you're talking about." Declan tried to give his friend a warning look, but Morgan leaned forward on the polished wood table, practically coming out of his seat.

"Don't you now. I know you've not been home before the wee hours of the morning in days, and I find you at my place before breakfast every morning." Morgan sat back in his chair and gave him a knowing smile. "Just look at you. You're even less well groomed than usual. Richards must be having a fit. You've got circles under your eyes. If I'd been meeting you for the first time, I'd assume you're ill."

"Well I'm not."

"Perhaps, but at this pace, if you're not, I soon will be."

He studied his friend. Morgan did appear tired. Even the touch of deviltry in his eyes had dimmed. They'd attended more entertainments in the last four nights than he had in the last two months.

His friend had insisted on accompanying him. He suspected it was out of worry, but there was nothing to worry about. He was fine.

"I'm sure Lady Lochsdale would be wanting to see you. Your engagement ball is little more than a week away." Morgan's exasperated voice carried over the refined muttering so typical at White's. It was expected that fortunes would be won and lost at the tables without the benefit of exuberant voices. He lowered his voice when he noticed the stares. "She must be wondering where you've run off to."

He glanced down at his drink. The amber liquid reminded him of Alex's hair. It was almost that exact color when touched by sunlight.

"Well, are you going to see her?"

"What?"

"You've not spoken to your betrothed in days, and I'm wondering why."

"I've been busy." In truth, he had been doing all he could to stay occupied. When he hadn't been watching his own house, hoping for a glimpse of Alex, he'd been going over reports with Adrian. Hell, he'd even taken his place one afternoon in the House of Lords, and the high drama of the posturing Lord Ruthby nearly put him to sleep.

"So, I'm to believe you're too busy to see the woman you're about to marry." Morgan appeared thoroughly disgruntled.

Loud murmurs mercifully drew their attention to the Betting Book ensconced in its normal corner. It was surrounded by a group of lords, the lure of a bet drawing them like the promise of a performance by a particularly risqué actress. Several of them cast furtive glances in his direction.

"The word's out about your pending engagement," Morgan said. "Lord Somby informed me Lord Duprey's entered a bet you won't marry the Countess of Lochsdale. I hear he's wagered quite a tidy sum."

"The bastard."

"He would be that, but you're not going to let him win,

are you?"

Declan took a long swallow of his drink and set it on the table with a decisive click. "What are you doing tomorrow?"

"I hadn't any plans."

"Would you like to attend Derby Day?"

"What's that got to do with...?" Morgan looked confused for an instant, then understanding crossed his well-drawn features. "Oh. I'd be pleased. I take it Lady Lochsdale will be joining us?"

"Yes."

A man hailed them from across the room. He held up a pack of playing cards. The leather mitten he used to protect his cuffs made his hand look like some macabre bird's head.

"Lord Chesterfield is looking to lose at whist again." Morgan shook his head. "You'd think he'd learn. Would you be wanting to play?"

"You go ahead. I've had the devil's luck with cards the last few days."

After Morgan left, he reached into his pocket and pulled out a crumpled note. He smoothed the creases out on the table, running his fingers over Alex's flowing script.

> *I asked you once if you would take me to Derby Day, and you told me my future husband would decide. As you are now in that position, I'm asking again.*
>
> *Regards,*
> *Alex*

No hint about how she was feeling. What did she make of his absence? Richards had surprised him with the note this morning, but it told him nothing except she wanted to go to a horse race.

Declan smiled. She had never been shy about what she wanted; it was one of the things he liked about her.

At least she'd done as he'd requested and kept to the house these last four days. He had only caught glimpses of her at the windows and once in the garden. He'd felt like a stranger, looking at a scene he longed to participate in.

He stood and stuffed the note back into his pocket. Morgan was right. Staying away from Alex was foolish. It made him to think about her constantly, like the immediate hunger you feel when someone tells you dinner will not be forthcoming.

He needed to put his relationship with her in perspective. The horse race was the perfect opportunity to prove he could manage his desires for one slip of a woman. Just in case he faltered, it was a public place, and Morgan would be there. What trouble could he possibly get into?

It was going well. Aside from the brief moment when he'd handed her into the carriage, Declan had managed not to touch Alex. Hell, he'd not even had to work at conversation. Morgan and Alex had kept up a steady dialogue for the last two hours.

Alex peered out the carriage window, her jaunty green hat brushing the curtains. "I didn't think there'd be so many people. Lord Derby only started this race a couple of years ago."

Morgan's voice took on a long-suffering quality. "An Englishman will always be finding a horse race to bet on."

"And the Irish don't?" Alex raised her brows in Morgan's direction.

"Ah, Wee One, I'm wounded." His friend proceeded to grab his chest in melodramatic fashion.

Alex grinned, shaking her head, then resumed looking out the window. "Where are all the horses? I was hoping to get a look at them before the race."

Declan realized she was right. There wasn't a horse in

sight. Brightly decorated booths marched side-by-side as far as the eye could see. All manner of wares were available for sale. He pretended to yawn in order to cover his smile. Leave it to Alex to be more concerned with horses than shopping. "They're stabled on the other side of the hairpin track. We can visit them later. We'll want to establish ourselves near the finish line. From that vantage, we can see the beginning, as well as the end of the race."

The carriage lurched to a halt, and they descended into a mass of humanity. The subdued attire of the Ton created a sharp contrast to the vivid colors worn by gypsies and hawkers. A main thoroughfare led to the track, and they proceeded in that direction, dodging people and stopping to watch a shell game. A wiry little man with nimble fingers deftly slid the shells in a circular pattern, trying to confuse the observers. He succeeded. His portly victim chose the empty shell, much to his chagrin.

Their little group thrust forward through the multitude until the smell of fish and chips wafting on the air made his stomach grumble. "Would you like something to eat?" He touched Alex's shoulder to get her attention. She started.

"I'm sorry. What did you ask?" Alex's voice was almost lost amongst the lyrical calls of the hawkers and excited chatter of the crowd.

He leaned closer to her, speaking as distinctly as possible. "Nothing of importance." He might as well not have replied. She was already looking back at a toy vendor, her eyes wide, as she watched the vendor demonstrate one of his marionettes. The man's movements were smooth, but the sharp angles of his face reminded Declan of one of his creations. He manipulated the strings of a small marionette, a jester clothed in a multicolored doublet, causing it to dance to an imaginary tune. At the conclusion of the performance, the little wooden jester gave a formal bow and blew a kiss to the audience.

Alex clapped, almost jumping up and down in her excitement. As soon as he could tear her away from the entertainments, he negotiated them to the edge of the crowd where they could at least hear each other.

"Isn't it wonderful!" Alex said. "I've never been to the races. Aside from a Season in London, Grandfather and I rarely left the estate."

Morgan smirked at Declan. "Ah, Wee One, it's happy I am Worthington suggested we come. He's been missing you something fierce."

Before he could open his mouth, Morgan excused himself and joined one of their mutual acquaintances. Declan had half a mind to drag him back by his elegantly tied cravat, but Morgan and his friend quickly blended into the press of race enthusiasts.

He was left alone with Alex, if you could call standing in the middle of a crowd alone.

It seemed like they were rooted to that spot, Alex looking at everything but him. Minutes stretched. He felt like his neck cloth was choking the life out of him and reached up to adjust it.

"Oh look." Alex attempted to move past him, toward some unknown goal, but in the crush, she was thrust against him. He put his hand on her waist to steady her. The innocent contact gave rise to the memory of Alex naked in his arms. A memory he'd been trying desperately to forget.

She looked up into his eyes, her lips slightly parted. He wanted to answer the longing and desire he saw lurking in her emerald gaze, but to do so would mean he would no longer have a choice. She would become a part of him—the best part.

A part he could no longer cast aside.

He brutally forced himself to look back at her with no emotion. A mask he'd perfected to cover the hurt his father had inflicted on a regular basis.

He'd become good at his ruse. She turned away, sucked into the throng, her bowed head no longer visible. He closed his eyes, willing his breathing to become even. When he felt in control again, he scanned the crowd for Alex, moving several feet in the direction she'd disappeared. She couldn't have gone far.

Why did he let her go off alone? He always seemed to do the wrong thing where Alex was concerned. Seeing a flash of dark green velvet ahead, he let out a deep breath. Thanking God his momentary lapse hadn't cost Alex her safety, he quickened his pace.

She seemed engrossed in something at the last booth on the lane. Of course it was a weapons vendor. When he finally caught up to her, he didn't let her know of his presence. He watched as she picked up a bone-handled throwing knife, testing the grip for her small hand.

The knife vendor was occupied with a comely serving wench at the other corner of the booth. The vendor smiled at the girl, but his black teeth and stringy shoulder length hair didn't have the needed appeal. The girl gave him a look of disgust and walked away. Disgruntled, the man turned toward Alex as she fingered the edge of the blade.

"Watch out there, that's sharp. You'd best look at something more suitable." The man snatched the knife, but when he got a good look at Alex, his voice took on a persuasive tone. "A mite of a girl like you couldn't possibly know nothin' 'bout throwing knives." He straightened his spine until he reached his full height, just slightly taller than Alex.

"If you really want to be learnin' 'bout throwing, I could show you. There's all manner of things I could be teachin' you." The man showed his rotting teeth as he tossed the knife from one hand to the other, his lecherous gaze on Alex. "Wouldn't want a pretty thing like you hurtin' herself."

Alex's back went rigid.

Declan stepped forward and put a warning hand on her arm. He knew the moment the vendor noticed him. Black teeth flashed a welcoming smile, but wariness draped the man like a shroud.

"My lord, might I show you a pistol?"

Declan found the man's ingratiating voice, as well as everything else about him, annoying. How dare he treat Alex with such disrespect!

"Perhaps you'd like to see a rapier. From the look o' you, I've no doubt you'd know wot to do with it."

"I'm really interested in throwing knives. The one you're holding, in particular." His strongest desire, at that moment, was to see it sticking out of the vendor's gut.

"A wise choice, my lord." The hawker held it up, running a tentative finger along the blade. "Right sharp, nice balance. You've got a good eye."

"How much?" The question was out of his mouth before he realized what he intended. It infuriated him that someone would deal with Alex in this manner. Hell, she could probably out-throw the half-wit.

He could feel the tension in her arm and knew it was taking all her control not to berate the ingrate, as he deserved.

"Two pounds, me lord. An' a bargain at that."

"I'm not sure." Declan turned toward Alex. "As this will be a gift for you, Lady Lochsdale, I'd like to know what you think."

Declan was amused when the vendor went red in the face and his jaw dropped open. He was half tempted to let Alex show the idiot what she was capable of, but there were entirely too many witnesses from the Ton in the crowd.

The muscles in Alex's arm relaxed. She turned toward him, a light of deviltry dancing in her eyes. "The workmanship seems solid."

She took the knife from the vendor's limp fingers,

turning it back and forth in her hand. "It's good steel. The chip carving on the handle has been smoothed to ensure an easy release when it's thrown." She gave a little shrug and handed it back, her voice laden with disdain. "It will do."

Smothering the desire to laugh, he considered what he was about to do. Hell, her grandfather used to buy her rapiers; surely he could buy her a paltry throwing knife. "I'll take it."

The vendor had the sense to sheath the knife and hand it to Alex after Declan paid for it. Declan gave the man an icy stare. The vendor dropped his gaze first and began to fidget, organizing the wares spread before him.

Alex slid the knife into a pocket. They moved away from the booth, Declan's hand in the small of her back, propelling her toward the track.

"Thank you."

"For the knife? It's nothing." He didn't want to talk about his gift to her.

Alex stopped and turned toward him, then put her hand on his arm. "The knife is beautiful, yes, but I really wanted to thank you for defending me. You acknowledged my skill with weapons and asked my opinion. No one's ever done that before." She dropped her eyes and studied the spot where her hand rested on his arm. "I know Grandfather was humoring me when he bought the rapiers I'd selected. He meant well. Most men act like the knife vendor."

"The man was a fool." Declan gazed down at her and shook his head. "And I'd be a bigger fool if I didn't recognize your abilities. Come on, the first race will be starting soon, and there's still plenty to see." He wanted to show her all of it, all the wonderful things she might have missed, all the things that had seemed ordinary until today.

They stopped by several more vendors, and Alex insisted on buying him a small statue of a horse carved from obsidian. It had a small chip in the base, but Alex pronounced it a perfect likeness of his stallion, Knight. He had it in his pocket, along with the fischu she'd purchased for Eleanor, and a wager. Alex had given him a pound and asked him to put it on *Edward's Folly*. If they'd let her, she would have placed the bet herself.

Making their way to the finish line, they slowly nudged toward the fence, until they could make out the turf course, its eighty-foot expanse meticulously groomed.

"We can't see the other side from here." Alex stood on her tiptoes to try and get a better view, but a hill blocked everything but the starting line on the other side.

"There's a hundred-foot climb in the first half-mile and then an abrupt turn on the downward slope called Tattenham Corner," he said. "You can just make out the sharp turn from here. If they get past that, the race becomes a question of speed. Look over to the right. They're lining up."

Alex wiggled in closer to the fence, trying to see around a rather large woman with a hat to match. "I see them. Which one is Edward's Folly?"

"The chestnut with white stockings."

A man with a booming voice that wasn't hinted at by his girth announced from a platform, "The tapes are up."

Almost immediately, a hush fell over the crowd. Even the horses stilled. Collectively, everyone seemed to hold their breath until they heard, "They're off." The roar of the crowd appeared to propel the horses forward, clumps of turf following in their wake.

He studied Alex as she watched the turn where the horses would come into view. A sun-burnished curl had escaped its bondage and was now doing a languid dance on the curve of her cheek.

He liked her. It was as simple as that.

When was the last time he'd enjoyed an afternoon more? What she expected and what he could give were two different issues, but was that any reason for them not be civil?

Just because he made the decision not to love, especially the woman he was going to marry, didn't mean he couldn't like her and enjoy her company, did it? Like was not the same as love. So, he liked her.

The horses came into view. Each animal's muscles strained, while their hooves beat out a rhythmic pounding in the soft earth. Edward's Folly inched up on the inside, coming neck and neck with a large bay. Alex noted the larger horse struggling to keep pace. In the last moments, Edward's Folly leapt ahead, and a great burst of speed made him appear to fly over the finish line.

Alex couldn't believe it. In the excitement of the moment, she jumped up and threw her arms around Declan's neck, her feet not touching the ground. He caught her. She felt him stiffen for an instant, before hugging her to him.

Finding herself at eye level with the cleft in his chin, her legs dangling, there was nowhere else she'd rather be. She raised her gaze to his smiling eyes, eyes that were no longer guarded, at least for the moment.

"We won." She hugged him tight, then threw back her head and laughed. She felt the answering rumble in Declan's chest before his laughter poured out of him, hesitant at first, then gaining in intensity.

He twirled her around, their joy forming a cocoon, shutting out the crowd around them. "Yes," Declan shouted to the heavens. "We won."

"How badly do you want to marry Worthington?" Luther adjusted his cuffs, appreciating the double layer of lace at their edge.

"I don't know what you mean." Catrina perched on the edge of a pink striped settee that graced her pink and white morning room. Her hands fluttered over her organdy silk skirt, smoothing out imaginary wrinkles.

He loathed pink, almost as much as he loathed the woman who had decorated this room. Oh, she had ambition, and could be clever, but she was weak. Something he could use to his advantage.

With deliberate steps, he closed the short distance to Catrina. He reached down, cupped her chin in his hand, and waited until she looked at him.

"I think you know exactly what I mean. Haven't you heard? Worthington's going to marry my cousin." He tightened his grip. "If you'd kept him occupied as I asked, it never would have come to this." He rubbed his thumb on the skin near her mouth. "Such a lovely face. It really would be a shame..."

Fear crossed her features. They both knew that without her looks, she would have no prospects for a future.

He allowed Catrina to jerk her head out of his hand.

"I did as you asked. Worthington's mine. He's only feeling sorry for Lady Lochsdale."

"Sorry enough to marry her?"

"He's not going to marry her!"

Catrina's petulant voice grated on his ears. He raised an eyebrow in her direction, making certain the disbelief he felt showed on his face.

She dropped her gaze and toyed with the lace on her overskirt. "You're wrong. You've been listening to rumors."

"Have I? Alex told her maid, who happens to be in my employ, that the announcement is going to be made at the ball this Saturday."

"He wouldn't." Catrina stood and practically knocked him aside as she headed for the door. She stopped short of opening it and turned. Bitterness robbed her face of its beauty. She took a deep breath, then let it out slowly. "The Countess can't have him. I've worked too long and hard for this proposal. I've put up with his cold arrogance for almost a year now. He owes me his name."

"I'm in total agreement with you." He gave a slight shrug, his palms turned upward. "The question is, what are you going to do about it?"

"I'm not sure yet, but you needn't worry. I'll see to it he doesn't marry her."

He drew his snuffbox from his pocket and took a pinch, then waited. Catrina fidgeted with the pearls at her neck until he closed the box with a snap.

Catrina jumped.

He did so enjoy the little things. Smiling, he replaced the box and brushed at his sleeve with one long-fingered hand before looking at Catrina. "Might I suggest a solution?"

Wariness crossed her face, but she returned and seated herself on the chair closest to the door. "Continue."

"My spies tell me Worthington hasn't been spending much time at home. And his valet is willing to tell anyone who'll listen about an agreement he overheard between Lady Lochsdale and Worthington." He paused, savoring the brilliance of his plan. "This, combined with an item I now have in my possession, should work to our advantage."

From his pocket, he drew a small obsidian statue of a horse, his thumb lovingly caressing the chip on the base.

He gazed into Catrina's eyes and gave her a slow smile. "I understand it was a gift."

Chapter 19

Alex felt like a child on Christmas morning.

"You can look now."

Declan's voice competed with a cacophony of sounds and smells she'd know anywhere. She opened her eyes. For a moment, the bright sun blinded her, but then her vision cleared. They stood near their carriage at the edge of a rough, planked dock.

People milled about in front of them: sailors loading vessels, prostitutes clad to entice, travelers saying farewells to loved ones. A nearby vendor sold medals and charms for a safe journey. Not far from there, a man hawked mementos of England to foreigners.

The array of noises was as varied as the throng. Gulls cried their displeasure as the fishmongers beat them away from their wares. Voices flowed and ebbed with the calls of vendors to each new passerby. Sails snapped in the wind. Barrels and crates creaked as they were hoisted aboard vessels. They all blended to become a kind of music Alex hadn't heard in years—music she'd missed.

"Thank you." Alex turned toward him, tears in her eyes. "Grandfather refused to let me spend time on the docks. I think at first he was afraid I'd run away, and later, he didn't consider it proper."

"I had no idea I took a risk in bringing you here." Declan's eyes and voice held an uncharacteristic note of mischief. "Do you promise not to run away?"

"And where do you think I'd run to?" She turned to him, and her voice lost its teasing quality. "Especially when

I'm finding more and more reasons why I should stay."

Declan ignored her subtle compliment. Acknowledging it would only encourage her attachment to him. Instead, he pointed to a ship barely visible in the third berth. "I thought you might want to stow away aboard that vessel."

She turned, and her quick intake of breath told him she had finally seen the reason for their journey.

"The *Merry Elizabeth*. Oh Declan, how?" Alex looked as if she were seeing a ghost.

"Captain Malachy sent me a note yesterday when he heard about your grandfather."

"Paddy? Paddy's now the captain?"

"Your grandfather put him in charge of the *Merry Elizabeth* shortly after you came to live with him. Padric Malachy has been a fine captain. He's waiting for us." He started to propel her toward the dock, but she held back.

"Did you tell him I was with you? It's been so long." She twisted the bracelet on her wrist. He reached over and put a hand on top of hers, his fingers stilling her movement.

"He couldn't wait to see you."

With a firm hand in the small of her back, he negotiated a path for them through the crowd, until they stood at the bottom of the gangplank. Paddy waited at the top. His legs were planted, as if even now he steadied himself against the roll and pitch of the ocean. When he saw them, he opened his arms.

Lifting her skirts way above what was proper, Alex dashed up the gangplank, her footing as sure as the twelve-year-old girl he'd known all those years ago. She flew into Paddy's arms, burying her face against his chest.

Declan followed at a more sedate pace, giving them a moment together. When he reached the ship, he met Paddy's gaze over the top of her head.

The captain's grizzled face showed the years he'd spent in the sun. Lines etched the corners of his watery blue eyes.

Delcan thought the wrinkles appeared deeper than the last time they'd met. Even his hair and closely cut beard were now totally iron gray instead of salt and pepper. He'd aged, but he still carried the spark of integrity and wisdom that had led Declan to suggest Paddy would make a fine captain.

Holding Alex as if she was his daughter, Paddy rocked her back and forth, murmuring endearments. He nodded to Declan. "Thank you for bringin' her."

Paddy held Alex an arms length away and studied her face. "Yer grandfather done right by you. Yer all grown up right proper like. Sure I was that I'd never be seein' you again and now, here you are."

"Where have you been all these years?" She captured his hand and clasped it in both of hers. "No one told me anything about you or *The Merry Elizabeth*. How long are you staying? What about the crew?" When she took a moment to breathe, Paddy stopped her.

"Hold on now. In time, we'll be answerin' everything. Right now, I have someone I want you to meet." Paddy motioned to one of the interested bystanders gathered in clusters around them. "Tommy, you might be rememberin' Alex here, bein' as her father were your first captain."

A strapping young man with sandy colored hair and freckles stepped forward. He had a plain, open face, with a smile that was disproportionate to the rest of his features.

Alex went forward and grabbed his hand. "I remember you. You were our cabin boy."

He pulled himself up to his full height, puffing out his chest. "I'm a bowsun now."

"So you are." Alex smiled at him, and the young man blushed to the roots of his hair.

"I thought you might be showin' Alex around." Paddy gave her a wink. "Or is it 'Lady Lochsdale' now?"

"It's Alex, and I'd love to." She turned back to Declan. "Do you mind?"

"Not in the least. Paddy and I have some catching up to do." Declan fought the impulse to call Alex back. He couldn't possibly be jealous of a green boy. Just the same, he'd make his meeting brief.

By the time he'd discussed the manifest for the next shipment to India and filled Paddy in on the situation with Luther, two hours had passed. When they came to the fore of the ship, they found Alex, her panniers gone and her skirt tied up between her legs. She and Tommy were engaged in a contest of skill.

Declan groaned and Paddy chuckled as they watched Alex wield her knife in expert fashion.

Her blade landed in the center of the barrel lid with a thunk, right next to her opponents. "As you can see," Declan said, shaking his head, "she more than remembers the things you taught her."

Home. Alex glanced here and there around the captain's cabin. The heady aroma of tar, damp wood, and stale smoke was achingly familiar. The large cot and heavy wooden table were still nailed in their accustomed places, ready to brave the pull of gravity when the ship climbed a wave.

Seated in her accustomed spot at the table, she could almost believe she'd never left, except that Paddy and Declan sat in her parent's places, and she was no longer a child.

Her index finger traced the initials "AK" carved in the tabletop. She'd been confined to the cabin for two whole days when her mother discovered what she'd done. It had been worth it. At least a part of her remained.

Her father's sea chest no longer graced the corner. It had been an ornately carved wonder with claw feet, but the current captain preferred a plain, strong crate, like the man himself.

Sitting back from the remnants of the mid-day meal, Paddy lit his pipe. "Are you sure you'd be wantin' to marry this one here?" Using his pipe stem, he pointed at Declan.

"Yer father would want me to be sure it was love you'd be feelin' for him."

"I love him. Yes." She could hear the "but" implied by her response. She didn't want to admit to Paddy that her betrothed didn't love her. She glanced at Declan's impassive face. Why didn't he say something?

Paddy gazed at her for a long moment as he worried at his beard with calloused fingers. "Good, I'd not be wantin' to fight one of my prize pupils."

She put her hands to her chest, mock indignation in her voice. "I thought I was your prize pupil."

"That you were." Paddy gave her a wink. "But your betrothed caught on quicker than any man I've known, him not bein' born to the sea and all. Still, it's glad I am you've not forgotten what I taught ya. Speakin' of which."

Paddy got up from the table and crossed the short distance to the chest, then threw back the lid. The smell of sandalwood tickled her nose. She smiled. After all these years, it must still be his favorite scent.

He drew out what appeared to be a knife sheath with thin leather straps attached. "I bought this several years ago. It reminded me of you." He shook his head, and the lines around his eyes became deeper with his grin. "You were always complainin' you couldn't get to that blade of yer's fast enough. I thought this might help." Paddy returned to the table, shoved the plates aside, and laid the tangle of leather in front of them.

"It's a knife sheath." Declan picked the gift up, then turned it over in his hands. "How's it worn?"

Paddy glanced at Alex as if he expected her to answer Declan's question, but she'd never seen anything like it. She gave a slight shrug.

His bushy eyebrows raised, Paddy gave her a reproving look and shook his head. "I thought you'd be knowin'. It's a *neck* sheath."

"Really?" She'd never actually used one, but from what she'd heard, they gave the advantage of added speed when drawing your blade. She grabbed it from Declan and tried to untangle the straps.

Her clumsy fingers finally managed to free the loops. She stood and slipped the harness on, then buckled the supple leather under her breasts. She adjusted the straps until they felt secure across her shoulders, then reached down to retrieve her new knife from her boot. With a feeling of satisfaction, she tucked it into the sheath that lay between her shoulder blades. Her hair tended to get in the way, but with a little practice it shouldn't hinder her.

"Course, she'd be wearin' it under her clothes." Paddy's face lost its normal jocularity, and he gazed at her, concern clouding his eyes. "It's not much, but I'd be feelin' better if you wore it. Least wise until the weddin'."

The threat of her cousin hung unspoken in the air. She didn't want to think about Luther. It had been a perfect day up till then. "Thank you, Paddy. Don't worry. I'll wear it." She gave him a hug. "But I'll never learn to use it if I don't practice. Let's go try it."

She headed out the door and up the ladder before Paddy or Declan could stop her. When she returned to the contest area on the foredeck, she was glad to see their target still hung on the mast. Several of the sailors from the morning acknowledged her as she paced off the distance from the barrel lid.

The man she'd beaten in the morning gave a little bow. His mustache, the predominate feature on his face, turned up on the ends. She suspected that passed for his smile. You'd never see his mouth under all that hair. She grinned in reply, then turned to face the target.

On her first few attempts, long strands of hair took flight

with the knife. She normally threw underhanded, which would have been awkward from the neck sheath. With this new overhand style, she couldn't get the correct rotation of the knife. Between the pain of yanking out her hair and the new throwing style, she didn't hit the center once.

She shoved up her sleeves and tried to focus on the middle of the barrel lid. Declan rested his hand on her arm, just as she started to throw. The blade spun out of control, veered to the left, and landed in a sack of grain that hadn't yet been stored below.

"Now see what you've done." She shrugged off his hand, then retrieved her blade. She hadn't thrown that wild since she was eight years old. Her embarrassment added to her frustration.

"Come along, my lethal tigress, it's time to go." Declan stood, arms folded, acting like he expected to be obeyed.

"I need to practice. I'll return later." There was no reason she couldn't stay. She'd be safe with Paddy.

In three steps Declan covered the distance between them. He picked her up and cradled her in his arms as if she were a child.

"Declan, put me down. I can walk." She squirmed, to no avail. The obstinate man simply tightened his hold.

"I'm well aware of that, but this way I'm sure you won't stow away." A glint of humor and desire swirled in the depths of his gaze. She became aware of the increased rise and fall of his chest. At that moment, only Declan's ragged breathing and dark edged blue eyes existed.

The screech of a gull broke the spell, and he looked away, his gaze coming to rest on her feet. "Besides, you're ruining your slippers."

She looked down at her stained footwear. Tar from the decks had left a sticky residue all over the delicate satin. She didn't care. The damage was done. He should set her down, but somehow she didn't want him to.

Declan glanced over at Paddy. "When you find the rest of her things, would you send them along?"

"That I'll do, my lord."

As Declan moved forward, the air filled with cheers from the sailors on *The Merry Elizabeth*. Paddy grinned, and gave her a wink. She buried her heated face in Declan's shoulder as he carried her down the gangplank. Why the hell had she allowed him to do this?

A little voice in her head answered.

Because you wanted him to.

Alex reached back under her hair and slid the knife out of its sheath in one smooth motion, adjusting the tension of her grip as the blade made an arc over her shoulder. She focused all her concentration on the wooden target about thirty paces away.

The weapon flew from her fingertips, hitting the center of the block with a thump that could be heard over the birds and rustling noises of the walled garden.

She'd hit the target seventeen out of the last twenty times. Not too bad, considering she'd only been practicing the last three hours. The activity had helped calm the nervous energy she'd felt all morning whenever she thought about the ball tonight.

"Excuse me, my lady."

She turned to see Declan's butler, Williams, at the entrance between two giant shrubs. Even from here she could see the thin line of his mouth and his disapproving stare. With a sigh, she waited for him to approach, wishing Edgar were here. No matter what she did, Oakleigh's butler always remained unruffled. Williams stopped before her with a slight incline of his head.

"Yes?"

The butler handed her a calling card. "There's a Lady Catrina Edwards to see you. I've put her in the drawing room."

"Now?" She glanced at the card, then down at her old gown, the faded color not even close to its original bright blue. She wouldn't have time to change, but it might have been worse; at home she would have been wearing her breeches.

"Are Lady Bradford or Lady Anna in residence?"

"No, my lady, they've gone to Madame Colette's for a final fitting on their gowns for tonight."

"And Lord Worthington?"

"He said he would be returning late this afternoon."

Just her luck, she'd have to see Catrina alone. By now, Declan must have told her about the engagement. Unease curled itself through Alex's body. She doubted Catrina would be gracious about losing him, but there didn't seem to be any sense putting off the inevitable. "Tell her I'll join her shortly."

After he left, she retrieved her knife and practically ran up to her bedroom. As usual, Mary couldn't be found, so she wouldn't have been able to get into another gown anyway. She pinned up her hair to the best of her ability and pinched some color in her cheeks. It was still half an hour before she entered the drawing room.

I should have changed.

Catrina sat ensconced in one of the parlor chairs, looking like a queen at an audience. Her light lavender gown had beadwork on the bodice, with a cream colored damask underskirt. The double ruffle of lace at the edge of the three-quarter sleeves covered the majority of her arms. Too bad Alex couldn't say the same about the neckline. The gown dipped down to reveal a substantial amount of bosom.

Catrina rose with polished ease, holding her hands out to Alex. "Lady Lochsdale, it's so good to see you again."

Alex moved forward and tentatively took Catrina's hands. "It's nice to see you as well." She couldn't help it that her response sounded less than sincere. This was not the greeting she'd been expecting. Perhaps Declan hadn't told Catrina about the engagement after all.

She tugged her hands out of her guest's grasp, then motioned for her to sit. Catrina waited until she'd taken a seat on the settee, then sat next to her.

Catrina glanced at Alex with a slight, apologetic smile, her hands resting primly in her lap. "I realize I shouldn't have come, but I just couldn't wait to thank you."

What did Catrina have to thank her for? Had she missed something? Catrina gazed at her expectantly, but she didn't even know what they were discussing. She gave a slight shrug. "I'm not sure—"

"I understand this is going to be a big night for you." Catrina adjusted a ruffle on her bodice and smoothed the lace flat. "It really is so gallant of Declan."

"What is?" She wasn't good with riddles, and an inner voice was warning her she didn't want an answer to this one. She should have known it would have something to do with Declan. The unease increased when she realized Catrina was unusually free with Declan's first name.

Catrina scooted closer to Alex, dropping her voice to a whisper. "Oh come now, Declan told me all about it."

"About what?"

"Your agreement. It really is noble of him to come to your rescue." Catrina gave a patient little sigh. "I didn't even try to talk him out of it. He feels such responsibility for you because of your grandfather."

Responsibility? It wasn't only responsibility, was it? She felt a tightening in her chest.

"Of course," Catrina continued, "I was devastated that we wouldn't marry, but I understand his reasons, and I support him however I can." She slipped a handkerchief out of her pocket and dabbed the corner of her eye. "It made it much easier knowing that after the birth of your heir, you'll be returning to the country. At least I'll have Declan here with me."

Alex wanted to tell her she was wrong. Declan couldn't mean to stay in London with Catrina. But how did the woman know what she and Declan had discussed? Alex searched her memory, but didn't remember telling anyone she'd agreed to go away after the child was born. "How did you know about our arrangement?"

"Declan told me." Catrina gave her a sad little smile. "We share everything. He was so apologetic. It just broke my heart, so of course I told him I understood."

Catrina patted her hair, a habit Alex found infuriating under normal circumstances, and then reached over to lay her hand on top of Alex's. "I want you to know he'll be well looked after when you've left. I realize you've become friends in the last few months."

Friends? She made a conscious effort to take slow, even breaths. Is that all they were? She'd been a fool to think enjoying each other's company meant anything to him. Just because Declan had started being nice didn't mean he was coming to care for her. Bitterness welled up in her as she remembered the nights she had lain awake, hoping he'd come to her. Now she understood why he hadn't. The nights must have been reserved for Catrina.

Alex forced her face into a polite mask. "I appreciate your concern." She stood and managed to get the appropriate words past her lips. "I'm glad to know he won't be alone. If you don't mind, I have some things to attend to before this evening."

"Of course." Catrina rose, appearing to barely touch the polished wood floor as she headed for the door. At the last moment, she turned and searched the pocket of her gown for something. "I almost forgot. Declan left this at my house the other evening. Would you return it to him?"

"As you wish."

"Thank you." She laid a silk bag on a small table near the door and swished out, her panniered skirts making a slight rustle as they brushed against the sides of the doorway.

Alex stood there listening to the mantle clock beating away the minutes of her life. Perhaps this was all a misunderstanding. Declan would be able to explain how she knew of their agreement. Catrina's animosity toward her was never a secret. It must be some sick game she played as revenge for ruining her plans.

Feeling a little better, she crossed to the table and picked up the bag. She untied the string, letting the cloth slide over the contours of a black obsidian horse. Against her will, she checked for the chip on the base.

It was Declan's statue.

Her fingers tightened around the legs. She'd given it to him, and he'd left it with *her*. There was no other way it could be in Catrina's possession.

She lifted the piece over her head, prepared to shatter it against the wall, but she couldn't do it. Instead, she hugged it to her chest and sank to the floor, tears making a silent course down her cheeks. There was no hope he'd come to love her, no hope at all.

Chapter 20

Declan couldn't suppress a feeling of apprehension. He suspected it wasn't only due to his announcement this evening. Fingering the note in his pocket, he climbed the worn stone steps of Bradford Hall. What could possibly be so important that his cousin called him away from last minute details for tonight?

A footman opened the door before he'd had time to knock. He observed the servant as he guided him through the turning passageways of the hall.

Unless you searched for unusual details, you'd never notice him. The man's face lacked any distinguishing features. Everything about him was average. With the prerequisite wig and footman attire, he'd be impossible to describe.

He didn't doubt Bradford chose his servants with this in mind. They did more than answer the door, but he wished to hell, this one had let him knock. He found it unnerving.

The footman preceded him into the study, announced his arrival, then left, shutting the doors behind him. Bradford stood behind his desk, shuffling piles of papers, while Morgan sprawled in the chair by the fire. At Declan's entrance, his friend and cousin exchanged a look of concern. Morgan's eyes were the most telling. For once they were totally devoid of mischief.

The knot in the pit of his stomach tightened. "What is it?"

Bradford looked at him, steady gray eyes luminous in the dim light. "Luther has put a petition before King George."

"A petition for what?"

"He's trying to do away with Queen Elizabeth's dispensation. If he succeeds, he won't need Lady Lochsdale. All her estates, as well as the title, will go to him."

"Can he do that?" He couldn't believe the petition would succeed. Of course, the king wasn't aware of Addington's questionable past, a past that might have included killing the other members of Alex's family.

"I'm afraid he can. We both know our illustrious king is not stable. His advisors are busy trying to keep the country going. In the scheme of things, this is a minor problem." Bradford crossed to one of his many bookshelves, found a decanter, and poured a good amount of amber liquid in it before handing it to him. "They may suggest the king pass it to keep the peace."

He took a sip of his drink and waited for the brandy to warm his throat. "I don't understand. Why would his petition create a problem?"

His cousin leaned back against his desk, being careful not to disturb the piles. "Addington has been instigating trouble. It seems some of the more traditional lords don't like a title and the management of estates falling on a woman's shoulders. They've been putting pressure on the king to sign his petition."

Declan dragged his fingers through his hair. Alex could lose everything. She'd had to give up one home already, how would she handle this? Granted, with their marriage, she'd always have a place to live.

With her estates gone, she could never leave him. A feeling of excitement washed over him, only to be squelched by a sobering thought.

She would never be the same if everything were forcibly taken from her. He couldn't deny it was a seductive idea, but if keeping her with him meant destroying her dreams, it wouldn't be worth it. He didn't want her to change. "There must be some way we can stop the petition."

Bradford indicated one of the piles on his desk. "I haven't gathered enough evidence to prove anything to the king. It could be two weeks, or never, before I get the information we need. We're running out of time."

Morgan cleared his throat, drawing their attention. "I have an idea. It might take a bit o' doing, but if it could be saving the Countess of Lochsdale her lands, then I'm thinking you should try it."

His friend had a look in his eye Declan had come to know well. He was almost afraid to ask. "What?"

"You should be taking her to Greta Green. Tonight, before the king has time to sign the petition." Morgan appeared entirely too pleased with himself.

"How's that going to help?"

"I'm thinking the king won't be apt to sign the lands over if she has a husband."

Bradford stopped tapping his index finger against his chin and stood. "He's right. Even the staunchest conservatives in the House of Lords will see you as taking the reins."

His cousin rubbed a hand over his face and continued. "The only other option is to advise the lords of your engagement and hope for the best. But everyone knows engagements can be broken, then they'd be right back to a woman in control. They might opt to support Addington's claim, over the *possibility* of a man in charge." Bradford shook his head, giving Declan an apologetic look. "Several of the lords feel strongly about this issue. I doubt they'd be willing to wait."

"It looks as if I don't have a choice."

"Not if you want Lady Lochsdale to keep control of her title and estates." Bradford crossed behind his desk and jotted something down on a piece of paper. "Contact this man when you get to Greta Green. He'll know how to procure the papers you'll need. The sooner you get her there, the better."

His cousin gave him a wry grin. "I'll make sure the relevant lords are made aware of your wedded bliss in the morning."

Wedded bliss. How in the hell was he going to talk Alex into this? Maybe he shouldn't say anything. He could steal into her room and take her away. She'd already agreed to marry him. What difference did it make when they said their vows?

His dreams, both waking and sleeping, had been filled with the silkiness of her skin and the soft curve of her lips. In spite of that, he'd made a conscious effort to control his desire.

He wasn't like his father. Alex could walk out of his life tomorrow, and he'd continue on as normal. He had to believe that.

Did it really matter that each day he enjoyed her company more? She kept him off balance, reminding him life was to be lived, not just passed through.

The evenings had been the hardest. Memories of Alex wrapped in a blanket, her hair tousled and dancing with firelight, tormented him. He'd solved his problem by staying out so late his exhausted body could crave nothing but sleep. He'd proven he could stay away from her. When the time came, he'd be able to let her go.

But that was somewhere in the distant future. Now his self-imposed celibacy was coming to an end. His manhood stirred in anticipation. Tonight she would be his.

She had to leave.

Alex paced back and forth in her bedroom, trying to make sense of her tangled thoughts. Images of Declan, naked, as he stood by the fireplace kept intruding. His body sculpted in light and shadow, the curtain of his hair covering his face as he studied the fire.

It had been foolish to think she could heal his past. Choking on a small sob, she sat on the bed, dragging the covers to her chest.

Should she stay, sharing as many of those moments as possible before she bore him his heir, or should she leave him to the woman he wanted to marry? The woman who would in no way threaten the wall he'd built around himself.

Could she accept the humiliation? What would it be like to walk into a ballroom knowing the Ton's gossip consisted of her husband's latest indiscretions? She squeezed her eyes shut and lay back on the bed. How could she pretend everything was fine? The pain of it would tear her apart.

Did he feel responsibility and nothing more? An hour ago she would have said he was coming to love her, but Declan's continuing relationship with Catrina told her quite clearly he had no intention of letting that happen.

She'd been an amusement for him these last few weeks. But his attentiveness had seemed so real. Did he care about her even a little? She hoped so. Would he forget her when she was gone? A knot formed in her stomach.

Perhaps.

You'll come to hate him. She ran her hands over her face, then dragged her fingers through her hair. If she stayed, she would come to resent his indifference. She didn't want to hate him, any more than she'd wanted to love him, but you didn't always have a choice. For both their sakes, she needed to walk away. If she were lucky, one day she'd be able to think of him without pain.

She sat up and turned the bracelet on her wrist as she pondered her options. If she returned to Oakleigh Manor, Declan would only track her down and make her marry him. His pride and imagined debt to her grandfather would never allow him to let her be.

Eleanor would be on Declan's side, even without knowing they'd made love. She'd see it as a sensible solution, not realizing the damage a one-sided relationship would inflict on her.

Then there was Luther's threat. No, she couldn't go to

Oakleigh, at least not yet.

Perhaps she could find a way to blend into London. At least for a little while, until Declan searched for her elsewhere and it was safe to return home.

Once she got to Oakleigh, she'd need to find a husband if she intended to stay. She hugged her stomach, the thought of someone else touching her, as Declan had, made her feel ill.

The problem was, she didn't have any contacts here. She suspected Lady Bradford, Anna, or Morgan would be willing to help, once they knew the circumstances, but it wouldn't be fair to put them in the middle. No, she had to do this on her own.

If she was going to keep her estates, she needed to marry. But where could she find a husband at this late date? What she needed was time, and a place to hide.

She crossed to the window and watched the servants scurrying to and fro in the garden as they strung the Japanese lanterns for the ball. All she wanted to do was go home to Oakleigh Manor. The only home left to her after...

A shiver of excitement passed through her. Was *The Merry Elizabeth* still in dock? Paddy would understand and help her to escape. They could set sail before anyone missed her.

Fear, regret, and hope swirled within her until she wasn't really sure how she felt about leaving. Her plan might work, but if she went forward with the activities this evening, Declan would become a laughing stock when she left. She'd need to leave tonight, *before* the engagement.

She crossed to her writing desk, slipped a sheet of parchment from a drawer, then removed the glass stopper from the ink. With short, even strokes, she penned a note to Paddy explaining the situation and asking for his help, preferably tonight.

As she dusted the missive, she thanked God that her mother had insisted those who wished to learn to read and write on board *The Merry Elizabeth* be given the opportunity to do so. Paddy had been proud about his ability, and it would stand her in good stead now.

For once, her maid answered her bell. "Mary, would you have this taken to the captain of *The Merry Elizabeth* right away?" It was already the middle of the afternoon. If she heard from Paddy in the next couple of hours, she'd be able to go tonight. "Have the messenger wait for a reply and let me know as soon as he returns."

"Yes, milady." Mary bobbed a curtsey and headed for the door.

"And Mary, I'd appreciate it if you wouldn't mention this to anyone. It's concerning a surprise for Lord Worthington."

Mary glanced back over her shoulder. "As you wish, milady." She scurried from the room.

There, that should keep her maid from spreading any tales until she could leave. The waiting would be the hard part. God willing, *The Merry Elizabeth* was still in port.

She didn't know how much her already taut nerves could take. At the bottom of her wardrobe, she found the shirt and breeches, which had lain unused during her trip to London. They would be useful if she hoped to slip through the dark undetected.

Concentrating on the details of her departure, she sorted through what money, jewelry, and clothing she should take, then secured them in a bundle and stuck them under the bed. The task kept her from thinking about what she was doing.

And, whom she would be leaving behind.

"You've done well, Mary." Luther rubbed his fingers along the soft edge of the parchment as he read Alex's missive a second time. "You were correct in your assumption I would find this valuable."

Mary's plain features brightened at the praise. "I had

no idea wot she wrote, but she seemed right upset. I been watching her after Lady Edwards left, just like you told me to."

He studied the pathetic servant in front of him. What made her so desperate for money? Ultimately, he supposed it didn't matter. Greed was a useful weakness. It always amazed him what a human being would stoop to for the glitter of gold. "Wait a moment."

He left her standing at the door as he strode across the shabby carpet, heading for his desk. His mouth narrowed into a thin line as he surveyed his surroundings. They were demeaning for the true Lord of Lochsdale. Threadbare curtains hung at the windows, matching the rest of the furnishings in his solitary room. It was all he could afford.

At one time The Sage Knight had been a respectable inn. Now it was no longer frequented by Society, their interest caught by grander, newer inns in other parts of London.

He hated the place. Even his clothes, his beautiful clothes, had come to smell of the stench of the kitchen as odors wafted up the back hall.

With quill poised, he considered a moment before scribbling a reply to Alex's note. It was mandatory he get his hands on her tonight, before the Announcement.

Catrina had obviously done well. Even so, the man he had posted to watch the house after his accomplice's little visit had been for naught. He'd hoped Alex would run blindly out of Worthington's home and he could easily take her. Leave it to the bitch to be unpredictable, but this might work to his advantage yet.

He hoped Alex didn't know the captain's writing. In a few brief sentences, he penned instructions to meet by the back gate of the garden at eleven tonight. He crossed to the maid and handed her the folded missive. "Take this back to Lady Lochsdale and make sure you aren't seen."

"Yes, my lord." Mary continued to stand in the doorway,

tugging on the fringe of her tattered shawl. "Beggin' your pardon my lord, but could you tell me when I might be receivin' me money?"

Outrage caused his breath to quicken. When he was lord at Oakleigh Manor, he'd never allow anyone to question him again. He gave her a look he'd used effectively on many a cowering servant, including the women he'd taken to his bed. "I've told you. As soon as I wed Lady Lochsdale, you will be amply rewarded. Now go."

Mary turned to leave, but he laid a restraining hand on her arm. The soft white of his skin appeared refined compared to the rough wool of the woman's shawl. Satisfaction swept through him. His was a gentleman's hand.

"I would suggest you leave Worthington's household after you deliver the note. Can you imagine his fury if he finds out you had anything to do with this?"

Apprehension filled the woman's eyes, and he smiled. "I see that you do. I'll be in touch when I have your money. Until then, I suggest you keep out of sight."

He watched as the servant disappeared around the corner of the hallway. Her speedy retreat and slightly hunched shoulders were a testament to his control.

Sauntering down the main hallway, he began to whistle a soft, tuneless song, the notes reverberating in the empty space. Now to find the landlord, so he could provide a messenger. A meeting with Spider in person would be a risk, but it was necessary. Even if Worthington's men were following him, it didn't matter. He'd eluded them before.

Mary's usefulness was at an end, and he didn't want anyone able to prove Alex had not come with him of her own free will.

Spider should be able to take care of Mary in time to help him in the garden. He smirked, remembering Spider's outrage at Alex's escape. There was no doubt he'd want to help with her recapture.

In spite of the very satisfying progress concerning his petition, he didn't intend to let his little cousin go unpunished for the way she had treated him all these years. As his wife, she'd have many long nights wishing she'd shown some respect.

The little fool had played right into his hands. He'd intended to use *The Merry Elizabeth* to make his escape. In fact, that part of his plan had already been put in motion. It's not as if he were stealing the ship. It already belonged to him, but now his intended bride would go with him.

Of course, if his petition were granted, there would be no need to make her his bride. He slipped out his snuffbox as he approached the main room of the inn. Raucous laughter filled the air. He inhaled a pinch of white powder, waited for the slight tickle in his nose to subside, then entered the room, attempting to ignore the menial laborers around him.

A small smile played on his lips when he noted the wary looks from the men at the table closest to him. He returned the thin silver box to his pocket and stared at them. They looked down. These men knew how to respect their betters. Pleased, he rearranged his embroidered turned back cuffs.

His little cousin had better hope his petition didn't pass. If that happened, Alex would have to be very nice to him if she wanted to stay alive.

Chapter 21

Alex's grip tightened on her bedroom doorknob when she noted who stood in the doorway. Thank God she'd hidden Paddy's reply under her mattress. Declan hadn't been near her room in weeks. Why now?

Try to act normal. She wanted to throw Catrina's revelations in his face. But if Declan suspected anything he'd tighten his security and force her to go through with the marriage. Damn stubborn men and their sense of duty.

"May I come in?" Declan used his index finger to pull at the cloth around his neck.

Obviously he'd dressed himself again. Richard's formal cravat was missing, and in its stead Declan had tied a neck-cloth with a slightly crooked knot. She fought the urge to push his hand away and straighten it for him. She'd miss watching for signs of Declan's ongoing battle with his valet.

He studied at her quizzically, and she realized he expected a response. "Oh, of course. Please, come in." She stepped aside.

He smelled of outdoors and sandalwood. The smell evoked vivid memories of their one night together. Damn him, she didn't want to think about that night, especially now.

Looking around the room, his gaze came to rest on the peach gown she'd tossed on the bed. "Is this for tonight?"

"Yes." She crossed to her dressing table, leaving the door open. That way, they weren't truly alone. Oddly enough, it was *her* reaction, not her visitor's, she was worried about.

"Good, these should compliment the gown." He

pulled a long slim box out of the interior pocket of his coat. The case's worn brown leather lid opened with a muffled click. He held it out for her to inspect the contents, his face unreadable.

She drew in a quick breath. Nestled amid the dark green satin lay a double strand of perfectly matched pearls. The gold clasp had been fashioned to represent two winged lions. Their interlocking wings formed the fastening mechanism.

Part of her knew she should tell him she didn't want them, but she still reached out and ran her fingertips over their creamy surface. It was an illusion, but they seemed warm to the touch. "They're beautiful."

"Will you wear them tonight?" He removed the pearls from their nest, returned the case to his pocket, and stepped closer to her. "They were my mother's. She wore them to her engagement ball." With his free hand, he turned her to face the mirror. "Lift your hair."

As if in a trance, she did as she was told. How could she accept gifts from him knowing she wasn't going to stay? "I really shouldn't wear them."

"Why not?" He fumbled with the clasp, his fingers tracing little circles over the nape of her neck.

She swallowed. "I, um, wouldn't want to lose them."

"You won't. Besides, the ball's here." Amusement quirked the corners of his mouth. "Or have you forgotten?" The necklace fastened, he began to turn the pearls so the lions would rest in front.

She wished he wouldn't touch her. It was hard enough to be indifferent when he stood in the same room. Somehow, she needed to re-establish her anger. She shut her eyes. *They could never have a future. Declan was never going to let himself love her.*

The thoughts didn't make her angry. Instead, she felt empty, as if part of her were missing. She wanted to argue with him, but what could she say? Beg him to love her?

Two months ago she would have fought, but now she knew drawing her verbal rapier wouldn't change anything. The hurt he'd suffered at his father's hands ran too deep. Catrina would always be there, coming between them, giving him somewhere to run when he felt himself getting too close to her.

No. She couldn't summon anger, only sorrow at falling in love with a man who refused to return her feelings. With a sigh, she opened her eyes as Declan reached around her to adjust the clasp on her chest.

Their eyes met in the mirror, and his hand stilled above her breast. The luminous pearls made even her drab practice gown appear elegant. But their glow paled in comparison to the desire turning his eyes a smoldering blue.

"Magnificent." His hand trailed upward to caress the pearls, then slipped under them, rubbing the sensitive skin. She gave up trying to feign indifference. She dropped her arms and leaned back into his embrace. He brushed her hair aside, tracing a warm, moist path down her neck with his mouth.

Making a soft sound in her throat, she turned into his embrace. Just one more kiss. She deserved a good-bye kiss, didn't she? This stolen moment would be a memory to cherish. It would help her through the bleak years ahead.

When he claimed her mouth, she tried to respond with all the love she felt. She wanted him to remember this moment, wanted it to be different from all the rest.

He reacted by drawing her tightly against his body, his desire for her all too apparent. The tips of his fingers massaged up and down her back as he started to move them in the direction of the bed. She knew what he intended, but it no longer mattered. Nothing mattered but the feel of his lips on hers and the heat burning her body wherever he touched.

She rubbed against him, the tips of her breasts stimulated through the thin material. Aching to get as close as possible, she wrapped her arms tightly around his neck, then tentatively thrust her tongue into his mouth.

"Lady Lochsdale, do you think—? Oh." Lady Anna made a strangled sound.

Alex tore herself out of Declan's embrace. How could she have forgotten the open door?

"I'm sorry." Lady Anna's flushed face still showed surprise. She tried to look at anything but them. "I didn't know. The door was open, so I…"

Declan seemed to find the whole thing amusing. "It's fine, Anna. I was reminding Lady Lochsdale what she might expect with me as her husband."

Poor Anna appeared even more flustered. Alex shook her head in exasperation. He was entirely too arrogant, yet she couldn't help smiling to herself. "Actually, Lady Anna, Lord Worthington came to give me a necklace to wear this evening."

The mention of the necklace had the desired effect. Anna immediately focused on the pearls she made a point of running between her fingers.

"I've never seen anything like them." Anna's eyes filled with curiosity. "Where did they come from? Has Mama seen them?"

Alex laughed. "They were Declan's mother's. I'm sure Lady Bradford has seen them before, but I suspect it's been a very long time." She glanced to Declan for confirmation, and he gave a slight nod.

As she suspected, the necklace was yet another part of his mother's past he'd unearthed for her. At least she seemed to have helped him make peace with his mother's memory. Hopefully, that would continue once she was gone.

She attempted to undo the pearls. "Here, help me get them off. You take them to show your mother."

Anna rushed over, and between the two of them, they managed to open the intricate clasp. She didn't dare let

Declan help. Her body still pulsed from their brief interlude.

"I'll bring them right back." Anna bolted from the room, making sure to shut the door firmly behind her.

No sooner had Anna left, then Declan started toward her. Alex held up a hand to keep him at bay. "I think you'd better go. I need to get ready for tonight."

He stopped and gave a slight bow. A devilish light played in his eyes, reminding her of a little boy with a secret. "As you wish. But it's only a reprieve." He headed for the door, but turned before passing through. "Alex, you will hold to our agreement, won't you?"

She swallowed, sweat breaking out on her palms. Did he know about her plans? Was he toying with her? "Why do you ask?"

A slight frown marred his features. "I want to make sure you still intend to marry me, no matter when it happens."

Now it was her turn to frown. What did he mean by *when it happens?* "I thought this marriage was a matter of necessity."

"It is." He opened his mouth to say something, then closed it again. "Just remember that."

There were guards at every door. Alex wanted to stamp her foot, but in these flimsy slippers and the way her luck was running tonight, she'd probably hurt herself. Why did Declan have every entrance watched? Luther wouldn't dare show his face tonight. All these precautions were going to make her escape much more difficult.

Scanning the crowd for Declan, she readily found his standard black and white evening attire amid the myriad colors in the ballroom. He stood with Morgan and Adrian, their heads together in earnest debate. Good, whatever occupied him this evening meant he had less time for her. She'd seen him briefly before he'd been whisked away by Williams with some last minute details. Hopefully, she'd avoid him all together before she left.

"Are you enjoying yourself, Lady Lochsdale?" Lady Bradford opened her ostrich feather fan and waved it back and forth with languid strokes.

"Yes." She didn't have time for polite conversation. She needed to consider another escape route, and time was running out. But, she couldn't be rude. Not after everything Lady Bradford had done for her. "Thank you for helping organize tonight. I hadn't expected so many of the Ton to attend."

Lady Bradford glanced around the crowded ballroom, an impish smile on her lips. "Gauging from the glum looks on several matron's faces, word must be out about your engagement."

That explained the cold glances she'd been getting from some of the older women. She wished she could tell them there wasn't going to be an engagement, but unless she came up with another way out of the house, she'd have no choice.

"When do you think Declan will want to make the announcement?" She tapped her lace fan against her fingers with rapid little movements, her foot mimicking the rhythm.

"I overheard him ask the orchestra to play something special at midnight." Lady Bradford gave her a warm smile and patted her arm. "I'm so glad you'll be joining our family. I know your relationship with Declan hasn't always been easy, but you'll see, it will all work out."

"I'm sure it will." She squirmed with guilt. She would miss Lady Bradford and Anna. Strange as it seemed, she'd actually begun to feel she could fit in here, but that had been before her visit with Catrina. "If you'll excuse me, the heat is unbearable tonight. I think I'll get some air."

Escaping Lady Bradford with an apologetic smile, she made her way through the crush of people, her oversized panniers hindering her progress.

Thank God Paddy's note said to meet him at eleven. Now Declan would be saved the embarrassment of explaining why his betrothed had left him.

Even without the engagement, she knew he would still try to find her. Shuddering at the consequences should he succeed, she tried to picture him in a rage. It wasn't something she would want to witness, especially if it were aimed at her. Her best defense was not to get caught.

French doors loomed ahead, opening onto the garden terrace. Two men dressed as footmen lurked nearby, their gazes on those coming and going.

She passed through the doors and gingerly crossed the flagstone terrace, trying not to stub her toe on the occasional uneven stone. Japanese lanterns created pools of light with flickering darkness between them.

It became a challenge to avoid the random couples occupying the benches as she made her way to the farthest end of the terrace, near the back of the building. She leaned out over the stone railing, studying the back of the townhouse.

There didn't appear to be any activity in this area, as the gardens didn't surround the side of the house to the back. Layers of darkness stretched before her, obscuring all but the largest objects. Good, she'd never be seen. The trellis appeared to be her only option.

Confident once again, now that she had a plan, she retraced her steps and entered the ballroom. Her gaze immediately sought Declan, standing perhaps twenty feet away. As if he could feel her presence, he looked at her and smiled.

Her heart constricted. She wanted to remember him like this. That devilish grin of his stealing her breath. His smoldering look brought every aspect of their recent kiss into sharp focus, causing her body to tingle. She reached up and ran her fingers over the pearls, coming to rest on the cold metal lions.

Declan excused himself from the knot of men he'd been conversing with and headed her direction. Her gaze was locked on his, or she would have seen Catrina approaching.

Resplendent in white, her nemesis took Declan's arm, propelling him in a different direction. He appeared unwilling to accompany her, but Catrina said something to him she couldn't hear over the din of music and voices. Catrina rested a hand on his chest, a slight pout on her lips, her look imploring.

He glanced back at Alex, giving her an apologetic smile, before allowing Catrina to lead him into the throng. His gaze remained locked on her until he was swallowed by the swirl of dancing couples.

She watched the spot where he had disappeared for several minutes, feeling as if she were frozen in place. She could picture years of that moment, watching on the fringes, as Catrina led him away. Despair welled up, but she squelched it, preferring anger. What right did he have to play with her emotions? She had a choice.

He didn't love her.

She needed to accept that and go on.

As if a spell had been lifted, she turned and headed toward the hallway. Nodding to acquaintances along the way, she managed to make it to the corridor. The main staircase for the third floor was to the right, so she went left. It wouldn't do for anyone to see her go to her room. If Declan found out, he might come to see what was wrong.

She turned a corner and came to the end of the hallway. A meager candle in a sconce lit a small servant's staircase. It was deserted with the ball in progress.

After she removed the candle from its holder, she looked both directions then turned the latch at her waist. Her wooden panniers collapsed with a small clicking noise, like the rattle of sticks in the wind. Thank God she'd insisted on these with Colettee. With one last look around, she gathered the extra material to her skirt over one arm and headed up the narrow stairs.

It felt like hours before she successfully reached her room. She sheltered the candle's flame from drafts with her hand as she lit her lamp on the nightstand, then checked the time on the mantle clock. Ten thirty. She'd better hurry if she was going to meet Paddy. The longer he had to wait, the greater the likelihood they'd be caught.

Unwilling to waste time, she reached for the knife in her boot. With a little maneuvering, she managed to slice the laces up the back of her gown and tug the garment off until it pooled on the floor. She stepped out of the peach silk circle and untied the panniers, which joined the pile of clothing. She ran to her wardrobe, her chemise fluttering about her legs.

With unsteady hands, she dressed in her breeches, shirt, and boots. Her neck sheath chaffed a bit when she rolled her shoulders, but she didn't care. Two weapons would be better than one. She knew from experience that the docks could be a dangerous place.

She crossed to the bed and slid her bundle out from under the mattress. The top of the sack was secured with rope, and she used the excess to tie it around her waist, then slid her belongings around behind her so they wouldn't get in her way.

Now, to get out of the house unseen. She went to her window, unhooked the latch and peered out. The spicy smell of roses wafted upward from the trellis that climbed the brick wall.

The garden paths were located on the left, sparsely lit by lanterns. To the right, about even with her window, were several rows of trees, randomly spaced to create the illusion of a forest.

No one from the garden would see her in the dark, but someone might be close enough to hear her. With luck, she'd avoid any trysting lovers who found the lure of the trees too irresistible.

She swung one leg over the windowsill and straddled the wall. With a last look around her room, she tried not to think about Declan, but the image of an angelic Catrina leading him away fixed itself in her mind.

On a deep breath, she reached out, grasped the trellis, then yanked on it with all her might. Relief washed over her when the framework didn't move. She'd counted on the lattice being securely anchored to the building.

Refusing to look down, she dragged herself over until her feet could find a purchase in the wooden grid. The trellis went to the roof, but she was fortunate the roses only reached the top of the first floor. Even so, she suspected she'd be sorry she hadn't worn gloves. Splinters from the rough wooden slats were already digging into her palms. What would the roses do?

She lowered herself a few feet at a time, testing each new step for possible breaks. The first two floors were relatively uneventful. Even the dizzying height didn't bother her, as long as she didn't look down. But the roses proved to be everything she'd feared. They tore at her clothing, impeding her progress and causing countless cuts on her hands, arms, and legs.

Time was slipping away. She had to get down now. Paddy couldn't wait. Still about ten feet from the bottom, she launched herself into the air and landed with a thud in the soft mud. Muck oozed up between her fingers. The welts from the roses started to sting, and her backside felt wet and sore, but at least she was free.

She got to her feet and brushed her hands on her breeches, then crept through the trees toward the back of the garden. Paddy's note said he would meet her by the rear gate. The new moon provided little light to illuminate her path; even the open areas were no more than varying degrees of shadow.

As she approached the wrought iron gate, a dark object lay in her path. Odd, why would the gardener allow something to block the exit? She bent to move the obstacle.

It was a man, face down and very still.

Wrongness settled into the silence around her. She listened, but didn't hear anyone nearby. With an unsteady hand she turned him over. A sticky substance covered her fingers, and the metallic odor of blood hung in the dew-laden air. She bit back a wave of nausea. Even as she checked, she knew there wasn't a pulse. The man's pale face appeared perfect in death, almost luminous, like marble freshly polished.

Paddy would never have done this. Her heart thudded in slow, deliberate beats against her chest. Where was the killer? Her muscles bunched as she propelled herself forward, intending to jump the body and dart for the gate.

Two arms wrapped around her from behind, effectively pinning her elbows to her sides. She opened her mouth to scream. A foul tasting rag was shoved past her lips, nearly choking her. In spite of her efforts, a small amount of bitter liquid trickled down her throat. She recognized the taste of laudanum.

With her dwindling strength, she tried to kick her captor's shins. One of her blows connected. A grunt of pain followed, but the arms didn't loosen.

She squirmed. Her breath felt as if it were being squeezed out of her body. Lethargy swept over her. She couldn't fight anymore. Lights flashed bright spots behind her eyelids.

"That's enough. We don't want her dead. Yet."

A silken voice penetrated the encroaching darkness. She fought to put her scattered thoughts together. A name rang alarm bells in her brain seconds before she passed out.

Luther.

Chapter 22

Where was she? Declan scanned the swirling dancers and mingling guests for the eighth time in the last fifteen minutes. It was almost midnight. Alex's mahogany locks shouldn't be hard to spot in this room full of colorless women.

He never should have let Catrina drag him away from Alex with one of her dramatics. He shoved his way through the crowd, heading for the exit. Startled expressions greeted his progress. Perhaps she'd gone to her room. It was the only place he hadn't checked.

As he passed into the hallway and came to the staircase, a strong sense of foreboding caused him to take the stairs two at a time. At the top, he traversed the short distance to her room.

After a sharp knock on the door, he waited several moments. "Alex, are you all right?" When he didn't receive a reply, he turned the knob. It was unlocked.

He entered the empty bedroom to find a lamp burning. Someone had been here. Scanning the room, he saw a pile of clothing on the floor. On closer inspection, he realized it was the dress Alex had been wearing this evening.

Apprehension filled him as he searched for clues as to her whereabouts. Her bed was made. Everything seemed in order. The pearls he'd given her caught his eye. He crossed to her dressing table and saw the note addressed to him. He broke the seal and studied its contents.

Declan,

I can't marry you. Please don't try to find me.

Alex

Can't marry him? He re-read the note. She was being stubborn. She may not *want* to marry him, but she damn well was going to.

Anger warred with fear for her safety. Her timing couldn't have been worse. He had to find her before Addington did.

He stuffed the note in his pocket, left the room, and hurried down the stairs. At the bottom, he stopped long enough to ask a servant to find Morgan and Bradford and bring them to the library.

Pacing the area in front of the library's stone fireplace, he tried to make sense of Alex's actions. What had changed since she'd agreed to marry him? He'd thought they were getting along admirably. Granted, she'd seemed distracted this afternoon, except during their kiss.

Her response to his kiss had haunted him all evening. He'd hoped it represented a mutual hunger, an indication she might not be adverse to a speedy marriage. Instead, it was goodbye.

Looking somewhat exasperated, Morgan burst into the room. "And what is it your wanting to see me about? You're supposed to be announcing your engagement. Don't tell me you've changed your mind."

"An engagement requires a betrothed. Mine appears to be missing."

"What?"

He handed Morgan the note. "She's gone."

"What might you have done to her?"

"Dammit, Morgan, I'm not such a blackguard. I haven't

done anything."

Morgan didn't respond, but his raised eyebrows told Declan he didn't believe him.

Bradford entered bearing a large envelope. "Shouldn't you be...?" He looked at both their faces. "What's happened?"

"Your cousin managed to scare Lady Lochsdale off. I'm thinking wherever she's gone, it's not safe."

Bradford's incredulous look was almost comical. "She couldn't have left without one of my men reporting it."

"You don't know Lady Lochsdale." Every muscle in his body felt tight. Where could she have gone? He needed to do something. "Have your men search the grounds as unobtrusively as possible. She might still be on the property."

"I'll check on Addington's whereabouts as well." Bradford headed toward the door, then stopped and turned. "A servant handed me this. It's addressed to you." He gave it to him and left.

Morgan went to the liquor cabinet and poured them both a drink. He accepted the proffered glass and sat behind his desk, then took a long swallow. Alex didn't know anyone in London. She was out there somewhere.

Alone.

He toyed with the envelope fashioned from folded paper. It felt heavy, as if it contained more than correspondence. The crest on the wax seal seemed familiar, two rampant lions back to back. He grabbed his bone-handled letter opener and slit the closure. The envelope sprung open and rows of diamonds poured out, making a constant tapping sound as they hit the polished wood desk.

Alex's bracelet.

"What is it?" Morgan leaned forward to get a better look.

With an unsteady hand, he picked up the diamond-studded mesh band. The lamp's light bounced off the jewelry, sending points of light skipping across the desk.

"It's Lady Lochsdale's." He handed the bracelet to Morgan and smoothed out the letter, then slid the oil lamp closer.

Lord Worthington,

By now Lady Lochsdale and I shall be well on our way to Gretna Green. Lady Lochsdale has agreed to be my wife. Please don't try to follow us. I'm sure you wouldn't want to distress her. You've done enough. This is the way it was meant to be.

The arrogant bastard hadn't even signed his name. He passed the note to Morgan. When had he last seen Alex? Perhaps ten-thirty? If so, they only had an hour head start.

Morgan perused the note, his brow furrowed. "She'd not have gone with Addington of her own free will. Would she?"

"No." His voice sounded harsh. She'd never agree to marry a man like Addington. A man who was capable of anything. A man who may no longer need her alive.

For the first time in his life, he felt fear. Until this moment, he'd never had anything to lose.

Existing. That's all he'd been doing before Alex. In spite of his resolution, he was irreparably tied to a slip of a woman with a penchant for danger. He sat back in his chair and closed his eyes. God help him—he was in love with her!

"Worthington, are you all right?"

He opened his eyes. "No. Dammit. I'm not all right. I'm in love with her."

"Are you now?" Morgan gave him a superior smile. "It's glad I am you're finally admitting it. I was beginning to wonder if you'd ever realize the obvious."

Let Morgan gloat. It was a relief to finally acknowledge

he loved her, but this was not the time to examine what a mess he'd made of things. Her life was at stake. "If Addington harms her in any way, I'll kill him slowly, not quickly as I plan to do."

Morgan's smirk faltered. "I'm hoping it's not too late."

"If they went by carriage, I'll catch them." He stuffed the bracelet in his pocket and hurried from the room, not bothering to see if Morgan followed.

Bradford met him at the entrance to the ballroom, his face grim. "Two of my men are dead. We found them by the back gate."

Morgan handed Bradford the note. He scanned it briefly, then passed it back to Declan.

"So, he's made his move," Adrian said. "It seems he anticipated us."

Declan crumpled the paper, his hand curling into a tight fist. "I'm going to get her back. Bradford, do you think you can find some way to delay Addington's petition for a few days? Right now, it's all that's keeping her alive."

"I can try. It should be easier now that he's no longer here to influence the lords."

"Do what you can. As for the ball, would your mother see to things here?"

Catrina wove her way through the crowd toward them. Her too bright smile flashed, a sure sign she wanted something.

He ran a hand through the hair at his brow. *Not now.* Whatever she wanted he couldn't give her, and he didn't have time to deal with her tantrums.

"Are you leaving?" Catrina moved closer, taking his arm. "You can't depart when your home is filled with guests. What would people think?"

"Lady Lochsdale is missing," Bradford said. "Lord Addington has her, and we believe he's going to force her to marry him."

Refusing to look at her, he shook off Catrina's hand and started to leave. "If you'll excuse me."

"Lord Worthington, wait." Catrina took his arm again. Her voice carried a note of desperation. "Maybe it's for the best. You wanted to marry her off. Lord Addington would make a fine husband."

He turned and glared at her. "I'm not letting Addington have her. She's mine. Do you understand?"

Catrina released his arm and stepped back as if she'd been struck. "Why? You couldn't be in love with her." Bitterness edged her words. "Lord Worthington doesn't know how to love."

Declan couldn't keep the contempt from his voice. "Maybe I never had the right teacher." He turned away. Had he actually considered tying himself to this woman?

"I'll not let you marry her." Catrina's high-pitched voice could be heard above the music. "The letter warned you not to follow. Go ahead. Try. You won't catch them." Her last comment came out in a strained whisper. "Then you'll have to come back to me."

He froze, then turned slowly to face her. "How did you know I'd received a letter?"

Confusion marred Catrina's flawless features. "You must have mentioned it. I mean...well...how else would you know Lord Addington was responsible?"

Barely able to contain his fury, he moved very close to the flustered woman, leaned down, and whispered in her ear, "I want you to tell me everything you know. Now. If you don't, I shall see to it you are ruined in Society."

Catrina's face turned whiter than her gown. "You wouldn't."

"You should never underestimate what a person will do for love." He took her upper arm in a firm grip. "Spreading a few rumors won't be difficult. And coming from me, they'd be believed. You'd be lucky to marry a baronet. Are you willing to take that chance?"

Alex rolled her tongue around the inside of her mouth, attempting to moisten it. She wrinkled her nose. Had she slept with her mouth open?

The smell of salt air combined with the soft lapping of water made her think of *The Merry Elizabeth*. Paddy must have found her. Everything would be all right now. She was safe.

She opened her eyes and counted the number of rough-hewn planks that comprised the overhead. There should be forty-seven. She lost count around the center where some of the boards had warped. Odd, the little game used to be simple when she was a child, but she couldn't seem to concentrate. What was wrong with her?

"You're awake. I thought perhaps Spider gave you too much laudanum." Luther's voice didn't carry any concern.

She sat straight up. Her head began to pound, and pain radiated through her ribs, causing tears to well up in her eyes. She bit the inside of her lip to keep from crying out, but barely felt the self-inflicted injury. The drug must be dulling some of the pain. Her mouth was going to hurt like hell when it wore off. Holding as still as possible, she stared at her cousin who sat at the captain's table, the remnants of a meal scattered before him.

He wore a white waistcoat and jacket of brocade with white embroidery adding a flourish to the edges. His breeches, hose, and shoes were of white silk. Even his blond hair had been powdered white. It hurt her eyes to look at him in the dimness of the cabin.

What did he remind her of? She chewed on her bottom lip as she tried to dredge up the memory. Of course. She had to bite back a giggle. He looked like a cut diamond she'd seen once when a jeweler called on her grandfather. The large gem had glittered on its black background, just as Luther now shone in his plain surroundings.

She shook her head slightly. Even diamonds had flaws, and Luther was more flawed than most. His faults weren't reflected on the outside. She was sailing too near the wind with someone as unpredictable as her cousin. She'd best remember that.

"Nothing to say?" Luther raised an eyebrow. "What happened to my sharp-tongued cousin?"

"Where's Paddy?" To the right of the bunk she could hear breathing, but didn't dare turn to see who was there.

"In a safe place," Luther said. "He didn't seem inclined to let us use *The Merry Elizabeth*, so my colleagues did a little convincing."

"If you hurt him, I'll—"

"You'll what?"

In spite of the pain, she reached for the blade in her boot. It was gone.

Luther gave her an arrogant smile. "I remembered your weapon from our last meeting and took the liberty of removing it."

Did he know about the neck sheath? She rotated her shoulders until she felt the rough leather rub against her back. It was still there. Thank God. The movement helped to clear her head so she continued rolling her shoulders and taking deep breaths. She needed her wits about her.

"As my wife, you won't have need of your toy."

Repugnance washed over her. "I'll never marry you."

"You're wrong."

Luther's unfocused gazed caused a shiver to run down her spine. He was mad if he thought she'd agree to his scheme.

"Oakleigh Manor is mine." Luther's hand clenched the

stem of his goblet. "I intend to have it with or without your help. As soon as King George signs my petition to set aside Queen Elizabeth's dispensation, I'll have everything."

Her momentary panic eliminated the last of the cobwebs from her brain. Could he do that? But if he was sure of the petition, why kidnap her? No, he must still need her. At least for the moment.

"I wish Mother could see me now." He picked up his napkin and dabbed it at the corner of his mouth. "She used to tell me I would be Oakleigh's lord one day."

"Oakleigh doesn't belong to you. Lord Worthington will never allow it."

"Ah yes, the guardian. I'm afraid he won't find you until it's too late. We'll set sail before he realizes the carriage he's chasing to Scotland is merely a decoy. After our marriage, he'll no longer be involved." He stood, circled the table, and pulled out a chair. "Come here."

She stayed where she was.

Luther gave a lingering sigh and nodded to whomever stood near the bunk. Spider appeared in her line of vision and yanked her to her feet. The sudden movement took her breath away.

Before she could steady herself, Spider backhanded her. The blow sent her sprawling on the bunk. Her mouth stung. The taste of blood made her want to gag.

She lay on her back, the pain in her chest forcing her to take small, quick breaths. With great effort, she turned her head and glared at Luther.

"I'm afraid my companion is still rather upset." Luther smiled and shook his head. "The last time you met, you left without saying goodbye. He's not nearly as patient as I am." Luther held out his hand. "Join me?"

By sheer willpower, she managed to sit up and wipe the blood from her mouth.

Spider loomed over her, his putrid breath mingling with

the smells emanating from his unwashed body. His small, wiry form and bulging eyes hinted at his name.

"Not so high an' mighty now, are ya? Here, let me 'elp ya." He extended a dirt-encrusted hand.

She slapped it away and dragged her aching body to a standing position. Luther held all the cards. He wouldn't kill her, yet, but he'd have no reservations about seeing her beaten. If she couldn't walk, she couldn't escape.

"I knew you'd see it my way." Luther stood by and watched her struggle, a small smile playing on his lips.

She crossed the short distance and fell into the chair. The pain in her chest wasn't as bad now that she had started to move.

If Spider was here, then the man who'd practically squeezed her to death was probably onboard as well. She scanned the room, trying to minimize her movements.

Spider stood in the corner, smirking, but aside from Luther, there was no one else in the cabin. *Only two?* The rest were probably up top. Once Luther and his henchman left, she could retrieve her knife. And then what?

Luther moved in front of her. All she could see were the crystal buttons on his waistcoat. He grabbed her chin, tilting her head up. His gaze bored into hers for a long moment. Melancholy gave his perfect features an almost poetic aura.

"Why couldn't you have loved me? It would have been so much easier." He reached down and brushed a curl off her cheek with his other hand. "I had cleared the way for us, just as Mother suggested."

She had to keep him talking until she could figure out what he was planning. "What do you mean 'cleared the way'?"

He dropped his hands, stepped away from her and gave a slight shrug. "Your father and grandfather had to go. You understand that, don't you?"

A core of cold fury formed inside of her. Could Luther

have had something to do with their deaths? Half of her wanted to ask him, the other half wanted to get as far away from this moment as possible. Her voice came out in a whisper. "What have you done?"

"You already know. Thieves *were* hired to kill your father, but by me. Spider almost didn't make it back." Luther raised an eyebrow in his companion's direction. "Worthington gave him the scar on his forehead as a reminder not to be careless."

Rage filled Alex. A good, clean rage that kept her from falling apart at the knowledge she'd lost all she'd held dear because of this one man and his minion.

She wanted them both dead.

The strength of the compulsion surprised her. She'd never before wanted to kill another human being. The knife sheath was now a weight between her shoulders. She clenched her hands to keep from reaching for it. At this distance, she could kill one, but not both. Spider would be on her before she had the chance to retrieve her blade.

"And how did you kill my grandfather?" Her voice was as raw as the emotions rasping over her soul.

"Lord Lochsdale's death was his own fault." Luther gave a slight shrug. "I tried to convince him of the advantages of a match between us." He shot her a reproving look and shook out the lace at his cuff. "You didn't help. If you'd shown some interest, he never would have had his accident."

"Why did his horse throw him?" She didn't really want to know, but she needed something to focus on other than the compelling urge to stick a knife in the man.

"Snakes. It's amazing how skittish horses seem to be around them. I find reptiles fascinating. Have you ever considered the sensuality in their languid movement?" He pulled out his snuffbox, inhaled a pinch, then dabbed at his nose.

"But I digress. You'll be glad to know your grandfather

didn't die right away. He asked about you." Luther's dry laugh filled the tiny cabin. "For some reason he was concerned for your welfare. I tried to assure him I'd take care of you, but... he got excited. I'm afraid I had to put a stop to his ravings."

Luther's matter-of-fact tone made it clear that killing held no horror for him. Unless she found some means of escape, he'd have no regrets about seeing her dead. Of course, he didn't dare hurt her yet. She had time. But could she endure days and nights with her family's killer? Her mind refused to accept the possibility.

Where was Declan? Was he truly on his way to Scotland?

She reached for her bracelet. It, too, was missing. She glanced down, loss and anger blending. Luther met her gaze when she looked up, a triumphant smirk on his face. Raising her chin, she squared her shoulders and refused to drop his gaze.

A calm settled over her. Declan wouldn't be fooled by Luther's ploy. He'd come for her. He had to.

Luther bent down and took her chin between his thumb and index finger, his face inches from hers. "So you see, I've gone to a great deal of trouble for us to be together."

She gathered what moisture she could and spit. The thin saliva sprayed across the side of his face.

He stiffened, his light blue eyes reminding her of pieces of steel. With very deliberate movements, he straightened and jerked a handkerchief out of his pocket to wipe the spittle from his cheek. "Tie her arms behind her back."

Spider grabbed her from behind, yanked her from the chair, and dragged her to the bed. She tried to break his hold by kicking backward, but he dodged her blows. He was quick, but not very strong. If her body hadn't taken such a beating earlier, she probably could have broken free.

He wrenched her arms behind her back and tied her tightly, then bent to whisper in her ear. "Yer in fer it now, miss high an' mighty. Mind, if yer real good, he might let you live." He fondled her backside out of view of Luther. "Did you know he lets me hav' his entertainments after he's broke 'em in proper?"

She shuddered.

"That's enough, Spider." Luther removed his coat and retrieved a knife from the chest.

She recognized her blade.

Luther joined them. "Leave us. It's time my cousin and I became better acquainted."

Spider gave one last knowing smile and scurried from the room.

After the door closed, she turned to Luther. His hand shot out and knocked her to the bunk. She lay on her back, arms beneath her, looking up at him. It was best not to move. She guessed he wanted a struggle. If she could just free her hands, she could get at her knife.

He positioned himself between her legs where they dangled over the side of the bed. Running his finger up and down the knife's edge, he gave a slight nod.

"Sharp. I approve." He stilled his movements and studied her, his face pensive. Very slowly he started to tap the tip of the knife to his chin, as if debating some deep mystery. "Now we come to an interesting dilemma." He tilted his head ever so slightly, his speech matter-of-fact. "I intended to teach you some respect, then rid myself of you. Permanently. But what if King George doesn't sign my petition?"

He reached down, sliced the cord holding her shirt together at the neck, then ran the tip of the blade between her breasts. The cut stung and a red trail welled up, but the scratch wasn't enough to cause serious injury. He was toying with her. Testing the limits of her pain.

He raised an eyebrow.

If he wanted a reaction, he wouldn't get one. She

wouldn't be his amusement. Nothing felt real. It was as if she wasn't a participant in this bizarre scene, merely an observer.

Luther reached down and cupped her breast, twisting her nipple through the thin silk. The pain forced her to draw away from him, but he shoved her down with the other hand, and placed the knife under her chin.

After a squeeze of her breast that made her grit her teeth, he let go, then leaned over and cupped her cheek with his hand. The cold blue of his eyes, so close, sent tendrils of apprehension through her. His voice was soft, melodic and warm where it played on her face.

"My proud cousin. Everyone has a gift." He ran his fingertips along her cheekbone. "Mine is instilling fear. You'll never know whether our time together will bring pain or pleasure."

He traced the tip of the knife just under her chin. She tried to turn her head, but he pressed the weapon into her skin, cutting a path to her jawbone. Warm blood oozed along her neck.

"Shall we get started?"

Chapter 23

"Is it sure you are this is the only way?" Morgan gazed at the mooring cable closest to them and craned his neck to find the spot where it disappeared into *The Merry Elizabeth*. He cast Declan a worried look. "I'd not be wanting to fish your broken body out of the water."

"There's no other option." Declan gave his friend a smile he hoped appeared more assuring than he felt. Damn, he hated heights. "You just make sure the men are ready to cross the gangplank when I've taken care of the watch."

"What if they're ready for you?"

"If Catrina's information is correct, they won't be."

"Don't go picking a fight without me. I'm not happy to be depending on the word of that banshee."

"Neither am I, but we don't have a choice. Judging by the loose rigging and tilting yards, I'd say someone other than Paddy is in control of the ship." He studied the brooding wooden vessel overhead. "Alex is here. I can feel it."

The early morning mist concealed them as they huddled behind crates and barrels on the dew-slicked dock. The predawn stillness, broken only by the rhythmic sound of water slapping against the hull, contrasted with his rapid heartbeat.

He waved to his cousin a short distance away. Bradford, flanked by two others, turned and walked into the swirling white fog. He gave them a couple of minutes to position themselves at the head of the dock. Addington might try to slip by them, but he'd find no escape by land.

"It's time." With a last glance at Morgan, he crept to

the edge of the wharf, attempting to stay in the shadows. He scanned the ship for any sign of movement, but aside from the men at the entry port, all was quiet.

The mooring cable felt rough as he yanked it to verify how securely it had been lashed to the pier. He worked quickly, taking shallow breaths, as the stench of fish, garbage, and God knew what else drifted up to him.

His rapier banged against his thigh as he drew himself, hand over hand, up the heavy rope. Raw patches developed on his palms as the hemp fibers dug into his flesh. He wished for the calluses he'd developed eight years ago and cursed silently as the wounds came into contact with the salt-encrusted cable.

At any moment one of the watch might look toward the stern of the ship. Caution warred with the need for speed. If he fell now, he'd either drop the thirty feet to the water or break his fall on one of the fenders holding the ship from the dock. He didn't relish either option.

His hands cramped. He needed to finish this. Now. With a final burst of energy, he crossed the last five feet and hauled himself over the rail. He lay there for a moment, attempting to get his bearings in the dim light. A small boat nestled against the railing to his left with the bulk of the quarterdeck in front of him.

With soundless movements, he gave the dingy a wide berth. Livestock were often kept in crates aboard the small boats. It wouldn't do to alarm the animals.

Clad in a black shirt, breeches, and heel-less leather boots, he blended into the shadows. Working his way around the horse block, he came to the wheel. The companionway blocked his path and beyond that, the ladders were partially obscured in the early morning mist. Masts and ropes stuck out of the swirling white like trees long dead in a swamp.

He fought the impulse to rush down one of the ladders. Alex was most likely being held in the captain's cabin below him. The need to see her, alive and well, overcame him.

His brave Alex might push Addington too far. The man wasn't sane. He might decide to kill her without confirmation of his success with the petition.

What would he do if Addington harmed her? He swallowed. Even the possibility she might be dead tore at him, like a crow with its prey.

So this was the kind of emotional torture his father had endured. For the first time, he understood what his father had gone through. He could almost forgive the man. Almost.

In the last few minutes, the mist had become less substantial. Urgency propelled him forward. Keeping low, he scooted around coils of rope, eyebolts, and barrels, then positioned himself next to the mainmast fife rail and peered down to the main deck. Three men stood at the entry port. A hulking giant, a short, stocky man with a cap pulled low over his forehead and, a small, wiry individual with a whiny voice that carried up to Declan.

"I just left 'im. I tell ya, she's in fore it. Ain't never seen old cold-eyes riled." The glee in the man's voice made him want to climb down and shake the bastard, the way a dog would a rat.

The man with the cap shrugged. "Right sorry to hear that. She's a purty little thing, but I finds it best not to mix in the doin's of the nobility. Ye might want to remember that."

"Yer just afeared of him. Me an' Lord Addington hav' an understandin'." The wiry man puffed out his chest and jerked his head at the quiet giant. "Com' on, Pete. We don' need no lecture by the likes o' him."

They took the ladder near the hold, leaving the man with the hat on deck. The rest of the crew must still be asleep below. He'd better get this over with. The sun already edged the horizon.

Creeping along the railing, he approached the ladder. He could drop the short distance to the main deck, but the noise would alert his prey.

The unwary sailor searched his pockets and brought out what appeared to be a piece of driftwood and a small knife. He turned, resting his elbows on the rail near the gangplank. Declan descended the ladder, watching for any sign the man might be aware of him.

Once he reached the main deck, he hurried to close the distance between them. The man barely had time to turn before Declan landed a blow to his jaw.

The force of the impact flung the sailor against the rail, his wood and knife skidding across the worn deck. He stirred once, then slumped with his chin on his chest.

Declan dragged the unconscious man behind a crate and returned to the gangplank. He pulled a white square of cloth from his pocket and waved it high overhead.

Without waiting to see if Morgan approached, he turned, tossed the cloth on the deck, and headed for the ladder. As he peered down into the opening, a ragged looking sailor loomed out of the darkness below. He ducked out of sight. Too late. The early morning light must have been enough to show the man he wasn't part of the crew.

A bellow reverberated through the ship. Declan fell back to join Morgan and his men at the entrance. Sailors in various forms of undress scampered up the ladders on each side of the hold. Most clutched swords, though he saw a scimitar or two among them. With grim relief, he realized none of the men looked familiar.

Morgan covered his back as Declan fought to gain one of the ladders near the hold. If he could break through, he doubted there would be many men below to hinder him.

As though guessing his intent, Luther's men swarmed in front of him. He barely had time to run one man through before another took his place. His arm was beginning to ache, and he wiped the sweat from his eyes.

Between adversaries, he stole glimpses of his

surroundings, hoping Alex might find a way from below deck. Shafts of light cut through the clouds illuminating pools of blood staining the white wood beneath their feet. Moans from the injured, shouts, and the clanging of metal against metal filled the air.

One man, no more than a boy, lay nearby with a knife protruding from his shoulder, the blade pinning him to the mast at his back. The lad's glazed eyes stared up at him out of a cherub face.

He turned away. Addington would pay, first for Alex, then for the poor he preyed on to do his bidding. Where was the coward?

A glint of metal high above the confusion caught his attention. Addington hurried across the quarterdeck, dragging Alex, a knife at her throat.

She was alive.

He wanted to sink to his knees in relief, but his burly adversary made it impossible. With a desperate parry, he disarmed the man and sank his blade into a meaty forearm. The man squealed with pain and charged like an enraged bull. Declan sidestepped and shoved the man into a barrel. His opponent's head shattered the wood. He twitched once, then lay still.

Before another of Luther's men could take his place, he turned to Morgan and gestured upward. His friend's eyes widened as he caught sight of Addington and Alex on the deck above.

Addington would undoubtedly try to take one of the small boats. He caught Morgan's attention, and they moved away from the thick of the battle as he hurriedly explained his makeshift plan to his friend.

The two fought in the direction of one of the ladders leading to the quarterdeck. Once they'd reached their destination, Morgan nodded to him, turned toward the starboard railing and melted into the mass of men and swords. He headed for the ladder and took the steps two at a time, thankful the main part of the battle still raged near the bow. At the top, he peered over the edge.

Addington attempted to launch a boat with one hand, while trying to maintain his hold on Alex. She wasn't making it easy for him, in spite of the knife at her throat. Even with her hands tied, she twisted like a sail caught in a crosswind. He swallowed. There wasn't another woman who could compare to her, but her courageous attempts at escape seemed merely a distraction for Addington. His foppish appearance disguised a strength he had underestimated.

After a quick glance to make sure no one else accompanied Addington, he grabbed the railing and hauled himself onto the deck, then proceeded toward the struggling couple with care. As he drew near, he could see a thin line of dried blood cutting a path down Alex's neck. Her swollen right cheek already showed purple and red against her pale skin. The ties for her shirt dangled, exposing a red welt between the tops of her breasts. He fought to control his rage.

"Addington." He roared the name. His shout hung in the air, easily heard over the waning battle.

For a moment his adversary held still, surprise and uncertainty in his eyes, then he yanked Alex in front of him and pressed the knife deeper into the skin below her chin. "Stay away."

He stopped.

Addington smirked and put his other arm around Alex, resting his hand several inches below her shoulder. "I'd be very careful if I were you." He gazed at Declan, then moved his hand downward, encompassing her breast. "It would give me great pleasure to kill her." He saw Addington's fingers tighten around the mound of flesh.

Alex's expression didn't change, but her chest moved rapidly under Addington's hand. He fought the urge to lunge at him. If he did, he knew she'd be dead before he could cover the ten-foot gap. He needed to stall for time.

"You're making a mistake." Declan lowered his rapier, and assumed a non-threatening stance. "If you kill her, King George may wonder about the circumstances of her death. He might even refuse to grant your petition."

Addington gave a slight shrug. "I would tell the king we were attacked. My poor future wife was a casualty of battle."

Sweat broke out on Declan's palms. Alex held perfectly still, her gaze locked on him. He could see the trust in her eyes. She thought he would save her. He looked away, dreading what he had to do. "There's no need to kill her. The king would grant your petition if *I* backed you, as her guardian, of course."

"Why would you do that?" Addington's eyes narrowed, and the knife against Alex's throat relaxed a little.

"I have no need of her title or estates." He prayed he sounded reasonable. "If I marry her, I acquire the wife I need to provide my heir, and I satisfy an old debt to her grandfather." He kept his gaze focused on Addington, afraid to see the look in Alex's eyes. He forced a smile. "Besides, it goes against the nature of things for a woman to hold a title. Don't you agree?"

In his peripheral vision, he saw a flash of dark blue near some crates to his left. Thank God, Morgan had made it.

Addington appeared thoughtful. He brought Alex closer and spoke in a loud whisper. "I'd always intended to make you pay for the way you've treated me."

Declan gave a slight shrug and schooled his features to feign indifference. "If you do, other members of the Ton may not be willing to give you their daughters. With your title and wealth, you could look higher than an earl's granddaughter." The comment hit its mark.

A calculating gleam appeared in Addington's eyes,

then his mouth drew into a thin line. "I'm not a fool. Once you have the girl, you'd never back me. You're saying this because you're in love with her and would try anything to get her back."

What was keeping Morgan? He should be in place by now. Addington wasn't going to stand here forever.

Declan forced a smile to his lips. "I'm sure you're aware of my reputation with the ladies." His condescending voice would have made Catrina proud. "They consider me a cold fish. I've yet to succumb to their charms." He smoothed the folds of his cravat as if he hadn't a care in the world, then raised an eyebrow at his adversary. "Do you *really* think I'd be enamored of a woman who dresses like a man and has a tongue as sharp as her blade?"

To his relief, Morgan straightened up from behind the capstan, then ducked under the bars used to wind the cables onto the giant barrel. He crept forward to within eight feet of Addington's back.

"What assurances would—?"

Morgan yelled behind him. Addington's eyes widened in surprise at the sound. "What?" He twisted and jerked his captive with him. The movement threw the two of them off balance. In his struggle to remain upright, Addington dropped the knife from Alex's throat.

Declan's voice split the air.

"Alex, run."

It was the moment Alex had been waiting for. With a strength born of fury, she brought her heel back and connected squarely with Luther's shin. Startled, he doubled over, and released her.

Morgan grabbed her arm and yanked her sideways. He gave a small grunt as she connected with his chest. They swayed for an instant before he got his feet under him.

She turned away from Morgan's waistcoat at the hiss of two rapiers being drawn from their scabbards. The sound had always given her a sense of anticipation; now it filled her with dread.

Her gaze sought Declan. How much of what he'd said was the truth? She'd been hurt and angry, but those emotions seemed to fade as she realized he stood, dark and proud, with his rapier held at the ready. His face wore an expression she'd never seen. It seemed to have lost its humanity. Even the muscle in his jaw stood still.

She felt Morgan run a blade between her hands and cut the ropes that bound her. Rubbing her wrists, she stepped forward. She had to stop this. Morgan stepped around her.

Declan held out his hand, palm facing them. "He's mine."

It wasn't so much the action, but his tone of voice that made them stand their ground. She turned to locate her cousin.

Luther stood, fair hair shining in the sunlight and hatred glowing in his eyes. In one hand he clutched the dagger she knew only too well and in the other his rapier. With a show of arrogance, he stuck the knife in his boot, then nodded to Declan.

As a young girl, she'd watched Luther practice his fencing skills. He excelled, but even then she recognized it was not the love of the sport but the love of the kill that gave him an edge.

There were no niceties exchanged. Her cousin came at Declan with purpose. In spite of the aggressive attack, Luther's moves were calculated, his parries clean and precise.

Both men seemed to be trying to contain their movements. The ship's cluttered deck, full of an assortment of ropes, eyebolts, and buckets, could cause the duel to be lost by distraction, rather than skill.

Their blades danced in the sunlight. Luther was smaller in stature and quick, but his extension couldn't compete with Declan's. Her cousin would attack, retreat, attack and retreat.

Like a cat that toyed with its prey, staying just beyond his opponent's lethal blade.

They'd pinked each other several times. Blood didn't show on Declan's shirt, and she had no idea how badly he'd been injured. Unlike Luther, his expression didn't change when his opponent's sword cut through the material on his chest.

Her cousin danced around Declan, vivid red ribbons etched across his white waistcoat like the claw marks of a wild animal. None of the wounds appeared to be very deep, but his movements started to show hesitation.

The sounds of sporadic fighting below, and the screech of the gulls above blended with the pounding of her heart. There was nothing she could do as the lethal battle continued. Even if she'd wanted to, she wouldn't have been able to step into the fray. Morgan's hand rested on her arm for more than support.

The opponents twisted and flexed as each tried to gain an advantage. Thrust, parry, thrust, parry in endless succession.

Luther began to take more risks. *He must be tiring.* She understood his strategy. The incredible bursts of speed were his attempt at ending the duel before he grew too tired to defend himself. It's what she would have done.

The urgency of Luther's attack put Declan on the offensive. Again and again, he beat back Luther's desperate lunges. Declan's parry fell short at an unusually quick thrust, and Luther's blade passed through his sword arm. Luther pulled it free, a smile on his face.

The wound barely slowed Declan, but she knew he couldn't keep up this pace. She wasn't aware that she'd started forward until she felt Morgan tugging on her arm. Sweat broke out on her palms.

Declan was running out of time, and she suspected he knew it. He began to press his advantage. Keeping his blade at full extension, he forced her cousin backward. They battled past the companionway to the wheel. Luther's smile faltered.

Blood dripped from Declan's arm as he backed his opponent up as far as the fife rail around the mizzenmast. Luther thrust high. Declan caught the point in the material between his left arm and chest. The tip tangled in the fabric. Her cousin desperately tried to extract it, but Declan's blade slid through his chest, between the rails, and into the mast. Luther's eyes went wide with surprise.

Declan yanked his blade free and kicked Luther's fallen rapier away from his body. He twisted, his gaze searching the ship until he saw her.

She couldn't read his expression. What was he thinking? Relief and uncertainty fought for dominance. Her foolish actions had caused this. He had every right to be angry.

Declan stood looking at her. It was then she noticed Luther looming up behind him like a bloody ghoul. Rage distorted his features. Her cousin's unsteady gait brought him within striking distance of Declan's back. She could see the glint of her dagger in his hand.

In one motion, she swept her blade from its neck sheath. *Please.* The word echoed in her mind as the hilt flew from her fingertips.

Declan jumped to the left, his eyebrows raised, as her weapon sped past his right shoulder and landed in Luther's throat.

Her cousin fell forward, the dagger still clenched in his hand.

Nobody moved.

Declan was the first to recover. He glanced back at Luther's body, then strode over to her and gently touched her injured cheek. She heard the air leave his body for one long moment, as if he'd been holding his breath till then.

"Alex, I want to break our agreement."

She backed away from him. All the old hurt and anger resurfaced. It was foolish of her to think this would change anything. With Luther gone, he was free to marry Catrina and force her into marriage with someone else. Pain shot through her. "Does killing Luther wipe away your debt to my grandfather? I thought you *needed* me to produce your heir."

He grabbed her upper arms, his grip surprisingly strong in spite of the blood she could see soaking his shirt. He waited until she looked up, then stared into her eyes, desperation and something else in his gaze. It was the "something else" that made her heart beat faster. "What I *need* is to have you never leave me again. If you so much as go riding, I intend to be at your side."

"But I thought—"

He gave her a slight shake, as though admonishing a child. "I'm in love with you, and I'll not risk losing you again. I'll marry you tonight if I have to."

Hope filled her like a sail unfurled to catch the wind, but then she remembered his comments about her unladylike conduct. "I want to help with my estates, and don't expect me to give up fencing and daggers. It's who I am."

The tension went out of his body, and he smiled that secret smile that warmed her insides. He lightly grasped her chin. "Why would I want a predictable society lady when my hoyden is so entertaining? Besides, how can I argue with a skill which saved my life?"

He gathered her to him, melding their bodies and lips as one.

Morgan's smug voice reminded them they weren't alone. "I'm thinking she's been thanked enough. We need to see to the men."

Startled, they both glanced over at Morgan. His brown eyes twinkling, he executed a small bow. "After all, we've a wedding to plan."

Epilogue

My dearest Alex,

If you are reading this, perhaps you have forgiven me. I couldn't tell you about Declan. You would have fought me if I had. I love you both, and I knew you belonged together. Try not to be too much of a trial for him, my dear, but perhaps a little spirit is not such a bad thing. You brought joy to my life, Alex, as I'm sure you will bring joy to Declan. Take care of each other.

Alex lowered the letter her grandfather's solicitor had given her at the wedding feast. He'd been instructed to present it upon her marriage to Declan Devereaux, the Earl of Worthington. The poor solicitor had raised his bushy brows and asked if she and Declan had been betrothed a long time before their wedding. At her negative reply, he'd shaken his head, shrugged, and handed her an envelope.

She smiled. Her grandfather had known them well. Left on their own, they would never have given love a chance. She sighed, dropped the letter to her lap, and leaned back in the bedroom chair, listening for sounds from the crib where her six-month-old son slept.

Her husband had challenged Luther with more calm than he'd shown when faced with her pregnancy. He'd refused to leave her side during the long months and insisted on the best doctors, not being satisfied with one man's opinion. It had been difficult, but she'd endured it because she understood what he feared.

Declan entered the room, his steps a whisper of sound on the plush carpet. He wore his traditional black, which was even more of a trial for Richards now that he was often covered with white cat hair.

Last Christmas, he'd given her a longhaired white kitten with the collar she had thought lost around its neck. Since that time, *Guardian* had not been far from Declan's side. She could usually find him wrapped around the back of her husband's neck. Alex understood the attraction. She liked wrapping her arms around his neck as well.

Declan crossed the room to peer into the cradle. Some day he might stop looking at their child with awe, but she hoped it wasn't any time soon.

She joined him there, locked her hand in his, and gazed down at their son. His curly auburn hair stuck in damp tendrils to his forehead. Dominic Devereaux, the Earl of Lochsdale and future Earl of Worthington, lay fast asleep, one of the few times his blue eyes weren't open and studying the world around him. She reached in the cradle and brought the blanket up to her son's dimpled chin.

It scared her to think how close she'd come to losing this life with Declan. Thank God her cousin and his minion could never hurt them again. Lord Bradford had caught Luther's accomplice trying to escape from the pier. She hadn't gone to Spider's hanging. It was enough to know her father's and grandfather's deaths had been avenged.

She led Declan away from their son and through the entrance to the adjoining bedroom. After she shut the door, she turned to face him.

"You promised you'd fence with me today."

"Did I?" Declan's blue eyes shone with mischief. He walked over to the bed and put Guardian on the counterpane, stroking the cat's fur with long, luxurious movements. He straightened and gave her an appraising look that sent shivers up her spine. "What do I get if I win?"

"Why, I'll do as you ask, within reason, of course."

At his crestfallen expression, she laughed and skirted his arms as he reached for her. She went to the wardrobe and removed her breeches and shirt. The enclosed garden would be lovely this time of day. Besides, Declan knew they'd end up here afterwards. They always did.

"What if I don't wish to be reasonable?" Declan's voice became intimate, a warm, low resonance that seemed to permeate her being. "Shall I describe some of the things I'd like to do to you?"

She felt heat rush through her body. The man was distracting her. "Win first."

"Is that a challenge?"

Declan approached and proceeded to act as her lady's maid, sliding the clothing from her body with slow, sensuous movements. She stood still, relishing the feel of the cloth against her skin. At last, she stood naked. Declan moved behind her, then reached around and ran slightly roughened hands down the front of her, starting with her breasts. "Before and after," he breathed into her ear.

With a smile, she gave into temptation and leaned back against him. She knew when she'd met her match.